PEACE RIVER

Spirit Dance Books™

By Jaclyn M. Hawkes

What readers are saying about Jaclyn's books:

Jaclyn, just finished your book. Made me get all choked up for a bit. And that kissing in the corn patch—oh my! You have truly done a great thing. Thank you.

Charlie M. in Georgia

Jaclyn, I wanted to take a moment to let you know how much I enjoy reading your books! My favorite is The Most Important Catch, but I do love the other two as well. Please continue to write interesting, clean, and uplifting stories. We need your influence in the literary world.

Cindy C. in California

Acknowledgments

Thank you to my wonderfully willing critical readers who tell me what they truly think, even when it isn't pretty. Thanks also to my team at Spirit Dance Books LLC. You worked sometimes around the clock to help get this book out on time. I so appreciate all you do.

And, of course, thank you to my family for supporting my need to write. You are incredibly patient, as well as adorable and I love you.   Jaclyn

Peace River
By Jaclyn M. Hawkes
Copyright © November 2012 Jaclyn M. Hawkes
All rights reserved.

Published and distributed by Spirit Dance Books.LLC
Spiritdancebooks.com 1-855-648-5559
Cover design by Jordan Youngberg Design

Printed in USA

First Printing November 2012

Library of Congress control number 2012953136

ISBN:0-9851648-1-6

ISBN-13:978-0-9851648-1-2

Dedication

This book is dedicated to my husband, who looks so darn hunky in his cowboy duds and has chosen to keep me, in spite of my very expensive love of horses. He trained the best horse I ever owned and then helped me bury him when he got old. He's a lot like the hero in this book—soft spoken and strong.

This book is also dedicated to my rodeoing neighbors, who sometimes drive all night Saturday night to make it home to fulfill their Sunday responsibilities. They are good, hard-working, honorable neighbors and friends, and I have the greatest respect for them. I wish I could ride half as well, or be half as tough. Rodeo is definitely not for wimps.

Chapter 1

Woodland Hills, California

Her running horse could be heard long before she appeared out of the mist. In the half light of dawn and the wisps of fog drifting off the river behind the track there was first the cadenced hoof beats and then the horse's rhythmic, even breathing. Finally, like an obsidian ghost appearing through a veil, the great black horse materialized and raced ahead, his gait so smooth he seemed to barely touch the earth with each massive stride.

She rode as if she was part of him, their motion fluid, his black mane streaming past her face in the wind to whip against her jockey helmet. He appeared and blew past in a matter of seconds and then disappeared again into the mist where the track curved into the distance. For a moment there was again his breathing and hoof beats, until these too faded into the half light and it was as if the sleek ebony spirit flying down the track had never been.

Flagstaff, Arizona

The sweet sad strains of 'This is where the cowboy rides away' came on over the PA system as the lights started to come back on in the grandstands. Slade Marsh and Rossen Rockland listened from behind the bucking chutes where they were packing the last of Slade's bull riding gear. The rodeo was over and the last of the fireworks had faded from the night sky leaving only the sulfurous smell and the mess the local youth groups would clean up first thing Monday morning.

It was the last night of this rodeo and for both of them it had been a profitable weekend. Together they'd taken first place in the team roping, and Slade had also been in the money bulldoggin' and riding bulls. It had been a good rodeo but now Slade was tired.

He zipped the duffle bag closed and stood up, stretching tired muscles. There was dust on his jeans from where he'd landed in the arena dirt after his ride, and his black cowboy hat would never be the same after being stepped on by a nineteen hundred pound Brahma bull. At least the bull had only gotten the hat. He'd been aiming for Slade.

They stopped to untie their horses from the outer rail and headed back across the rodeo grounds toward the trailer that was home to them on this rodeo circuit. Leather reins in hand, they paused when they realized a street dance was starting up in the area directly ahead of them. Giant speakers that had been set up on the lawn chose that moment to emit a series of crackling static and then throbbing country music. Their horses were veterans of enough rodeos that all they did was twitch an ear and wait to see what the two cowboys would ask them to do.

"We're old, Rossen," Slade stated it matter-of-factly. Rossen simply turned to look at him with one eyebrow quirked as Slade went on, "We are. Just look at us. Saturday night, good music, beautiful girls under the stars. And what are we doing? Trying to figure out a way to get past this crowd without being seen so we can go home, put on some liniment and go to bed. It's true. We're old."

Rossen grinned. "You may be old at twenty-seven but I'm still only a whippersnapper at twenty-six. I'm in my prime."

Slade had to work not to limp. "My backside hurts. Actually, most everything I own hurts. I gotta quit riding bulls."

"Better your backside than your head." Rossen laughed and added, "Backsides are optional, heads aren't. Although Jesse probably wouldn't agree. You're

3

right. You'd better quit riding bulls."

Slade groaned and said, "Jesse. Now you can see why we're avoiding the dance. It'll be a meat market. Let's try going through the south parking lot and cutting through the warm-up arena."

As they trudged across the lot, Rossen said, "Someday, Marsh, we're gonna meet some girls we actually look forward to being with."

"I just hope we're not too old to enjoy them."

Rossen chuckled. "Hey, we enjoy girls. Sometimes they make us laugh."

Slade answered in a voice devoid of energy. "Sometimes they just make us tired."

"Sheesh, you're negative. I have half a mind to drag you back to that dance just to perk you up." They skirted a row of cars waiting to exit the parking lot, their horse's feet clip-clopping on the pavement.

Shaking his head, Slade said, "Can't dance tonight, I smell like a cow pie."

Rossen let out a laugh. "I gotta teach you to be more selective on your landings."

"How 'bout if you just teach me to stay on until I can jump down nice and easy?"

"How 'bout if I just teach you to stay off the bucking stock?"

They reached their trailer next to the row of stalls where they kept their horses, then tied them up to start stripping their saddles and bridles. After brushing them down and getting them settled for the night, the men headed back to the big six horse trailer with living quarters.

Rossen went in to see about scrounging up a late dinner while Slade loaded their gear into the tack storage, then settled his tall frame on the trailer step to take off his spurs. Rossen's head appeared inside the screen door. "Nuked pizza okay?"

Slade sighed. "After I learn to dismount bulls, I'm gonna learn to cook." He leaned back on his elbows with a soft groan.

 Rossen stepped past Slade and folded his 6'2" length into an old lounge chair. "Might be quicker to learn to like frozen pizza."

They sat in the dark in companionable silence until the bell dinged on the microwave. Slade went in and came out with two plates and two bottled waters. Handing one of each to Rossen, he sat back down on the step and tentatively started on his pizza.

They were quietly eating when they were approached by a pretty brunette in a low-cut, cropped tank top stretched dangerously tight over her well-endowed chest, and with tight, low-rise jeans, and cowboy boots.

Walking up, she said, "There you two are! I've been looking for you at the dance." She turned to Slade. "You said you were going to come swing dance with me. We talked about it this afternoon, didn't we? I thought we had plans."

Her voice had just enough whine to grate on Slade's nerves. Trying for patience, he looked up at her and replied, "I'm sorry. I didn't realize you thought that. I'm not much of a dancer anymore. Two left feet I guess."

Putting both hands on her hips, she said, "I know that's not true. I've seen you dance. Come on! There's still plenty of time." She took both of his hands and tried to pull him up off the step, nearly dumping his plate. "It'll be fun!"

"I don't think so, Jesse. Not tonight. I'm exhausted. In fact, if you two will excuse me, I'll go have a shower, wash the arena dirt out of my hair and hit the hay." He stood up, stepped into the trailer and firmly shut the door behind him.

From inside the trailer he heard the whiny tone again. "Oh, now why does he always do that? He's such a party pooper! Hey! What about you, Rossen? You can come dancing with me!"

"Naw, I'm right behind him. Some other time, maybe. By the way, you rode great tonight. It's too bad you knocked that third barrel down. You'd have been in the money." A second later Rossen followed Slade into the trailer, saying over his shoulder, "Night, Jesse."

Slade peeled off his shirt and kicked out of his boots on the way to the shower. In the tiny bathroom he ruefully examined a skinned mark on his shoulder where the bull's hoof had barely missed him as it stomped on his Stetson. That was way too close for comfort. He'd just about decided that after the National Finals Rodeo this year, he'd quit the bulls for good.

He studied his image in the mirror. Dark, almost curly hair, probably a little too long, and just now dusty.

A hint of five o'clock shadow below brilliant green eyes with a trace of fine lines around them. Smile lines? Or just too many years and too much sun?

Sometimes he wondered why he was still out here. Wasn't this the exciting life? Danger and adrenaline? Action? The roar of the crowd? He looked at the man in the mirror. Something was missing. He was still out here searching for something. He just wasn't sure what.

He showered and put liniment on the sore spots he could reach and went to bed. Maybe tomorrow he could find some enthusiasm.

He took a big breath and let it out in a sigh as Rossen spoke out of the darkness, "How can she even breathe in that shirt?" That little hint of humor somehow made Slade feel better.

When Slade woke up, he couldn't remember what he'd been dreaming about, but he felt strangely at peace. For whatever reason, last night's unrest was gone and he felt that everything was all right. Maybe his life was going in an okay direction after all.

Rossen was already up and loading the trailer to get on the road to the next rodeo. They had two days to drive eight-hundred miles and get their horses settled in to rest. They'd checked and fueled the truck the day before so all that was left to do was secure everything for the trip and load the horses. Then they had to find fast food again for breakfast.

As Slade bit into another rubber breakfast

sandwich as they traveled, he grimaced. "This diet is going to kill us long before the bucking stock. What do you 'spose these eggs are made of?"

Rossen glanced across the truck and said mildly, "It's probably best not to ask those deep philosophical questions while you're driving." He pulled out his cell phone and started to retrieve his messages, giving Slade an abbreviated play-by-play between bites.

"My mom says hi, and she loves us.

"Joey has a girl she wants me to meet.

"Ruger says Fancy foaled. He says the baby is ugly and has crooked legs, and that he wants to buy it immediately. I'll just bet it's ugly!

"The rodeo secretary in Laramie says we missed the deadline for the draw but since it's us, she'll let us register late if we do it today. What a sweetie. I think she likes you."

Rossen paused and made a disgusted sound. "Dang! How did Angelique get this number?

"And the saddle shop in Evanston has my saddle repaired." He snapped his phone closed. "I wonder who gave Angelique this number?!"

Slade raised a hand defensively. "Don't look at me! You're on your own as far as trashy women go. I've got problems of my own."

Rossen opened his phone again and pulled up a number. "Ruger, its Rossen. What'd we get?" Slade could only hear Rossen's half of the conversation, but it sounded like Rossen's mare had had a dandy baby. Rossen ended that call and then phoned the rodeo office

8

in Laramie to arrange their entries. He and the rodeo secretary talked back and forth and then Rossen pulled the phone away from his ear and asked, "Marsh, bulls or broncs? And are you gonna bulldog?"

At Slade's nod with three raised fingers, he returned the phone to his ear. "He'll ride saddle bronc, bulls, and bulldog. For Thursday and Friday . . . no, make that Friday and Saturday. We won't be pulling in 'til late Thursday and we're getting too old for those photo finishes. Our horses hate us when we come peeling in, unload and rush straight into the arena. Great. Thanks."

He put his phone away and mused, "We need a secretary. We need a cook. We need a gopher. Maybe we shoulda let Joey come with us when she offered."

Across the truck Slade shook his head. "Your sister is a killer mechanic, but I remember her salty Jell-O. And even Joey couldn't get a handle on our schedules."

Rossen laughed. "No. No one could actually do that. But she is a pretty dang good bowler."

Slade smiled and shook his head again. "I'll try to keep that in mind for the next time I need a dang good bowler." He rubbed the back of his neck. "What we really need is a masseuse." He leaned forward and flexed his back.

Smiling, Rossen teased, "Hey, that little redhead in Cheyenne offered. As I remember, you turned her down flat. In fact, I think you actually blushed! I didn't think it was possible!"

Slade looked a little embarrassed and said mildly, "Yeah, well that's not all she offered. She'd had way, way too much to drink, and I think she was like that song about how tequila makes her clothes fall off. And she didn't have enough on to start with."

Rossen waved a hand. "She wouldn't have been a good masseuse anyway. Too skinny. I like all my masseuses to be large and Svedish, with those nice sweet roll on-each-ear hairdos like Princess Leia."

Slade chuckled. "Okay, so all we have to do is find a nice large Swedish girl wearing sweet rolls on her head, who's a massage therapist, an organizational whiz, a gopher, and a chef, who would be willing to travel around the country and live in a trailer with two men she doesn't know and four horses. Right. I'll get right on that."

Chapter 2

As Carrie pounded past Eli and his son Dante leaning on the rail in the predawn light, she could almost sense Eli punching the stop watch. Even though the great stallion had long since retired from racing, there was still something almost mythical about his amazing speed. She let him run for the pure love of it and let her mind and body simply be in the moment. She could never have explained this feeling. The horse and the wind and the mist. The way her body blended with the rhythm and motion, the magic of the half night, half day. She could even smell it. A potion of the river bottom, the mist, and the track. The ultimate cadence. Here and now there was just her, the horse, and the wind.

At length, Ebony slowed of his own volition. They jogged the track one more time, and then she walked him to cool him down. As she rode back toward the paddock, the sun slipped over the hills to the east and a new day had come.

Her mornings started the same every day. This magical time on the track with no troubles or cares was a renewal that recharged her spirit. She could face anything afterward with a full heart and a happy attitude.

She handed the still-sweating horse over to Eli at the rail, glancing around as she did so to see if Geoffrey Goulet was around. The son of one of her grandfather's friends, Geoffrey was actually very smart—just hopelessly self-centered. He was madly in love with her, and hung around the farm in hopes of having the opportunity to propose for the nine hundredth time. He was a nice guy, except for the fact that he was totally and ridiculously spoiled which made him a complete nincompoop. Dante actually referred to him as "Stupid Geoffrey," which wasn't very nice, but it did fit.

Grateful that Geoffrey was nowhere in sight, she mentally began to go over her day. With her college semester just ended she'd be able to catch up on a few things. Walking toward her house to start breakfast, she unbuckled her helmet and let her hair cascade down her back. Life was good and she loved living it.

Even with Judd around, life was good. Brushing off her riding boots on the scrubber mat on the sun porch, she glanced around to make sure there was no sign of him. What was she going to do about Judd? He'd always been hard to deal with, but lately things had gotten so bad that she knew something had to be done about him. Worst of all, he'd begun to hang around with some people at the track who were

12

rumored to be involved with organized crime. It brought an element of lawlessness to her very home that was incredibly troubling.

Thank goodness Judd hated mornings and was afraid of horses, especially Ebony Wind. Carrie thought to herself that it was wise for Judd to fear the great stallion. For some reason, the typically gentle beast hated Judd with a passion that scared even Carrie. He seemed a different animal whenever Judd ventured near, which was rare, thankfully. Carrie had seen outlaw horses before--those rare crazed individuals that seemed to have a blood lust. Ebony had acted just like that several times toward Judd. It was as if the animal could sense his meanness.

Carrie had been taught by her grandfather not to hate and she was by nature kind and gentle, but she continually struggled to deal with Judd. She used to hate him. At least she'd gotten over that.

Judd was her father, biologically, although she never considered him that. He had always been abusive. Carrie's earliest memories were of his raging tempers that would leave her mother bruised and battered. Carrie had no doubt her mother had died a young and broken woman because of Judd. She'd passed away six months ago when Carrie had just turned twenty.

For years, her grandfather had put up with Judd as well as possible because he was always threatening to take Carrie and her mother and leave. Everyone knew what would happen to them if he ever did, so the whole farm dealt with Judd for their sakes.

She'd never loved Judd—never even liked him and had changed her name the moment she'd turned eighteen and could legally do so without his permission. She'd taken her Grandfather O'Rourke's last name because she did love him with all her heart.

Thinking of her grandfather brought tears to her eyes. It had been two months since a training accident had taken him. His death so shortly after her mother's had hit hard, and the pain didn't seem to be lessening much. His absence was still heartbreaking. Wind Dance Farms would never be the same. Sometimes she felt guilty for missing him so much more than she missed her mother, who'd quit living long before her death. But her mother had become so removed from everything around her and her grandfather had been involved with everything.

She missed everything about her grandfather, his gentle spirit, his unbending character, his sense of humor, and his wisdom. How she desperately needed his wisdom in her life.

Eli, half owner and head trainer, was wise. He had the humility acquired from growing up a poor black farm boy, tempered with the strength that had brought him to pursue his dreams of the race track. He'd worked his way from stable boy to become the most trusted and competent right hand of the legendary Hugh O'Rourke, and with Hugh's death, Eli had become half owner. He seemed far more a father to Carrie than Judd had ever been.

Eli was wise, but he would never recommend she leave her home. More and more lately she believed that was what she should do. Because her mother never divorced Judd, the small house they had lived in became Judd's at the time of her death. It was right smack in the middle of the farm and so close to the main house it was practically attached. Her grandfather had tried to buy it back from Judd, but he'd refused. So, until something changed, they were stuck with him.

When Carrie's grandfather passed away, he'd left very clear and concise instructions concerning his estate. Carrie was to get the most valuable stallion, Ebony Wind, who'd won the Preakness and the Belmont a few years ago, as well as several other key races, and then had retired to become an incredibly successful racing sire. He was extremely valuable and was insured for $8,000,000. The other horses and the farm were to be left in equal shares to Carrie and Eli Johnson, with Eli calling all the shots until Carrie was twenty-one unless Carrie was married before that. In the event that Carrie married earlier, she and Eli would manage the farm as partners.

For that matter, Eli already had Carrie helping run the farm as partners and she knew he was very, very good. She would never have questioned his management.

Her grandfather had strictly stipulated in his will that under no circumstance was Denzel Judd to ever have ownership of any part of his estate, other than the small home. Everyone had assumed this clause would put an end to Judd's scheming--until his distant nephew Deek arrived.

Pausing on her porch, Carrie sighed and shook her head. Something had to be done, but food first. She was starving and Dante would be ravenous as usual.

Pushing Judd, his friends, and his alarming behavior out of her mind, she hustled around the kitchen preparing breakfast. Other than the racehorses, cooking was her next great passion and over the years she had come to truly believe that good, healthy food could solve most any problem. It brought people together and strengthened relationships. It brought good will, health and happiness. Her philosophy was, you have to eat, so it might as well be one of life's great pleasures.

As she was setting out dishes, she was gently picked up in a bear hug from behind and swung around in a circle in the dining room. Automatically, she said, "Dante, put me down. For a second I thought you were Geoffrey. I have to finish getting breakfast."

She squirmed in his arms and he put her down and followed her back to the kitchen where he snatched a piece of bacon and said mildly, "Haven't seen Stupid Geoffrey yet today and he couldn't lift you anyway." He chuckled as she absent-mindedly handed him glasses. Finishing his bite, he said, "You ever gonna tell that poor boy you'll marry him so he'll go away and leave us alone?"

"It would never work," she answered drily, "He'd just move in here. Don't you want me to marry

16

someone with a brain?"

Dante picked up napkins and condiments and switched gears. "That stallion is still as fast as our most promising colts. Do you know that?"

"I was the one riding him, remember? Of course I know he's fast." She reached around him to pick up the silverware. "So . . . who was the pretty girl in the little black sports car last night?" She looked up into his face with a teasing grin. "It's about time you settled down with one of the girls who are in love with you, isn't it? You need to hurry! I'm waiting patiently for nieces and nephews." He followed her back into the kitchen for the rest of their breakfast.

"There were two pretty girls in little black sports cars last night. Which one are you talking about? The movie star or the super model?" Teasing back, he took another piece of bacon and she swatted at his hand.

"Dante, I swear! Were there really two girls?"

"No, I was kidding. There was only one girl. She likes me. Dad said not to wait for him." He swiped a third piece of bacon.

"Of course she likes you. You're adorable! Now sit down and use your plate. I want to hear all about her. I've seen her a couple of times now and I need details!"

Between bites, Dante told her about his new girl. They teased back and forth until finally Dante pushed his plate back and folded his arms across his brawny chest and said, "Okay, out with it."

"Out with what?"

"Don't even go there. I know you better than anyone on the planet. What's got your pretty little mind so wound up this morning? You obviously didn't sleep well. You were out on the track even earlier than usual, which is ridiculously early anyway. You keep glancing over your shoulder like you expect ghosts. What's going on?"

"How do you know I didn't sleep well?" She continued picking at her food.

"Easy. You look like heck." Dante was grinning when she looked up. "So why didn't you sleep well?"

She sighed. "Judd's up to something and you know it can't be good. This distant nephew or whatever of his is here a lot. I didn't think much of it at first, except to notice that he's as scummy as the rest of that crowd, but Judd has apparently decided I should marry him. In fact, now I wonder if that isn't why he came in the first place."

She shuddered involuntarily. "The whole idea is revolting! Not only is he disgusting, but if he really is related to Judd, then unfortunately he's related to me somewhere. It's like incest or something as well."

Shaking her head, she continued, "I knew Judd was being too low key. I've wondered if something has been going on for a while. I overheard him on his cell phone the other morning talking to someone about confirming when they were bringing their mare over. Since when does Judd give a hoot about a horse?

"And then the other night there were cars coming and going in the middle of the night, and there was a

18

whispered conversation about knocking someone or something off. Honestly, Dante, I wondered if they were talking about killing someone! I know that sounds ridiculous, but it's true! Imagine hearing something like that from your own bedroom window!" She got up and started to clear away the breakfast to take it to the kitchen, then admitted more softly, "His latest friends really scare me."

She continued almost tiredly as they cleaned up, "We have to do something. I know we do, but I don't know what, or how to do it. I actually called the police yesterday to see about getting a restraining order. They said I had to prove he was an immediate threat before they would get involved." She put a syrup pitcher on the counter, slopping syrup over the side and turned to him. "What in the world are all the calls we've made over the years about him, if they aren't proof that he's dangerous?"

At this point Eli poked his head into the kitchen door. "Is it safe to come in here in search of a bite to eat?"

She smiled. "Come on in, Eli. We're just putting breakfast away while we're talking. Your plate is right there beside the microwave."

Advancing into the room, he said, "I couldn't help but hear part of your conversation. I've been meaning to sit down and talk to you about some things as well, but I think we should be more discreet."

Carrie realized he was right. They should have been talking somewhere more private. If Judd heard them, he'd raise a fit. They went into the dining room and shut the door and talked while Eli ate. The consensus was that Judd was definitely up to no good and his friends were dangerous. He needed to go, but none of them were sure how to accomplish his removal. Maybe they could offer to buy his house back again and this time he'd accept. They decided to think about things, and Eli would check with their attorney and meet back together that evening.

Judd had been much better to her when her grandfather was alive. He knew he had a cushy lifestyle here on the farm and rarely did anything to endanger that. Carrie also believed he knew her grandfather would never have allowed Judd to treat her the way he'd treated her mother.

Her mother had never done anything to stop Judd. She had had some twisted sense of responsibility about having to live with the bad decisions she'd made, namely marrying Judd. She'd refused to leave him or even press charges, and neither Grandpa nor Carrie could seem to help her change. They'd gone to the police numerous times, but her mother would never cooperate to have Judd punished and the legal system hadn't been too eager to force her. Finally, Carrie and her grandfather had quit trying because the bigger deal they made of it, the meaner Judd got.

However, her grandfather would never have stood for Judd abusing Carrie on his farm and Judd had known it. For years it had been a sort of tenuous truce where Grandpa let Judd live in the home he had given

20

to Carrie's mother with no responsibilities, and Judd let Grandpa and Eli raise and care for Carrie as they saw fit.

Carrie had spent most of her time out of the little home. One day, when she was twelve, after a particularly nasty tirade, she'd quietly moved into her grandfather's home and seldom went back to the little house, except to visit her mother. Over the years they'd learned to stay out of Judd's way, and toward the end of her mother's life they'd moved her over too.

Carrie was sure Grandpa and Eli were glad Judd had an aversion to the horse part of the farm. Had he ever tried to help with the raising and training, it would've been a fiasco. Judd had a raging temper with an incredibly short fuse and was hopelessly impatient. Animals and people alike steered clear of him as much as possible.

That suited Judd. All he wanted to do was drink, gamble, and stay out until all hours with his degenerate friends. Carrie had no idea where he'd gotten the money to gamble all those years, and she was sure she didn't want to know. Lately however, she believed he'd become a compulsive gambler, and apparently his source of funds couldn't keep up with his habit.

Since the death of her grandfather, he'd become increasingly more demanding and threatening, and Carrie knew something had to be done. Several times lately Judd had approached her as she crossed between her home and the farm buildings, or when she was coming or going. She always tried to be polite to him and most times they could be civil, but yesterday when he'd tried to tell her whom she should marry, she'd told him exactly what she thought. Things had gotten ugly fast.

Lately she felt more afraid, especially in her own home. Grandpa was gone and Eli lived in his own house with Dante, and while Carrie's home was securely lockable, she'd seriously considered starting to carry the pistol Grandpa had given her. Her grandfather had been a gun collector and had been proud of her prowess with the little gun. With Judd's house being so close to hers, and with his kind of friends, carrying it was starting to make more and more sense.

As they were leaving, Carrie heard Eli whisper, "Why does she look so hammered?"

When Eli and Dante headed back out the door toward the horses, Carrie went in and sat with her laptop at the kitchen desk to start checking emails and feed delivery schedules, as well as handling some registration business.

An hour later, the housekeeper had arrived, put away Carrie's dry cleaning, and was washing windows in the front entry. Carrie was still sitting at the computer when she heard Judd snarl something at the housekeeper as he walked into the kitchen. Carried looked up, panicked as he stalked in. It was obvious Judd had had a wilder than usual night.

She took a deep breath, striving to stay calm and not let her voice shake as she said evenly, "Judd, you can't just walk into my kitchen uninvited. Get out. Now. Before I call Eli and Dante."

He roared in anger and she winced as he swept everything on the countertop within his reach to the floor and roared again, "No! If every hand on this farm can walk into your kitchen, then your father ought to be able to!" If he hadn't been raging he would have sounded like a spoiled child as he continued to bellow, "You're going to wait on me at least as much as you wait on those stable boys out there. You treat them like they own the place and try to pretend like I don't exist." He glared around the kitchen looking for something else to shatter. Unfortunately, everything breakable was already in pieces on the tile floor.

Carrie continued to try to stay calm. "Some of them do own the place. And I have no intention of serving you. Get out. Now." She started to shut down the computer so she could get away from him, but it was still powering off when he started in again.

"No! YOU own this place and you need to act like it! And you'll start to show me some respect or I'll beat some into you! It's time you realize I *will* have some say around here!" He raised his voice even more. "What? Do you think you can just pretend I'm not here and I'll go away? There are going to be some changes around here, or you'll figure out that you shouldn't have trifled with Denzel Judd! I have people who would have no problem taking out a stable boy or two! I have ways of taking some control, if I have to. You'd be much better off just agreeing to marry Deek and going along with the plan. Not nearly as many people have to get hurt that way!"

Without realizing it, she had backed away from him until she was now up against the wall. She wasn't even sure what other horrible things he said to her as he continued to snarl in her face. She just knew that his threats were horrible and went on and on.

He abruptly broke off his tirade when suddenly there were several riders and hands in the kitchen doorway. They must have heard him clear from the barns. Each of them carried a pitchfork or shovel and wore a grim expression. Judd pushed past them and out the door and then a minute or two later Eli shoved his way through. He went to Carrie and put an arm around her shoulders and was starting to ask if she was okay, when she turned to the kitchen sink and was violently ill.

She'd tried to stay calm. When Judd had treated her mother like that, Carrie had learned things seemed to go better if her mother stayed calm. But the things he'd threatened! He'd actually threatened to kill those who lived on the farm if Carrie didn't do as he demanded! Eli and Dante--even the hands were at risk!

Eli wrapped his huge arms around her and she let herself turn her face to his chest and cry. She'd known things were bad, but she hadn't realized they were this bad! She didn't know how things had gotten to this point and she didn't know how to fix it. How grateful she was for Eli and Dante! How many times had they saved her like this? For years it was only Carrie or her mother Judd had threatened, but now he was threatening them all.

Finally, she raised her head and blew her nose on the tissue Eli handed her. Dante had come in and all the rest of the hands had left them alone. Sniffling, she shook her head. "I have to go, Eli. That's what this is all about. He thinks he's going to force me to marry Deek and he'll gain control of the farm."

At the mention of her leaving, Eli began shaking his own head and said with that soft drawl, "No one can make someone marry." He put his arm around her again and assured her over and over that this was her home and that she wasn't going anywhere.

He was right that Judd couldn't get away with it, but what would they all have to go through while he tried? These people had begun to seem like monsters. Eli didn't understand like she did. Judd would never just give in. And now with his friends . . . things were escalating.

Earnestly she tried to make him believe her. "Eli, listen to me. I either need to leave now, or I'm going to put the whole farm in your name and hope and pray that that's the end of it." But she didn't really believe it would be.

Eli quietly looked into her face and gently said, "Your grandfather wanted this farm to be in both our names. He died trusting it would be that way, and that's the way it will stay. They wouldn't let us take it out of your name legally anyway. Come. Dry your tears and we'll figure something out. The Good Lord is in His heaven, and He *is* in control. Remember His promise in Isaiah, 'And I will extend peace to her like a river.' Have faith. He will send His peace like a river. Somehow, some way, or maybe someone. With God's help we will be free of your father."

The tears started again. "Oh, Eli, you silly." She sniffled. "Judd's not my father. He never was and never will be. He's just some jerk who took advantage of an innocent and foolish girl. You're my father. You always have been. Don't you know that by now? I love you." She smiled through her tears and kissed his leathery black cheek.

He'd long used that particular scripture to encourage her to not give up hope on someday having a peaceful home without the anger and violence of Judd. She hugged him again and pushed him away. "Go. Get back to the barns. I'll clean up this mess, and then I'll come out to your office and work until lunch." She turned to Dante. "Maybe you could come and help me get lunch today. I don't really want to be in here cooking alone in case he comes back."

Nodding thoughtfully, Dante said, "Actually, I think I'll help you clean up and walk over to the office with you."

At first they were quiet as they swept up the glass and garbage, but she finally looked up into his eyes and asked, "You know I'm right, don't you?"

Their eyes held for a silent moment and then he admitted, "Yes, you should go somewhere safe for awhile. I just don't know how or where." Sometimes he was a tease, but she adored this tall, sweet man. They had grown up side by side here on the farm. He was six years older, but they were as close as any brother and sister could be. He continued, "Although, Dad's right. God is in control, and He'll provide an answer. Just keep praying. We'll find your river of peace."

Later that evening, Carrie could feel the results of her last restless night and earlier than usual morning. She was tired to the bone when she finally had all the loose ends tied up and headed for home. Thinking she was safely inside her house, her heart nearly surged out of her chest when someone spoke to her out of the shadows in her dimly lit hall.

It was Deek and she could smell the alcohol on his breath as he said, "Hey, Baby." His eyes were leering as he blatantly looked her up and down.

Backing from him, she asked, "What do you want?" She hoped she sounded more confident than she felt.

"Oh, I think you know exactly what I want." He reached out to touch her long blonde hair and she instinctively pulled away. Anger flickered in his eyes and he grabbed a handful of her hair and jerked her toward him.

She slapped him and he swore viciously as he yanked harder on her hair and twisted her arm up behind her back and snarled, "Now that ain't no way to treat your future husband, is it? I came here tonight so we could get to know each other a little. And you acting like this don't help promote romance." His breath in her face made her ill.

In fury, she ground out, "Let go of me and get out of here, before I call Eli and Dante!"

Through clenched teeth, he said, "You just call all you want, darlin'. There's not a soul except Judd to hear you, and I think you know he would love this!" He pushed her away and his voice became almost silky. "Don't you fret. Our time will come soon enough. I'm definitely looking forward to it." With another revolting grin, he turned away. "I have more important things to see to tonight unfortunately, but yes, I'm definitely looking forward to the future."

Carrie stepped into her suite, slammed the door and locked it behind her. For a moment she leaned her back against the door to catch her breath, and then rushed to make sure the windows were all shut and locked. She picked up her cell phone, speed dialed Eli and after a short explanation hung up with him and called the police.

Two and a half hours later, after having been politely told by the police that they would try to find Deek and question him, and since Judd hadn't been involved they couldn't charge him, Carrie shut the door behind them, discouraged to tears. The police didn't even seem to think there was a problem.

Eli had called a locksmith who had come and changed the locks in case they had a key to her house. Other than that, for the time being, they weren't sure what else to do except have Eli and Dante stay at her house for the night.

The farm had a security company and there was a night watchman who would keep an extra close watch on her house as well. More tired than ever, she told Eli and Dante goodnight and once again headed for her room.

She dug into the top of her closet and pulled out the slim black gun case her grandfather had given her. Removing the tiny pistol, she checked the loads, then carried it in to her bathroom, locked that door too, and slipped out of her clothing to shower. Deek had made her feel filthy.

As the steaming water pounded her tired body, she thought about the long talk she'd had with her dear friend Anna this afternoon. With lunch over, she'd gone to run a few errands and stopped in to see her childhood playmate and they'd reminisced.

She and Anna had been friends as long as she could remember. They'd spent a hundred afternoons playing dress up and pretending to be damsels in distress, waiting for their knights in shining armor. What Carrie wouldn't give for a knight to rescue her just now.

With a wry smile to herself, she remembered trying to talk Dante into being a knight, but he would have none of it. Shutting off the water, she began to towel dry as she whispered, "O Lady Lillian, where did I ever lose Princess Isabel?"

Dressed in a silky night shirt, she knelt beside her bed to fervently ask again for help in her life. "Please, God, help me find a way to keep us all safe and put an end to this." After she finished praying, she felt a warm peace seep into her heart as she climbed into bed and tried to let her tired body rest.

Forty minutes later, she felt on the bedside table for the third time to make sure her gun was still there beside her Bible. Weary as she was, sleep wouldn't come. Even with her comforting prayer, she was unable to rest. Turning on her side, she thought back to the counsel Dante had given her to 'just keep praying.'

It was her mother who'd taught her to pray. It was the one good thing that had happened to her mother when she ran away to find excitement as a rebellious young girl. When her days had been darkest, after she realized what a mistake she'd made in marrying Judd only to find she was pregnant and had also involved a baby, she'd met some young women missionaries. She'd only begun to learn about Christ's true church when Judd had become furiously angry and had forbidden her from ever seeing the two young missionaries again. They moved and she'd never been able to learn more. Later what little she'd learned she had told Carrie she knew in her heart to be true. She'd done her best to teach her small daughter all she could remember.

At first when Carrie's parents had come back to live at the horse farm, her grandfather had questioned the religion, but Eli had encouraged it and that was enough to make Hugh approve.

Through the years Carrie had often wondered about the two young missionaries. What had ever
30

become of them? She didn't even know which church the young women represented. She did know she was grateful for the beliefs her mother had taught her. They'd helped her to get through the toughest times of her life. Still wondering about the church she wished she could find out more about, she finally fell asleep.

Deep in the night, she was awakened again and was immensely grateful for Eli and Dante's presence in her house. She could hear voices coming from the back yard and crept to her window in the dark to find out what was going on. There were two men she didn't recognize, as well as Judd and Deek, having a quiet, but heated, conversation on the drive. Carefully, she silently cracked her window open and listened.

She could distinguish a word here and there, but had no idea what was going on until she very clearly heard one of the strangers threaten Judd, saying, "Come up with the boss's money or we'll have to do what he sent us to do." Judd actually seemed to be afraid of them and hurriedly assured them he'd have the money soon.

The stranger threatened further, "You'd better. If you don't have it soon, we're just going to nab the horse. You know we'd get as much ransom money for that big black as if it were a kid. You get this estate thing settled or we'll be back. Once we physically have her, Tony can have the attorneys do whatever they need to do to contest the old black man's claim to half, and then have her deemed permanently incompetent. The boss has a place just for people we need to keep around, but want out of the way." The two men laughed and climbed into a dark sedan and drove into the night.

Judd and Deek began to argue viciously and walked around the corner of the house in the dark. Minutes later Carrie heard another vehicle start up and drive away.

She closed her window and sat down on the edge of her bed. It was almost 4:00 in the morning, but there was no way she would get back to sleep again on this night. She put on a robe and sat in her chair in the dark, trying to come up with something, anything, that would end this nightmare.

The whole idea that someone could grab her, and physically force her to marry someone she didn't want to marry, then take control of her assets sounded ridiculous, until she came into contact with people like this. Whether they could make it stick legally when all was said and done wasn't nearly as big a concern to her as the thought of what would happen to her in the meantime. Dealing with Judd on a day-to-day basis was awful enough without the thought of basically being kidnapped and held at his and his criminal friends' mercy until the legal system worked it all out. She wanted nothing to do with any of them, ever. And now, he was threatening others and her magnificent horse as well.

Even after mulling it over and over, she could think of nothing. She always came back to the fact that she needed to quietly disappear for a time, and ideally, she needed to have Ebony Wind disappear with her.

Finally, as it got to be time to get up and go exercise horses, she came back to what Eli had counseled yesterday. God is in His heaven. He was aware of her troubles and He would provide a way. She knelt and prayed for help and then slipped into her riding gear, picked up her helmet and headed for the stallion barn. This morning racing in the dawn wouldn't free her spirit.

Chapter 3

When Slade and Rossen walked into a diner in a small rural California town, they were hoping for nothing more than a mediocre bite to eat. They were both somewhat disgusted with the way the day had gone so far. They'd done well at the rodeo in Flagstaff a couple days before, but things had gone downhill from there.

Rossen's hazing horse had thrown a shoe and then come up sore. They'd run over something on the highway that had flattened one of their rear dual tires and then flipped up and damaged the trailer lights. Then, after pulling off into this small town to make repairs, the local policeman had ticketed them for not having working trailer lights.

There wasn't a thing they could do but hang around while the repairs were made. They parked the trailer in the shade and it was the cop who recommended they grab a bite to eat in the diner while they waited.

They were seated by a pretty, dark haired, young waitress with a ready smile and a contagious laugh.

There was no one else in the diner at this mid-afternoon hour, so she stopped to chat with them occasionally and she'd brightened Kenney's day considerably. He was also encouraged when their food came and he found it surprisingly good.

Also pleased, Rossen said, "Mmmm, maybe this day is going to turn out after all!" He took another bite and seemed to savor it. To the pretty waitress, he said, "Ma'am, would you marry me immediately and go rodeoing with us, so we can eat real food like this and not die of our own cooking?"

Her laugh brought out dimples. "I just serve it. Which is a good thing, 'cause I'm a terrible cook and then you really would be at risk of dying!" She laughed again as she worked around the tables near them refilling the salt and pepper shakers.

Rossen shook his head in mock disgust. "Aw, I knew it. We haven't found anyone yet willing to travel around the country with a trailer full of horses."

****

Pacing in the kitchen a few minutes later, Anna became absolutely thoughtful. She did usually wear a smile, but as she remembered more about the conversation she had had the afternoon before with her dear friend Carrie, her face became downright pensive. She thought about another conversation she'd overheard just that morning.

Carrie's father Judd had come into the diner with

a man who had to be the disgusting nephew and another of their frightening cohorts. They didn't know her, but she recognized Judd. They were so slippery they were slimy. How sweet, beautiful Carrie ever came of such a man Anna would never know.

They sat at a table near her section, and talked in low tones about horseracing and gambling. The nephew made a comment about how Eli and Carrie would never go along with their schemes. Then Judd himself had said something about how it didn't matter if they went along or not. Lowering his voice marginally, he had said that once they'd forced Carrie to marry, they would take over management of the farm and just keep Carrie out of the way.

The way they all laughed, made Anna wonder what in the world they meant for Carrie. Anna knew Carrie had feared for herself from the time she was little and now was wondering if even her stallion was being targeted.

By the time the men left the diner their conversation had made Anna's heart sink. Carrie had always had trouble with Judd and it had gotten so much worse lately. They all knew exactly what he was capable of after the way he'd treated Carrie's mother. Anna hadn't doubted his hatefulness, but she'd been hoping that Carrie had just been tired yesterday and things hadn't really gotten this bad. After hearing their conversation, she knew Carrie had been right.

But what if Carrie could find a way to disappear? Anna wiped a few more ketchup bottles, praying silently to herself to know if what she was thinking was a good idea then, sure of herself, she walked back over to the cowboys' table.

****

Slade and Rossen were quietly eating when the pretty waitress approached and soberly asked, "Are you serious?" Several minutes had passed since Rossen's teasing remark about marrying a cook and for a second they both just looked at her. Slade wondered what had happened to the cheerful waitress to make her look so earnest, and what she was asking.

Breaking a tentative smile, she repeated, "Are you serious about wishing you could find a cook who would be willing to travel with horses?" Slade was a little taken aback, especially when she sat right down at their table and he was sure Rossen was, too.

Skeptically, Slade said, "I thought you said you couldn't cook. Are you offering?" He was disappointed. He'd really thought this pretty, happy waitress didn't seem like that type of girl.

Back pedaling, she quickly said, "No, no, no! Not me! I'm actually thinking about a friend of mine. Were you serious?"

Rossen answered almost disgustedly, "Girlfriend, the only kind of woman who would go traipsing off across the country with two men she doesn't know, isn't interested in the kitchen."

"No." Hurriedly, the girl shook her head.

"You're wrong. My friend would go and she's not that kind of girl. I'm sure it would have to be strictly business or she wouldn't even consider it. She's a great cook, loves to travel, and recently finished her spring semester at UC Santa Barbara."

She seemed to be warming up and became more enthusiastic. "Just yesterday she was telling me how much she wanted to get away, but didn't want to leave her horse. This might work out perfectly!" Her brown eyes were shining as she stood looking from one cowboy to the other. After a minute of silence, while Rossen gave Slade a searching look, she pulled her cell phone out of her pocket. "Come on! At least meet her. If you don't like her, no harm done."

"How do you know we're not muggers or politicians or something?" Rossen broke the tension with a grin and a twinkle in his eye. "For that matter, how do we know she's not a mugger or politician or something?"

****

She turned to study the two cowboys at length. Slade knew exactly what she was seeing. Even with the crease in their hair from the hats that were resting on adjoining chairs, they were both good looking enough.

Slade was quieter, was tall and dark with slightly curly hair and heavy shoulders. He was clean-shaven and the brown hands that rested on the table in front of him were heavily calloused. His bright green eyes were steady as he returned her gaze.

Rossen was also tall. Blonde hair bleached by the sun and blue eyes framed with tiny smile lines looked back at her with the same steady gaze. She studied them for a moment, apparently weighing something in her mind.

It had to be obvious that they were a little skeptical where women were concerned. It always seemed that they'd had more than their fair share of females who would like to mug them. The waitress scrunched her lips to the side as if she were considering, as she said, "Hmm, I can see how you two might need some protection from questionable women." Her teasing smile was back. "You are kinda cute. We may have to blindfold her to ensure your safety!" With that she laughed and dialed her phone.

****

As Carrie went about her day, her heart waffled between a sense of urgency and an inner calm. When she tried to rack her brain for a solution, the worry would build, but then a scripture from 2nd Timothy would slip into her mind, 'For God hath not given us the spirit of fear, but of power and of love and of a sound mind.' With that thought she would remind herself that God was over all and she need not fear. A warm peace would flow into her heart, a 'river of peace' that she knew was from God. She knew He was there watching over her and aware of her troubles. If she could just trust in Him and lean not to her own understanding, she knew He would provide answers to her prayers.

In her heart she knew that, but it was hard not to worry about those around her and even for her own safety and for her grandfather's farm. It was hard to be calm and wait on God. A sense of urgency filled her heart in spite of the fact that she knew God was over all. In fact, she felt like this feeling of being compelled came from Him. She wanted to do something. She felt like she needed to do something. Now! Today! She just didn't know what.

She tried to think more clearly. Could she just pack her things and load up a trailer with Ebony and somehow sneak out without Judd or his cronies finding out? She would need to involve as few people as possible, but all of their trucks and trailers had the farm logo emblazoned across them. Usually that was a good thing but it wasn't very inconspicuous.

And where could she go? How could she hide that distinctive horse for any period of time? How would she find a place to stay and somewhere to board him where he wouldn't be recognized? The truck logos and his face marking would give them away immediately.

Maybe she could buy a new truck and trailer, but even if she paid cash, the people Judd was involved with would know exactly what she was driving all too soon. And if she did get safely away, where would it all end? If the thought of the police and the laws and courts hadn't deterred Judd alone, how could she stop him if

Jaclyn M. Hawkes

he was now working with organized crime?

She was struggling again to hold that peace in her heart when Anna called.

Carrie wasn't sure what Anna was up to. She'd sounded so excited on the phone and then she'd called her Isabel, the old damsel-in-distress name from their childhood games. She practically demanded that Carrie drop everything and come to her work immediately to meet someone. Carrie was sure she'd met all her cousins and Anna hadn't talked about a new guy when they'd spoken last night, so what was going on?

Carrie walked into the mostly empty diner and waited by the front counter for Anna to respond to the sound of the bell on the door. The only people in the place were two men in the back part of the dining room working on heaping pieces of pie. They'd both looked up as the bell sounded and seemed to be openly studying her. Their expressions weren't flirtatious or aggressive, just frankly curious, and she discreetly returned their scrutiny.

Tall and clean-shaven, they were wearing button down shirts. They were both strikingly handsome and had open honest faces, deeply tanned skin, and the blonde one's hair was bleached by the sun. Her subtle inspection was interrupted when Anna came breezing out of the kitchen with a tall soda and fairly skipped over to Carrie.

"Hey." Carrie turned toward her friend and automatically accepted her hug. "What's up? What did you need that couldn't wait? Who did you want me to

42

meet?"

Whispering, Anna asked, "Um, did you happen to notice the two men in the dining room?" Her brown eyes were absolutely flashing.

Carrie lowered her own voice. "They are a little hard to miss, frankly. Look at them. Why?"

Anna whispered back, "Well, it's a very long story, but it begins with this. They're professional rodeo cowboys who are possibly looking for someone to travel with them and cook." She spoke faster and her excitement was obvious. "Carrie, they go all over and take their horses! No one here knows them! You could get safely away without Judd or anyone knowing!"

Carrie looked at her sharply in concern. "Anna, are you nuts?"

Anna's eyes and voice became earnest. "Carrie, I know this is going to sound weird, but I don't think those two men in there are here by coincidence. I feel good about them. I think they're the answer to our prayers." Anna looked long into Carrie's eyes. "I don't really want to have to tell you this, but you need to know. Judd and his nephew, and whoever else, really are planning to do something drastic. They were in here this morning and I overheard some of their plans. You need to leave now! And you need to get Ebony Wind safely away too! Come and talk to these guys. See if you feel like it's a good idea. This might be the perfect solution!"

Carrie glanced over to the two men. "Do you even know them?"

"No, I just met them, but I do know Judd! Come talk to them. See what you think. I've been praying about it and have a peaceful feeling about it, and I'm so afraid for you to stay."

Carrie hardly had to consider. She had to do something. Telling herself she could always say no if she felt it was a bad idea, she straightened her shoulders and walked into the dining room.

She walked purposefully up to their table and they immediately stood up. She was just extending her hand to introduce herself, when Anna interrupted her by saying, "Isabel, I'd like you to meet my new friends." Carrie caught herself just in time. She almost turned to ask her friend if she'd lost her mind and couldn't remember her name, when she realized why Anna was calling her Isabel. Of course, she couldn't just continue to be Carrie O'Rourke if she went. So, with barely a glance at Anna, she became Isabel.

The blonde one took her hand firmly. "I'm Rossen Rockland, from Wyoming, and this is my good friend and roping partner, Slade Marsh. It's good to meet you." Both men looked her square in the eye as they in turn shook her hand with their deeply calloused ones.

She turned to the darker one. "And you are from?" He had the most amazing green eyes.

"Rossen and I are both from Wyoming. Southwest corner of the state, up in the mountains." His manner was absolutely direct.

"And what exactly are you looking for in this

44

traveling cook position?" She might as well get right to the point.

"That's a good question." He paused to look at his partner. "Honestly, although we would love to have some help, we really never thought this was even remotely a possibility until just a few minutes ago when we were talking to your friend.

"You need to know from the get go, we're on the road a lot. We do over 100 rodeos a year. And, although our trailer is nice, and has slide outs, it's a trailer. It can be cramped, and it's pretty much guaranteed to smell like a horse." He wasn't apologizing, just stating a fact.

"I'm aware that horses smell, Mr. Marsh. That's not a problem. What I really need to know is, what you would need me to do? I guess what I am asking is what do you need help with, and is there a firm guarantee this job would be kept on a professional level?"

She detected the slightest hint of amusement as he replied, "In other words, are we planning to behave ourselves?" At her almost imperceptible nod he continued, "Yes, you have our word." They continued to look into each other's eyes.

Rossen and Anna were looking from her to Slade, then glanced at each other and Rossen raised his brows and shrugged his shoulders. He whispered to Anna loud enough that Carrie could hear, "This is the first time I've ever known him to have a girl insist he keep his hands *off*." He grinned, and said right out loud, "Okay, we'll be good, but can you cook?"

This time Carrie smiled and repeated Slade's phrase. "Yes, you have my word." She put out her hand to Slade. "Shake?"

He was still eyeing her like he wasn't too sure. Rossen elbowed him, "Dude, shake her hand, her word is good. Let's get down to the nitty gritty." He turned to Carrie. "Okay Isabel, How much money and when can you start? And please say soon, because our trailer should be repaired by late this afternoon and the sooner we can leave the better. We have a rodeo up north day after tomorrow and need to be in Reno the next."

It was as simple as that. Anna left to seat some new people who had entered and Carrie sat down at the cowboys' table to hammer out the few things they needed. None of them really knew for sure what they had in mind yet. Slade and Rossen wanted real food and maybe some odds and ends errands. Carrie needed to "travel" and take a horse with her. They all seemed to feel good about it and they made arrangements to pick her up the next morning at sun up.

Twenty minutes later, Carrie stopped to hug Anna a moment on the way out the door. They didn't need to say much. Carrie found herself brushing a tear off her cheek. "Thank you. I love you. Please don't tell a soul. I'll be in touch." Almost out the door, she turned back and whispered, "Anna, what's my last name?"

Whispering back, Anna said, "You'll think of something! Enjoy this adventure! They're the answer to your prayers. I know they are. Good luck." With one more hug, Carrie went on out the door, hoping that she truly had found the solution to dealing with Judd.

****

As the first light crept over the hills the next morning, Carrie carefully covered Ebony Wind with a light sheet and hood, then took the tiny exercise saddle she'd ridden and stuffed it into the bulging duffle bag she'd lugged with her. It'd taken her over an hour to reach the rendezvous point. It was a good thing Ebony had mellowed with the years because he'd never had to carry anything other than a rider. She'd tried to pack light but she'd ended up with quite a bag.

After struggling to get it to the barn undetected, it had taken her several minutes to successfully get it and herself up onto his back at the same time. He'd never seemed quite so tall. In the dark she'd slipped out of the yards and into a pasture that would take her to the far side of the farm and a gravel lane miles from the main road. She hadn't wanted to take a chance on being seen.

She'd left notes for both Eli and Dante where she felt sure they would be the only ones to find them. All she'd said was that she felt she had to leave for the safety and good of all. She would be in touch and that Ebony was with her. She reasoned the fewer people who knew anything the better.

Her emotions were a riot of feelings ranging from sadness at leaving her friends, to excitement about this new adventure, to fear she was doing something amazingly stupid, to hope that she could finally feel safe, to a calm and a sense of tranquility. This was the right thing to do. She knew it. As weird as that sounded even to herself, she knew this was right.

Although the cowboys weren't on time, she never wondered if they would come. She had always had a knack for discerning people's character. From that first moment she'd met them in the diner, she'd known she could depend on them and had this feeling of peace.

When she finally saw a plume of dust far down the valley where she knew it had to be them, she breathed a deep sigh. Logically she should be feeling absolute trepidation about literally trusting her life and such a valuable horse to these two men she knew almost nothing about, but in reality she'd never felt such a sense of relief.

****

"I hope she doesn't think we're not coming. I didn't realize it would take so long to reach the place. The gravel road slowed us down." Rossen was watching for the turn off in the first light of day.

"She knows we're coming." Slade was confident he was right. "I think she realized immediately that we'll do what we say we'll do. I don't think she would have even considered coming with us for a moment if she didn't believe that."

Rossen mulled that over in silence, and then agreed, "Yeah. She looked clear into my soul those first few seconds after we met her." Spotting the turn, he pulled off the lane and up to the waiting girl and her

48

horse.

They smiled a greeting and then little was said as they loaded up the huge horse completely hidden by his sheet and hood. With the animals secured, Slade hefted her bag into the living quarters. *Holy Cow! What did she have in here?* Although he did have to admit that one bag, no matter how large, for a woman was not much. After wrestling it through the door, he glanced around wondering where her truck was or who had dropped her off. Why hadn't they hung around to say goodbye?

Seeming to read his mind, she said, "I came alone across the pasture." He held the door of the truck for her, now even more curious about how in the world she got that huge duffle here. She didn't even have a saddle.

Not much was said as they got on their way. Country music was playing quietly and a few minutes later Slade was amazed to glance in the rear view mirror and see that the girl was fast asleep. "Apparently she was tired." He nodded toward the back seat.

Rossen followed his gaze. "Apparently she's not too worried about you and me, either."

Slade studied her in her sleep. Her hair was pulled back into some kind of twist the same way it had been yesterday and she wore plain jeans and a simple stretch T-shirt. Her sandals had been replaced by deck shoes and she wore small, dangly earrings. There was no other jewelry he could see except an elegant watch and, in fact, she wasn't even carrying a purse. Her skin was clear and tanned and she didn't appear to be wearing any makeup. Not that she needed any. Though she was blonde, she had thick dark lashes that rested on her cheeks.

No fuss, no fanfare. She had to be the most unassuming girl he'd ever met. She couldn't possibly be as wash-and-wear as she seemed.

Rossen watched him watch Isabel. He didn't say anything, just gave a mellow smile when Slade glanced up at him.

****

It must have been hours later as they pulled to a stop for gas that Carrie, now Isabel, finally opened her eyes. Both men in the front seat were looking back at her.

"Short night?" Rossen asked the question.

She sat up and smoothed her hair a little. "Several in a row. I guess they caught up with me. I'm sorry." Someone had put a pillow under her head and covered her with a small blanket. "Thanks for letting me sleep." She stretched and looked at her watch. "Three o'clock! Is it really three o'clock?"

"It really is. We tried to wake you around noon, but you were pretty out. We're gonna gas up. Do you want to grab something to eat here?"

She groaned. "Oh, I'm sorry I didn't make you lunch. You probably think I'm a complete flake."

Slade only smiled placidly. "We've survived for awhile. One more day won't hurt. But you probably need to eat, don't you?"

"Yes, thank you. Food sounds wonderful. Can I eat in your truck or should I hurry before we leave?" She was fishing around under the seat for a shoe that had slipped off.

He quietly reached back into the wadded blanket and handed her the shoe. "You can eat in the truck."

Putting it on, she climbed out and said, "I'll hurry. Do either of you want anything?

They both shook their heads and Slade said, "No, we're fine thanks." One of them began to pump gas while the other washed the windshield, and she stopped to check on Ebony on her way into the station.

Five minutes later she was back with her food and asked, "Could someone unlock the trailer? I'd like to grab a notebook out of my bag to make some plans, if that's okay." Rossen reached into the pocket on the back of the driver's seat and handed her a small spiral bound pad.

"Will this do?"

"Perfect." She climbed back up into the rear seat of the cab and buckled in. She was just starting to eat a chicken salad as the truck pulled back onto the highway and she looked around. They were on I-5 in central California and had made good time pulling a loaded horse trailer. As she ate she studied the two men in front of her. She was slightly mystified with why she'd felt so comfortable with them so fast. Usually she was slow to trust and always she was careful to the point of standoffish around men she didn't know.

She'd learned from Judd that some men were to

be feared and although she'd learned from her grandfather and Eli and Dante that some men were gentle and could be trusted, it usually took her a long time to feel comfortable around new people. She loved the hands at the farm, but had quickly learned that most men were interested in her either because of her wealth or the way she looked.

It must have been that she had a sense of rightness with them because she knew when she'd prayed about doing this that she'd felt such a sweet inner river of peace. She knew it would work out—she just knew. Somehow she had an innate sense it would all be okay with these two. They inspired confidence and trust. Just like Anna, she knew they were the answer to prayer.

She finished her salad and picked up the notebook and asked, "Can I pick your brains? What do you like to eat?"

For the rest of the afternoon they talked and planned for how to best take advantage of having some help traveling with them and she planned menus.

They told her they tried to end each day where there were stalls available so the horses could rest from the trailer. This didn't always work, but for the most part it did. They would pull the trailer in and park near the horses for the night. In the past they'd existed largely on fast food and frozen entrees, but were hoping Isabel could find a way to prepare real food in their trailer kitchen between stops.

Isabel hadn't seen the inside of the living

quarters, but from their description she didn't think this would be difficult. When they stopped, she could cook while they tended to their horses, and when she needed groceries or they needed errands run, they would unhook the truck and give her money. She would try to have lunches ready so they could eat in the truck as they drove, and on days they were actually at a rodeo, they would adjust things as needed.

Once she felt somewhat comfortable with what her responsibilities would be, she leaned back into her seat and watched the scenery until her head began to bob. When it did, she unbuckled her seat belt and stretched out full length on the seat with her head on the pillow once again.

The pillow smelled faintly of aftershave and she was surprised she hadn't noticed when she was using it before. She'd been so tired. At home she hadn't slept well for who knew how many days. She hadn't felt safe there for awhile. She didn't know if she'd ever felt truly safe there. Her whole life she'd never known when Judd would act up.

She felt safe in this truck and drifted off to sleep wondering which of the two in the front had lent her his sweet smelling pillow.

****

Denzel Judd had no idea when he dragged himself out of bed late that June morning that his life had quietly turned itself inside out in the darkness of the night. Half hung over, he scrubbed at the stubble on his jaws with a hand that smelled of cigarettes and tried to focus. Memories of the day before deepened the scowl permanently etched into his forehead and compounded the headache between his eyes. After confronting Carrie two days ago, he and Deek had lost a lot of money yesterday. Now he owed his bookie even more. How had they blown it so thoroughly? That stupid horse in the third race was supposed to have been a sure thing! He'd just have to speed up collecting something on that monstrous, black demon horse of Carrie's.

He tried to focus his eyes again on his watch to see the date. He thought there was supposed to be a broodmare arriving in the next day or two. What day was it anyway? He couldn't remember. And where was Deek? He couldn't recall him coming home with him, but then he couldn't remember coming home. He dug through the medicine cabinet in search of some mouthwash. He could hardly stand himself.

In the kitchen he considered food and decided on a drink instead. He was sure he had a bottle here somewhere if he could figure out where he'd put it. He couldn't recall that either.

A shower, shave, and Bloody Mary later, he was feeling marginally better. Sipping his drink, he watched out the kitchen window to the yards, wondering where everyone was. Typically there was more going on out there, and by this time he could usually smell Carrie cooking lunch. He could hear nothing from her house next door. Maybe he'd actually made it out of bed

54

before lunch. He was still having trouble focusing on his watch.

Deek apparently hadn't made it home. His car wasn't out there and he didn't think his bed had been slept in, although it was hard to tell from the stale pile of wadded bedding. He walked outside and seated himself at a patio table, then went back inside for a pair of sunglasses. This glare was killing him.

Dante led two of the colts out to the track rail and spoke to the Mexican riders for a minute or two before legging them up to the small exercise saddles. Then he stood at the rail to watch as they warmed up the horses on the back side of the track. Judd could occasionally see a glimpse of stable hands in the barns and runs as morning chores were finished and horses were brought out to exercise and then cool down.

The big oval paddock in front by the drive was conspicuously empty and he wondered why no one had brought Ebony Wind out to run loose there for the day. Now that was a horse, even if the animal did seem to hate him. Judd was the only one the horse had it in for. He never even tried to approach him anymore for fear the beast would come right over the fence at him. He'd take into him with a chain and teach that horse a lesson if he wasn't so stinkin' valuable.

Judd's attitude soured further when he contemplated the fact that no one else had any trouble with Ebony. But what did he care if he couldn't handle the horse, as long as it brought in the money he needed to get out of this mess with his bookie, Tony. He smiled a grim smile and rubbed his hands together in anticipation. Now that the old man was gone, he had to get on with his plan to run this place like he wanted. He needed to settle this issue of Carrie's marriage to Deek, then he could start legal proceedings to contest the old man's will to get Eli out of the picture. At that point he could really get the ball rolling.

Where was Carrie? He had yet to catch a glimpse of either her or the stallion.

A raised voice drew his attention to the gravel area near the office. He walked around the corner of the building to see a truck and trailer parked there, and two men he recognized as Eli and the owner of the mare he'd arranged to be brought in. He was right then, today was the day. He was rubbing his hands together again in anticipation of the breed fee, when what they were arguing about registered. The irate mare owner was shouting at a very calm Eli, "What do you mean the stallion isn't here? I've paid thousands in booking fees!"

Still calm, Eli stated, "I'm sorry, but we weren't informed of any of this. You'll have to take this up with Judd. He had no right to make any arrangements as far as this farm is concerned. He . . . "

Judd grabbed Eli by the shoulder and spun him around rudely, repeating the earlier question with an explosive expletive, "What do you mean the stallion isn't here? Where's the horse?" Eli quietly but coldly looked at Judd's hand on his shoulder and Judd hurriedly removed it.

Eli turned back to the other man. "As I was

saying, the stallion's owner has taken him away for a time. I'm not at liberty to say where. I will tell you that we're through breeding him for this season. If you need any further assistance, that doesn't have to do with Judd having accepted your money for breeding a horse he has absolutely no involvement with, find me. I'll be around. In the meantime, I have a farm to run." With that he strode off toward one of the barns.

Judd was still trying to process the fact that Carrie and the stallion were gone when the angry mare owner tore into him. So much for obtaining more money from him today.

Later that day, after the mare owner was gone and Deek had finally crawled home from wherever he'd been, he and Judd began to try to find out where and when Carrie had gone. Eli obviously wouldn't tell him, but it wouldn't be hard. It wasn't like you could hide a horse that famous and distinctive for long. And when they found her, she would pay! He was through messing around. She would marry Deek even if he had to kidnap her himself and drug her! They only had to keep her around long enough to make it all legal and assume control of the farm; then it didn't matter what happened to her. Locking her away wherever Tony had in mind didn't sound like a bad idea.

It never occurred to him that something could happen just as easily to him.

****

Eli walked away confidently, but in his heart he was worried. Carrie was as sharp as they came and it probably was better to have her safely away, but if they had no idea where she was, they could do nothing to assist her. Now, as far as he knew she was alone, and Eli was more aware than anyone else how dangerous the men were that Judd was dealing with. They made Judd seem mild. He and Dante had to find her and protect her before the others did. He knew worrying wouldn't help, so he prayed and then went into his office to call a friend who was a retired cop.

****

It was late when Slade, Rossen, and Isabel finally reached the county fairgrounds where they'd arranged to stall the horses for the night. Isabel led Ebony out of the trailer and to his stall and left him comfortably settled for the night without removing his sheet or hood. She helped feed and water the horses before she and the two cowboys went into the living quarters to get their own rest.

She was pleasantly surprised when she stepped into their home on wheels. The trailer was actually very nice and she found that although the kitchen was small, she would be able to work there quite efficiently. She'd expected it to be a bit of a mess as far as having been a bachelor pad, and was pleased to note that other than being cramped from trying to find a place for all their gear, it was clean and neat.

Slade and Rossen cleared off the bed in the top of the front where they'd been storing various odds and ends, and digging some linens out of a storage bin under one of their beds, helped her to arrange her own tiny kingdom up there. A curtain pulled across for privacy and after they showed her how the small bathroom worked, she felt like she had this trailer living thing down.

She'd traveled to races with her grandfather from time to time but they always stayed in luxury hotels. Her grandfather had never been a snob or allowed her to be one, but he'd always insisted they stay in nice places away from home to promote a prosperous image of Wind Dance Farms so people wouldn't hesitate to want to bring their horses there. He said it just made good business sense. Having never been one of those to actually stay near the racehorses at night, she was impressed with just how comfortable and efficient their trailer set up was.

One thing that stood out almost more than anything else about the trailer living quarters was a photo hanging on the wall over the table. It was a print of a river running through a mountain valley in the sunrise. It was the most serene image she'd ever seen. The colors of the sunrise reflected in the water and the sky and she immediately felt it was a tangible image of her river of peace.

When she lay down, she noticed the pillow she was using now didn't smell nearly as nice as the one she'd used earlier. It had turned out to be Slade who had so kindly lent her his earlier.

Still tired in spite of her naps, she prayed and went to sleep without even thinking about the little pistol she'd been carrying and sleeping with the past two days and nights.

****

Slade could swear he could smell bacon in his dreams. Bacon and sweet smelling perfume were all mixed up with images of huge horses in full battle armor. Somewhere in there was a beautiful girl wearing a pretty little pair of well-fitting jeans. Where had that come from? He almost never dreamed. When he did, he certainly never dreamed of a figure like that.

Slowly, as he came awake, he realized the bacon aroma was a reality and remembered discovering last night that his pillow held the lingering scent of perfume. When he'd put it under Isabel's head as she slept in the truck yesterday he'd felt a bit silly. Women usually got on his nerves and if he did something nice for one, they invariably took it as a come on. However, after he'd laid down last night and realized his pillow smelled of wildflowers and something else he couldn't quite place, he was glad he'd lent it.

As for the well-fitting jeans, he discovered those to be a reality too, as soon as he turned over to glimpse Isabel standing in front of the stove stirring something that smelled like heaven.

"Hey! I didn't know we had bacon!" Slade

pulled his gaze away from Isabel to look across the trailer to where Rossen's tousled blonde head had emerged from a rumpled sheet.

Isabel turned around to give the two of them a hesitant good morning and then turned back to her cooking. Behind her, she didn't see the look that passed between the two as Rossen nodded toward her and raised his eyebrows with an appreciative grin.

Slade shook his head. "We didn't have bacon. What have you been up to this morning, girl?" He agreed with Rossen's nod. That was quite a sight to wake up to. He wasn't so sure this was a good idea after all. From his perspective, that little pair of jeans looked like trouble.

A few minutes later, when they sat down to eat, when Rossen took his first bite, he all but gushed, "Marsh, we shoulda found this girl a long, long time ago!" Rossen's enthusiasm about breakfast made her laugh. It was a musical sound in the small confines of the trailer and it seemed to change the whole spirit of their little home on the road. When she'd assured them she could cook the other day she hadn't been joking. The breakfast was great!

They finished eating and she started to clean up as Slade and Rossen went out to start getting things ready for the road. Slade had wondered how she'd come up with the bacon and other ingredients for her breakfast. He didn't remember any stores nearby as they'd pulled in last night. Upon stepping outside he realized that she had, in fact, unhooked the trailer and taken the truck to buy groceries while they slept.

He and Rossen looked at each other in surprise and Slade asked, "How the heck did she do that by herself? That's a heavy trailer."

Rossen answered him sarcastically, "Hmmm, I wonder if she could be in good shape or something."

He elbowed Slade who replied almost worriedly, "Sheesh, you can say that again. What were we thinking hiring a girl to live right in the trailer with us?" He walked into the rows of stalls shaking his head. Rossen took a halter and stepped in with his rope horse, chuckling under his breath. Slade actually seemed flustered. Rossen laughed right out loud.

From the next stall down Slade asked, "What's so funny?"

Rossen chuckled out loud again. "You have women from one end of this country to the other, throwing themselves at you morning to night and all it does is get on your nerves. Then this quiet, mysterious college student shows up, makes you give your word *not* to touch her, does nothing more than wear a pair of jeans to cook in, and you forget how to breathe. I thought for a minute you were going to insist we take her right back home." He came out of the stall leading his horse and grinning.

Slade flipped at him with the end of a lead and said, "You keep this up and I will, smart aleck." They bantered back and forth as they loaded horses and presently Isabel came out and brought her horse around to load in as well.

Back in the truck and on the road again, they all three appeared happy with the way things were turning out.

****

When Isabel was cooking breakfast and turned around to say good morning when Slade and Rossen woke up, for the first time she wondered if she'd made a mistake. The sight of Slade bare chested and still half asleep took her breath away. His bed head was actually perfectly in style, and he looked far better to eat than the breakfast she was cooking. She found Rossen only slightly less striking. At least he was been wearing a T-shirt.

With a hurried "Good morning," she quickly turned back to the stove, completely flustered. *Holy Moly! What had she been thinking?* She'd been around men all of her life, and was, in fact, far more used to them than women because most of those working at Wind Dance Farms were male, but she'd never encountered anything like these two, and certainly not in their beds. She was so flustered she burned her hand taking biscuits out of the oven.

She studiously refused to look back toward them, and when they both appeared at the table, dressed and combed, a couple of minutes later, she breathed a sigh of relief. They were still very handsome but much less tantalizing fully clothed. She felt even more at ease with them when they prayed over their food before eating.

Over the next couple of days she grew more and more comfortable with them and began to learn how they did things, and what they did and didn't like.

It became apparent rather quickly that everywhere Slade and Rossen went they attracted attention from females. It only took Isabel a little while to figure out they had a friendly competition going about who got the most unsolicited phone numbers. One time as they all piled back in after gassing up, Slade stuffed a slip of paper into the ashtray on the left of the steering wheel. Rossen slapped the dashboard in front of him. "Dang it all! I was ahead for most of a week!"

Slade only gave a wan smile and focused on driving. Isabel had no clue what they were talking about and didn't ask. The next day however, when a woman in a little red convertible at the pump next to them struck up a conversation with Rossen, and Isabel saw her give him her phone number, which he then tucked into the ashtray on the passenger side of the cab, she began to get an inkling. The wild thing about it was that on closer inspection she saw that the ashtrays were overflowing with little slips of paper and cards.

She'd assumed they would behave like some of the horsemen she'd encountered around the track with occasional coarse language and suggestive comments directed toward her when her grandfather wasn't around. These two men thrilled her when not only did they always treat her with respect and deference, but they also quickly squelched a crude comment from a passing trucker at a truck stop while getting gas one day. She truly felt like Princess Isabel and any last reservations she had about her decision to travel with them melted away. She finally allowed herself to picture a future with hope instead of lingering fear.

She hadn't realized how uptight she had become at the racehorse farm until now when she found how much she was at peace. Now not only was her safety no longer in jeopardy, but she believed those at home at Wind Dance Farms would be safe from Judd's threats as well. Judd could no longer try to use her to harm the beautiful horse farm her grandfather had spent half his lifetime building. She was still cautious but she usually felt safe, especially when both the guys were with her. That night as she said her prayers, she decided for the first time to touch base back home. She needed to let them know she and Ebony were doing well and she wanted to tell Anna how grateful she was for her help. Not sure what was safe to use, she decided to email Anna a minimal message. She was sure that somehow she'd get word discreetly to Eli and Dante.

****

Looking back on that afternoon in the diner, Rossen couldn't help but be amazed at the turn of events. Before that, they hadn't even really thought about traveling with someone to help them. Now, five days later, they couldn't imagine not having the help. Their lives were more interesting, more organized and they were certainly better fed. The trailer that had before simply been a means to accomplish their work, now felt like a home. Isabel was indeed a wonderful cook and was also serious about feeding them as athletes. It was delicious, but she was also very good about nutrition.

She'd turned out much better than they'd hoped. She had none of the pushy, suggestive demeanor they often encountered from women. She never flirted, and though their relationship was casual as they were practically living in each others' back pockets, she was always polite and respectful.

The only thing that was at all weird was that although Isabel was competent and capable, sometimes he could swear he saw fear at the back of her eyes. Never when it was just the three of them, but sometimes just as she stepped out of the trailer, when she quickly looked around, or if someone surprised her or came up from behind. He knew Slade had noticed it too.

Several times Rossen had tried to ask her about her life and her family on the long and monotonous drives, but she hadn't volunteered much. She was from the small town in California where they'd picked her up. She was studying sports medicine in school. Her mother was dead, and she and her father weren't close. She casually mentioned that she liked horses but never attempted to ride hers. Neither Slade nor Rossen ever handled her horse. She was always careful to take care of him herself.

They'd never even gotten a glimpse of the horse without its sheet and hood. She never took it off and even exercised the horse covered, and they'd been surprised that their own horses almost seemed to be afraid of it. Granted, it stood inches over theirs, but they'd never seen their horses act that way before.

Probably the most amazing thing of all about her to Rossen was that Slade seemed completely okay with her. It wasn't that Slade was uncomfortable with women. He just didn't ever really quite trust them. Other than Rossen's mother Naomi, and little sister Joey, Slade never let his guard down around women. Not so with Isabel. From just a few moments after she'd stepped through the door of that little restaurant, a slender, young woman in jeans and sandals, Slade had seemed at ease with her.

Actually, the fact that Slade had even considered this whole deal surprised Rossen--surprised and pleased him. Rossen loved their life. The rodeo circuit was exciting and challenging and he loved the competition. He loved truly striving to excel. His partner was the best, their horses the consummate athletes, but deep in his heart he knew the real reason he was out here still and not home working the ranch and business with his parents and siblings was because of Slade.

Slade was one of the greatest men he'd ever known. Honest and hardworking, competent, generous and smart—he had it all. Except peace. Slade had been raised by a wonderful father who had worked hard to raise his children in spite of choosing a flake for their mother. He'd married Slade's mother before he really knew what she was like, and then spent the next eleven years trying to make up for that mistake. He'd finally quit trying to fix his bad marriage when his wife ran off with, of all people, a preacher when Slade was ten and his little sister Chante was six.

Rossen knew that Slade had known for years that his mother had been unfaithful, and he had known forever that she was shallow and self-centered. Still, her abandonment, and the fact that it had been a supposed man of God, had rocked Slade's world hard. Slade was still distrustful of religion and women.

His good father had picked up the pieces as well as possible. Slade had loved and respected him and adored his little sister, and they'd had a good life without his mother. Then, when Slade was twenty-one his father and sister had been hit and killed by a drunk driver.

Slade had never been the same. He'd simply gone on with his life. He was still going through the motions, and was, in fact, doing very well, in some ways. He was on track to make it to the National Finals Rodeo for the third year in a row in team roping and all-around. His ranch and his investments were doing great. On the surface everything seemed fine.

But Rossen knew he'd lost the light in his eyes. He'd lost his trust in people, especially women, and questioned his faith in a God he couldn't understand. He couldn't understand why God had let a drunk driver kill innocent people. He couldn't understand why He'd

68

taken the father and sister whom Slade loved and needed, instead of the mother who had only hurt him and left with someone who was supposed to be one of His shepherds.

Rossen didn't think Slade was even sure why he was here or what his purpose in life was. He had tons of friends, especially women, but still he seemed a little alone. He believed that almost all women were as shallow and selfish as his mother had been, and he had been proven right time and again. Rossen and his family understood and had basically adopted Slade long ago, but they had never been able to completely fill the void left in his heart and were still trying to get him to trust in organized religion again.

So, Rossen was still here, traveling the country and winning at rodeos. Always beside Slade, always dependable, always having a good time. And every once in awhile surprised and pleased.

****

Isabel climbed up into her bunk and slid the curtain over to obtain some privacy. As she slipped out of her jeans and let her hair down, she thought of her friends back home. She'd been gone for five days now and felt like she was beginning to be very comfortable with this new life. Slade had gotten her a new cell phone so they could touch base when they needed, and she was getting along well with them. So far they'd traveled to the rodeo in Redding and one in Reno, and tomorrow they'd be in Oregon for another.

She hadn't watched the first two rodeos. She'd still been worried about getting away and was trying to get used to this new life, so she'd stayed near the trailer while Slade and Rossen competed. She'd been very careful to keep Ebony well hidden. He was probably dying to get out and run, but until she figured out a way to hide him long term, she had to keep his presence low key.

Perhaps she could buy some women's hair dye and dye the distinctive lightning shaped marking that ran down the side of his face. ESPN had once done a piece about the marking and had made it pretty famous. Even without the lightning bolt he was huge and his coat glistened like black oil. She needed to find a way to get him to some barn in the middle of nowhere where he couldn't be discovered. She'd stay there with him, although she was afraid to be alone. She had the little gun her grandfather had given her, but she knew if she was ever found alone by the kind of men her father associated with, it wouldn't be enough.

During the long drives of the last few days, once she'd finally gotten enough sleep, she had been racking her brain to find a solution to this whole mess. Maybe she should figure out how to legally just sign the whole farm over to Eli and his family. Judd and his buddies would finally leave her alone and she knew Eli would always see that she was taken care of. She'd almost decided to do just that, but Eli wouldn't be on board, and honestly, it felt like giving up and giving in. Knowing this train of thought would do nothing more than discourage her, she tried to push the negative thoughts away and rest.

She could hear Slade and Rossen outside her curtain still moving around and talking quietly. The more she came to know the two of them the more she genuinely liked them. Rossen was a cut up and pretty much enjoyed life to the fullest no matter what he was up to, although sometimes she knew he was much more substantial under the surface than he appeared. He loved to read, and had a deep, quiet inner core that inspired total confidence in spite of his happy-go-lucky attitude. She hadn't been surprised to find out in their conversations that he had a degree in petroleum engineering and was actively involved in his family's oil drilling business back home on their Wyoming ranch. He had several brothers and a sister, and they sounded down right entertaining from the stories he told. He assured her she'd meet them as they traveled home sometimes between rodeos to tend to business.

Although she'd been inexplicably drawn to him from their first meeting in the diner, Slade had been a little harder to get to know. He never talked about his family, and Isabel didn't feel comfortable asking. Much quieter than Rossen, he didn't seem to be shy, but was more naturally reserved. It was a still-waters-run-deep kind of thing that was very intriguing. He had a wicked sense of humor that blended beautifully with Rossen's madcap goofing.

She'd never seen two humans who were better friends. They seemed to be able to almost read each other's minds. In some ways they were complete opposites, but that only served to enhance their friendship. Slade was absolutely competent and had an incredible grasp of a huge variety of interests, although it took awhile to come to know it. He was calm and gentle around his horses, and they seemed to perform for him almost without being asked. Slade was just quietly confident in a way that inspired confidence from those around him as well. Isabel innately trusted him, and had from the get go.

She'd started to help them with some of their paperwork and was amazed at what the two accomplished with a couple of cell phones and laptops.

She'd found that along with his rodeo, Slade ran a several hundred acre ranch in Wyoming and had extensive other investments. He had an older couple who stayed there and Rossen's brothers helped to run the place when Slade wasn't there, with occasional help from other locals.

Isabel cooked, kept the trailer as straight as possible in the small space, helped in the "office" and had done a couple loads of shirts and jeans for them. She'd found them interesting, resourceful, and completely incapable of a coherent schedule. They could do anything it seemed, except keep an organized calendar. How these two had been this successful on the road this long with their current system, or lack of one, amazed her.

She tried several ideas and finally they just came up with an oversized wall calendar that they both had room to write notes on and then together they would figure mileages, and purses, and pencil things in. Quite by mistake they found a system with her taking the wheel, and then with their heads together, and both cell phones out, they kind of got into a zone that seemed to work beautifully. After that it was a daily regimen, and both remarked several times how much smoother their lives ran under her influence.

After just a few days they all seemed to be comfortable, and once Isabel figured out that they ate like five times what she was used to feeding a jockey, she relaxed even more and began to enjoy the journey.

The one thing that still troubled her was the ports of entry. So far, the ones they'd passed had been closed. Some others they'd missed as they'd exited for one reason or another, but she knew that eventually, they would end up stopping, and she'd have to provide documentation for her horse. She knew when she just happened to mention who they were towing there was likely to be a fuss, especially when word got out that he'd disappeared.

She wished there were a way to avoid this altogether. Until she found the way, she waffled between feeling guilty for not being totally honest with Slade and Rossen after they'd turned out to be so good to her, and knowing she had to protect them from being involved in such a mess. At length she decided she'd better tell them. She'd do it sometime before the rodeo tomorrow. Somewhere along there she fell asleep and dreamed of long, lean race horses and cowboys.

****

Slade watched Isabel slip gracefully into her bunk. As he listened to her get ready for bed he thought of the last time he'd lived this close to a young woman. It had been six years since the death of his father and sister. The pain was less sharp now, but still deep.

Chante had been dark where Isabel was blonde, but in many ways Isabel reminded him of his sister. They both looked at him with that steady, calm, absolute trust in their eyes. They were both quick to smile and slow to anger. Both were practical and organized, but still with a touch of that different drumbeat. Isabel had climbed out of her tiny bedroom this morning wearing the wildest flowered capris he could have imagined. She could do anything they needed so far, and do it all well. She seemed wise beyond her years, and in spite of the hint of fear deep in her eyes, didn't hesitate to turn up a good song and dance around their tiny, tiny kitchen.

After five days he still knew so little about her. He and Rossen had just realized they didn't even know her last name or how old she was. They were both convinced that boredom was not the real reason she'd come with them. They were also convinced that whatever her reasons, they were valid. This girl was absolutely stable, he was sure of that. She was capable, but at the same time so completely feminine. Naturally beautiful, she didn't have a drop of that obnoxious, catty teasing most women used on him. He'd never known a girl he felt this comfortable with except his own sister. But Isabel definitely didn't seem like a sister. That was the one thing about her that actually did trouble him. He was drawn to her — like a quiet, but insistent magnet.

In the last five days, he'd completely lost the urge to eat out, go dancing after the rodeo, or hang out with the guys. In all honesty some of those things had begun to pale before she'd come with them. Now however, after the rodeo or when they'd made it to wherever they were headed for the day, he just wanted to come back to the trailer, sit on the steps or in the old lawn chairs and quietly watch the stars. She wasn't a big talker and neither was he, but the silence was comfortable. Without even knowing it, she was bringing him peace.

It had been a long time coming.

****

Rossen watched Slade watching Isabel again. Something told him that maybe Slade had finally found whatever it was he'd lost. He smiled to himself for his friend.

He lay back on his bed and linked his fingers behind his head to stare up through the small window at the moon and ponder. *Okay Lord, what have you got in mind for me? I'm trying to be patient, but I'd really like to settle down as well. Any ideas?* Just then a wisp of cloud blew across the moon and he thought to himself, *How silly that some truly don't know God is watching over us.*

75

He's so obvious sometimes.

****

Slade and Rossen woke to ham, whole grain blackberry muffins hot from the oven with real butter, fresh squeezed orange juice, and cold milk. The tiny kitchen had been straightened and Isabel's bed was neatly made. They could hear her outside talking to her horse as she lounged him in a circle. Opening the curtains over the table, they watched her as they ate.

Around a bite of his muffin, Rossen wondered, "What do you 'spose, Slade? Why did she come with, and why won't she take the sheet off that poor horse? I wonder when she'll either ride him or turn him out to run."

Slade washed his own muffin down with a glass of milk before answering, "Actually, first thing the other morning I stepped out just in time to see her finish sliding the sheet back on him. I think she'd been grooming him, although it was still so dark out I don't know how she could see what she was doing."

Rossen looked puzzled. "Maybe he has a skin condition and can't be exposed to the light. I wonder if he's contagious. Maybe we should ask." He was warming to his topic. "Or maybe it's just a dang ugly horse and she just doesn't want anyone to see it."

Slade was thoughtful. "If I hadn't come to really trust her, I'd almost wonder if she was trying to hide that horse."

Rossen swallowed another bite of muffin. "Nah, what would a nice girl like her have to hide?"

Later that afternoon, they'd cared for their horses, roped for awhile, confirmed their entries for that night's rodeo and checked their gear. They were sitting at the table eating the Asian salads Isabel had built for them before leaving to run a few errands. Rossen was clicking through the channels on their little TV and paused on TNN. It was a beer commercial so he waited to see what was being televised.

They'd both just taken a bite of their salads when the announcer came back on with a special report about the mysterious disappearance of a world class Thoroughbred stallion and his owner Ms. Carrie O'Rourke, granddaughter of the late Hugh O'Rourke, and owner of the beautiful Wind Dance Farms of Woodland Hills, California. The missing stallion had won both the Preakness and the Belmont Stakes, and had then gone on to be one of the most successful racehorse sires of their time. Slade and Rossen stopped chewing in unison as across the screen flashed a grainy picture of Isabel, followed immediately by footage of the several-million-dollar stallion Ebony Wind with the distinctive marking of a wild lightning bolt down the side of his sleek face.

Rossen stared and Slade whispered a mild expletive. They simultaneously erupted from the table to explode out the door of the trailer and sprint to the row of stalls where their horses were stabled.

Slade slipped quietly into the stall and approached the big horse in the sheet and hood. He gently slid a lead rope around its neck and pulled the hood. Neither man uttered a word; they just stared open-mouthed at the unmistakable jagged lightning strike. Slade pulled the thin sheet off the horse's body and almost hesitantly ducked to look under its belly.

In utter disbelief, the two cowboys stared at each other, speechless for several moments until sounds at the far end of the barn prompted Slade to hurriedly replace the sheet and hood. Ebony Wind stood quietly listening to the tall cowboy at his side swearing under his breath.

Slade took the lead rope off the big horse's neck and exited the stall, carefully shooting the bolt on the closure. He stood there while Rossen went to the trailer and returned with a hardened padlock to secure the stall door. Still speechless they walked back to the trailer and sat looking at their salads. Finally, Rossen broke the silence. "And I thought he was just ugly."

Chapter 4

Ten minutes later, when Isabel came breezing into the trailer, Slade and Rossen were still sitting at the table in shock and Slade was still wondering what they needed to do about their discovery. With her usual easy smile, she said, "Hi, guys!" She put down the bags of groceries she was carrying and went back out to bring in the clean laundry.

As she came in with the next load, balancing the laundry on her hip to close the door, she set the folded jeans on the table and said, "Sorry, I'm not really sure which ones are which." Laughing, she said, "Which can't be that big of deal because they are all exactly the same size, and style." She laughed again as she turned and started to put groceries into the cupboards.

Rossen began hesitantly, "Um, Carrie. We were, uh, thinking we should, uh . . . "

She turned and tossed a package of chocolate licorice to him. "Your licorice." She turned back to the groceries, humming to herself.

She suddenly stiffened, standing perfectly still for a moment, and then silently turned around to stare at the two of them with wide eyes. "What did you say?" She stood looking from one to the other, searching their faces.

Slade answered, "He said--Carrie, we need to talk." He wasn't necessarily angry but he certainly meant business. And he wanted to know why she had lied to them. He'd trusted her.

Hesitantly, as she left the groceries and came to sit at the table next to Rossen and facing Slade, she asked, "So . . . What's going on?"

"That's exactly what we were hoping you could tell us, actually." Slade knew his voice was cool. "During lunch we just happened to see a segment on TNN about a missing horse worth millions, and a missing horse owner worth more millions. Her name was Carrie. She looks a lot like you."

She let out a big breath and Rossen said, "We went to the barn, Isabel. We looked at the horse." His voice wasn't nearly as cold and accusing as Slade's. He continued, "I'm sure you have good reasons for what you've done. Even in the short time we've known you, we've grown to trust you." He was looking pointedly at Slade. "But under the circumstances we think we deserve an explanation. You do realize we can't drive around the country indefinitely hauling a horse worth millions of dollars, don't you? And if we'd known he was a stud, we probably would have done a few things differently."

She nodded, and a look of defeat crossed her face as she said, "Please forgive me for not being completely honest with you."

After a short pause that felt long, she went on, "Look, I know you probably won't believe me, but I'd already decided to tell you. I do have my reasons for not telling you. At first I didn't know you. I didn't know I could trust you. And now that I know I can trust you, I didn't think it very fair to involve you. But then I guess I already have, so . . . Last night getting ready for bed I was trying to figure out what to do about the ports of entry. Of all the things I tried to think through, the ports of entry have me stuck. I've thought and thought and come up with nothing. I could never falsify information to the government and it'd never work anyway. He's pretty distinctive. There's just no way. But I can't just waltz in and announce to the world where I am either."

She took a deep breath and continued, "I know I'm a burden to you. I realize much more than you what a responsibility the horse is, and I also realize much more than you that I could be putting you in danger. Give me a day or two to figure out what to do and I'll get out of your hair. I'm sorry for putting you in a bind, but I do have to tell that you'll never know how much you've helped me even just for these few days." She got up to go back to the kitchen counter and the groceries.

Slade sat silently at the table thinking. He hadn't meant to tell her to leave, and actually had no intention of letting her go. He just didn't know what to say, exactly. He hadn't had time to even fully comprehend this turn of events.

Rossen, on the other hand, got up to help her unload the groceries and got straight to the point. "We aren't asking you to leave. In fact, you can't, no matter what kind of a mess you're in. We can no longer function without you so we'll just have to find solutions.

"That being said, we can't just keep driving around the country with a stallion worth Fort Knox in the trailer. We'll get through this rodeo tonight and tomorrow. Then first thing the next morning, we're heading home to Wyoming to stash him away somewhere safe.

"Secondly, is there anyway you would feel comfortable with telling Slade and me exactly what kind of trouble you're in, so we could help?" He continued without giving her time to answer. "And thirdly, what the heck is your real name anyway?"

Carrie looked at her feet. "I never told you my name was Isabel, you know. Anna was the one who intimated that." She smiled a mellow smile. "You see, when Anna and I were little we played this game where we were damsels in distress, and our knights in shining armor came and saved us. Anna just knew I needed to disappear and she recognized you for what you are, two wonderful men I could trust to get me and this horse safely away. I needed Carrie O'Rourke to cease to exist for awhile, so Isabel was just a logical choice. I realized what she was doing and went along. I've never even figured out a last name."

Almost to herself she said, "You know the funny thing about it, I actually like it. I feel safer as Isabel, and

82

wouldn't mind keeping that as my name forever. Whether I stay with you or not, I can't just go back and be Carrie right now, so Isabel is great for me." The groceries were put away and Carrie came back to the table and sat down across from Slade. She looked up into his eyes as if trying to read his thoughts and he returned the gaze. She took a deep breath and began the necessary explanation.

"Denzel Judd, my father, biologically at least, is a violent and abusive crook who's lately become a compulsive gambler, among his myriad of other character flaws. He's also recently acquired some very interesting friends who do things like money laundering, drug dealing, and illegal gambling. You know, kind, gentle, trustworthy types. I believe he came by these friends by way of some huge gambling debts he can't repay." Isabel knew she sounded as bitter as she felt about her father. "It's a very long story, so I'll give you the bare bones version.

"He's been messing up my life from well before I was born. He lives in the house right next to mine on Wind Dance Farms that became his when my mother passed away six months ago. He's always lived there. I used to live there too until I moved over into my grandfather's house when I was twelve to get away from him. Let's just say he's never been good to me or anyone else, especially my mother, and if it hadn't been for my grandfather, my mother's father, I honestly don't know how I would have survived all these years at all. While my grandfather was alive, Judd was much easier to live with, for whatever reasons.

"But my grandfather was crushed against a fence by a colt two months ago and died the next day." She quietly brushed tears from her cheek and after a moment went on.

"Judd was pretty mellow for a couple weeks after his death and then got violently angry and completely disappeared for days. We didn't know where he was, but later found out he'd hired a private investigator to check out my grandfather's estate. I can't imagine why, but apparently he believed my grandfather was going to leave him something. Needless to say, Grandpa would never have left his property to the man who'd made my mother's life hell.

"Grandpa left Ebony Wind, the stallion you've been towing around this last week, he left him to me entirely, which incidentally, is quite a good portion of the estate. The rest he left half to me and half to his head trainer, Eli Johnson.

"Eli's the real father who has raised me all these years and I love him dearly. He's been with Grandpa since the very beginning of Wind Dance Farms almost forty years ago.

"Eli has control of my inheritance, unless I marry, until I am twenty-one in about five months. At that time, we'll have control together, which is a total moot point anyway because Eli's management and wisdom is what has brought the farm this far to begin with and I would never question his judgment, no matter how old I become.

"Anyway, not only was Judd excluded from any inheritance, there was also a clause saying that under no circumstance could he ever have ownership of any of Grandfather's holdings. I'm sure Grandpa put that in the will in hopes of protecting me from Judd. It should have put an end to his scheming, but for some reason Judd's become more demanding than ever.

"Now, I know this is going to sound crazy. It is crazy. It makes no sense at all, but somehow Judd thinks he can get me to marry some distant nephew of his, and he will somehow gain control of the farm. The nephew is a slime ball and when Judd realized there was no way I would ever choose to marry him, he began threatening to force me. Which is also crazy but I've come to believe he would try. His organized crime friends offered to help him and then put me somewhere where I'll be out of the way. I'm not sure what that means, but I am sure they were serious. That, along with threats against people at the farm and threats to kidnap Ebony, along with the fact that the police would do nothing, have made me pretty desperate.

"I tried to get a restraining order, but they basically told me no until one of them actually physically harms me again. "

Something in Slade's chest skipped a beat and he broke in, "Again?"

She nodded sadly. "Again. Judd's incredibly mean, that's why I moved in with Grandpa. He never treated me the way he treated my mother, thank goodness. My grandfather would have had child social services come and Judd knew it. My mother would never leave him or even press charges and would never cooperate with the police, so there wasn't much we could do to protect her, but they all protected me. They still do.

"That's why I finally knew I had to leave. Judd has started threatening to have people from the farm hurt or even killed if I didn't go along with his schemes. I don't know that in the long run he could ever get away with all of it, but I was afraid. The people he's dealing with are scary. Scary enough to make me feel like I had to go.

"I knew I had to leave, but I had no idea how to get away without Judd or the others knowing where I was. Especially after they started threatening to kidnap Ebony, I knew I needed to do something, but I really thought it would be impossible to hide him.

"Dante, Eli's son, kept telling me to keep praying as Eli had taught us, and that God would provide a way. Although I was trying to have faith, I was also having this feeling urgently telling me to go *now*. I realize now, in retrospect, that God knew you were coming, that He did have a plan all along, but I just didn't understand what it was. Thank goodness Anna did. I wasn't kidding when I said you were the answer to prayer."

She continued, "I'm sorry again that I didn't tell you. I'll make a call to a friend of mine at ESPN who follows racing, and ask him to do a follow-up story about how I'm fine and just out of town for awhile or something. Then I'll go somewhere."

When she finished the trailer was silent for what seemed like a very long time. Finally, as if not knowing what to do, she got up and walked to the door, running her fingers over the photo on the wall as she went, and said, "I'll, uh, leave you two to talk in private."

Slade caught her hand as she stepped past him to go out the door. She looked down and into his eyes as he softly said, "I'm sorry. I'm sorry for what you've been through, and I'm sorry for the way I behaved just now." She squeezed his hand and walked out the door.

For a few more minutes Slade and Rossen sat silently. Slade absent-mindedly drummed his fingertips on the table. Finally, he reached out to touch the folded laundry on the table and mumbled, "We had an heiress washing our jeans."

****

There was apparently an unspoken agreement not to bring up the subject of Isabel's real identity, or the situation behind it, for awhile that afternoon, as the three of them sat in old lawn chairs outside the trailer door. Isabel was making up a menu and shopping list for the next week as if nothing had happened and the world would keep right on spinning as it should. Her list making was actually very comforting. All three of them wanted the present arrangement to continue for a variety of reasons.

Isabel was happier and felt safer than she could ever remember and she'd come to enjoy both of them, maybe even too much. This life had become an adventure that she really wished was just beginning. She did miss the farm and her friends, but Slade and Rossen had far overwhelmed any feelings of homesickness with new emotions and experiences.

Slade was a little confused about why he wanted things to stay the same. In his mind he reasoned that it was the much improved food situation and the better organization, but there was another little voice in his head that dared him to admit that when she said she would leave, just for a moment he'd panicked. Somehow, in a way he didn't even begin to understand, the hole in his life that had gaped open since the death of his family, had been neatly filled up by this sweet, happy, runaway girl. He knew it to be true, but was a little hesitant to examine the fact too closely.

Rossen sat tipped back in his chair fiddling with a leather strap that'd come off a bridle the day before. He knew how Slade felt about Isabel. And he was trying to understand Isabel's perspective to this whole deal, but he made up his mind that no matter what the two of them thought would come to pass, he was going to do all he could to see that Isabel stayed safely with them. He knew without a doubt that Slade needed her in his life for now at least, and he suspected that Slade was exactly what she needed in hers. And quite frankly, life was better all around with her here, for him as well.

Each busy with their own thoughts, none of them even noticed as another girl approached until she was right before them. She unabashedly checked out Isabel with a disgusted look on her face and then said, "I heard you had a girl living with you, but I didn't believe it. I thought you two were the self-professed straight arrows of the circuit, but I guess not, huh?"

Isabel calmly looked up at the other woman without saying a word. The girl wore tight jeans and boots, with an even tighter shirt that showed off a very definitely female figure. She would have been quite pretty with less makeup and less scowl.

Slade and Rossen remained tipped back in their chairs as Rossen nodded and said, "Afternoon, Jesse." His voice was all but dripping with exaggerated warmth and he went on, "Isabel, may I introduce you to one of the most famous rodeo personalities on the entire circuit, Ms. Jesse Colvin." Rossen gave Jesse a wink. "Jesse, this is our good friend and lifesaver, Isabel."

Slade let the legs of his chair down slowly. A low, "Hey Jess." was all the acknowledgement the girl got from him, and Isabel could sense something going on here, but wasn't sure what. She looked up from her list in interest.

Rossen stepped in to defend all their honor. "We're not actually living together, Jesse, we're just living together. Know what I mean? Isabel here has simply and generously agreed to work for Slade and me in an attempt to help us pull our disorganized acts together. She's doing a fine job of it too, I might add, so please don't offend her by making nasty insinuations. She might run off, and we need her desperately." Rossen turned to Isabel and at that last sentence, flashed her his biggest and most irresistible smile.

She smiled back at him and Jesse made a rather unladylike sound and asked, "Why haven't you ever mentioned you needed some help? I would have been glad to help you. You know that." Slade was still studiously looking at his fingernails, or anything else but paying attention to Jesse.

Isabel was still trying to figure out what was going on as Rossen continued, "Oh, we knew you were much too busy, and besides, Isabel here was just a bored college student who needed some money and wanted to travel." Now both Slade and Rossen were looking directly at Isabel and smiling.

Jesse, sensing that she was missing something, looked from one to the other. Her sour face returned when her look rested on Isabel. "How exciting for you to have the chance to come rodeoing with them and do your *work*." She made it perfectly clear that she didn't think Isabel really did anything, then added, "Do you ride barrels?"

Isabel shook her head. "I have to admit that I don't believe I've ever ridden a barrel in my life." She smiled innocently up at Jesse and asked, "Is it fun?" Now it was apparently Slade's and Rossen's turn to take an interest in the scene going on. Rossen put his chair legs back on the ground too and leaned forward.

Jesse sputtered, "Don't you even know what a barrel race is?"

Isabel acted amazed. "You mean you actually race around on a barrel? That is remarkable! What makes the barrels go? I mean do you use motorized barrels or are they electric or is it like some sort of a stick horse or what?"

Rossen's grin got bigger and bigger. He turned to Jesse. "I'm sorry Jesse; she's a bit new to rodeo." Turning to Isabel he began to explain in exaggerated detail just what a barrel race was.

As he finished, Isabel exclaimed, "Oh good! That makes so much more sense. I couldn't even begin to picture how you'd actually ride a barrel around!" Slade apparently couldn't even begin to hide his smile. Thank goodness Jesse thought they were laughing over Isabel.

Just then a group of people walking by said they were going to go get a bite to eat and wanted to know if Jesse wanted to go. Upon seeing Isabel, they stopped and introductions were made again, this time in a much more civil manner. They all turned to go. Jesse turned to Isabel with a begrudging, "It was nice to meet you, Isabel. Maybe you'll get the chance to learn a little about horses with this job."

"I certainly hope so. It all seems so exciting." In a dreamy voice she added, "Maybe I'll even learn to ride barrels sometime. Slade, would you teach me?" With that last comment, Jesse stomped off in the direction of the others.

The three of them sat there grinning and when she was out of hearing, Isabel asked, "What's she famous for?"

With a completely straight face that completely cracked Isabel up, Rossen replied, "Being able to breathe in the clothes she wears."

Isabel actually had seen a barrel race, but it had been years and years before. Much more at ease now that she had no secrets from Slade and Rossen, she planned to attend the rodeo that night. Early in the evening, they saddled up and went over to the arena to warm up their horses. On their way, they dropped Isabel in the stands with a contestant's pass. Until five days ago, Isabel had had no idea how much went into this sport or how incredibly talented both man and beast had to be. She did know horses and she knew these were magnificently well trained. She could sense that what these rodeo men and women did had taken most of a lifetime to bring to this level of perfection. Well before the rodeo had even started, as she was watching the contestants warm up, she knew she was going to love it.

The Professional Rodeo Cowboys Association-- PRCA as Slade and Rossen called it, certainly knew how to put on an entertaining show, and the crowd was on its feet and whistling and yelling from the very first horse in the arena. They saluted the flag, the National Anthem was sung, and there was a beautiful tribute to America and the troops and veterans, complete with a group of performing horse women racing through with flags and patriotic music. Next was a parade of rodeo queens, decked out with their big hats and hair and flashy clothes. Even their horses sparkled with glitter and sequins. They streaked around the arena at

92

breakneck speed on beautiful, racy horses, smiling always as they blew by.

Then the events started. The roping was great! She especially loved the team roping. Watching Slade and Rossen compete together on horseback for the first time was an incredible thrill. It was almost like watching a choreographed dance or something. Their precision and teamwork were amazing, and she couldn't help feeling a sense of pride when they took first place and took their victory lap around the arena. In just a few short days she'd come to feel these were *her* cowboys.

The tie-down roping was interesting, although she sometimes felt sorry for the calves. The steer wrestling, or as the announcer called it, bulldogging, was just flat out unbelievable. She didn't ever remember having seen it before, and when the first cowboy jumped off that racing horse and actually threw the steer she laughed right out loud. She thought to herself, *These guys are nuts! Who comes up with these ideas?* Throughout the whole rodeo there was a ridiculous clown wearing huge, baggy Wrangler jean shorts held up by wildly colored suspenders, running around teasing the contestants and audience alike. He started in poking fun at the "daggers" and Isabel was astounded to realize that the team he was teasing was, in fact, Slade and Rossen.

She'd thought they were only ropers and realized she really didn't know much about what they did for a living. The announcer was saying they were headed to the National Finals Rodeo again if they kept competing as well as they had been, and she wasn't even sure what that meant. It sounded important. She probably ought to find out.

Her heart was in her throat for just a second as Slade dove off his horse. Almost immediately his steer was down and the crowd was cheering wildly and continued to cheer as Rossen swung his horse around and pretended to rope the clown who'd been teasing them. Leave it to Rossen to clown with the clown! The thought crossed her mind for the umpteenth time, *Why were these two men single?* They seemed to have it all. Were they just not the settling down kind? She'd only been with them a few days, but had yet to see any sign of a girlfriend. The cowgirls were missing out! These two were good men.

The first bareback bronc out of the chute ended her musing. Bareback bronc riding was exciting, but she quite honestly thought the cowboys were trashing their bodies for an adrenaline rush. Getting beat up like that for a show seemed incredibly foolish. And when the saddle bronc event began and Slade's name was announced she couldn't even believe it! She'd thought him far too intelligent to do such a thing, and found herself disgusted with him as she watched. *What a brain dead thing to do to such an incredible physique!*

She thought back to that first morning when he'd sat up in bed shirtless and his hair all tousled. Her heart beat faster just thinking about it. She'd hardly been able to look away and was sure he'd known it. She'd tried to be up and outside when they got out of bed these last few days. She was much less likely to gawk that way.

Pulling her mind back from memories of Slade's bare chest to his bronc ride, she watched him finish with the second highest score and held her breath again as one of the pick-up men rode up to help him dismount. Slade simply leaned over onto the pick-up horse and then slid safely to the ground as Isabel finally breathed. She decided she definitely appreciated the job the pick-up men did and knew they were easily some of the best riders out there.

She ultimately did see the barrel racers and as Jesse came out and knocked over the first barrel, Isabel felt bad for her. She may have been a bit of a ditz, but the girl could ride. Isabel admired her talent and guts.

The last event of the evening was the bull riding. She'd seen some of this on TV on Saturday afternoons and, frankly, she didn't like it at all, but it held a certain morbid fascination. These riders made the bronc riders look intelligent. At least the broncs didn't try to kill the cowboys after they were thrown!

Several of the riders wore thick vests the announcer called a flack jacket, which he explained was like a bullet proof vest to protect the cowboy's vitals. Some also wore neck pads, mouth guards and helmets. Even with all the protective gear it still seemed to her to be a crazy, dangerous way to make a living.

There were actually two new clowns who were introduced as bull-fighting clowns. They had the important job of trying to protect these overly gutty cowboys from the aggression of the bulls. She had to remind herself that jockeying was also very dangerous, but she rationalized that at least winning a race seemed to have a point. This was just foolish.

Three or four men had ridden their bulls when suddenly almost right in front of her the rider was thrown. As the whole crowd gasped, she knew instantly something wasn't right. Strangely, it made the entire scene around her appear to go into slow motion with every detail heightened.

Instead of being thrown clear, the rider's hand hung up in the rope, and as the bull continued to spin and buck, making deep grunting noises with every impact, the bull rider was whipped around like a rag doll. The sheer violence of the bull only accelerated and even the smell of the arena dirt was more pungent. No one in the crowd seemed to breathe as the bull-fighting clowns dove in, trying to free him and stall the bull, but it felt like days before the rider was finally freed.

As one, the crowd continued to hold their breath as the obviously wounded young cowboy couldn't move fast enough to escape the bull that immediately turned on him. The scene slowed even further as the huge bull closed the meager distance, dirt flying with every digging, determined stride. It caught the cowboy in the back with its horns and threw him high into the air. As soon as the cowboy landed, the bull began to grind him into the arena dirt with its massive head.

The bullfighting clowns were still there whooping and slapping, trying to distract the bull and pull the cowboy to safety, but the bull would not be deterred.

Seemingly minutes later, although it could only have been seconds, when the bull was finally pulled away by a pickup man who had roped its horns, the cowboy lay piled up in the dirt not moving. An ambulance quickly drove into the arena from a back gate and the young man was carefully moved onto a stretcher and put into the back.

As the vehicle pulled away, lights flashing, leaving a somber and strangely silent arena, all the earlier excitement of the evening faded, leaving Isabel sick to her stomach. Trying for a deep breath, she shuddered involuntarily. Tears welled up and coursed quietly down her cheeks as she left her seat and wended her way through the crowds and the cars and vendors, back to the trailer to let herself in.

At first she climbed up on her bed and closed her eyes, but as soon as she did the scene would replay itself over and over in her head. She climbed back down and tried to keep her mind on the late dinner the guys had requested. Tears still dripped down her face as she grated cheese for the Alfredo. What a horrible waste of a life. She had no doubt that the young cowboy had died that night. There was no way a body could survive that kind of abuse.

Slade and Rossen were watching the bull riding from an area behind the chutes. As soon as Slade saw the bull catch the young rider, he knew they needed to get to Isabel. She was sitting almost directly in front of the wreck and this was her first rodeo. They were trying to reach her through the crowded grandstand when they saw her get up and leave, and Slade groaned. He had hoped tonight would be a happy experience for her. They hadn't really settled whether she would stay or go, and he wanted her to stay badly enough that it almost scared him. Even if she did go, he wanted her to take good memories of the rodeo life with her.

When they finally made it back to the trailer, she was quietly sobbing into the pasta sauce she was making. Slade took one look at her and knew she needed to be held, but he'd given her his word. Rossen gently rubbed her shoulder as they told her the young cowboy had indeed died on the way to the hospital.

No one really felt like eating, so they put the dinner away for another day and got undressed and went to bed.

Rossen and Slade knew she was crying behind her privacy curtain, but didn't have a clue how to deal with it. They could only imagine what she'd seen. It had made them sick and they were clear across the arena and had dealt with this kind of thing before. Listening to her cry was killing them, and when she finally drifted off to sleep she still breathed with an occasional little sob.

Deep in the night, Slade was awakened by her moans and could tell she was having a nightmare. Unsure of what to do, he hesitated for several minutes until finally he stood up against her bed and pushed the curtain back. Just as he went to touch her to wake her, she whispered, "Oh, Dante, he died. He died." She began to cry in her sleep.

Slade hesitantly brushed the tears aside as he softly spoke to her, "Isabel. Isabel, wake up." He gently rubbed her arm until she began to wake. He could feel exactly when she went from bad dream to half awake fear. She stiffened and jerked away and instinctively he knew she was going to scream.

She cried out in such fear it made the hair on the back of his neck tingle. He spoke her name again and the scream died out when she realized who it was. There was incredible relief in her sleepy voice as she breathed, "Oh Slade, it's you." Half asleep, she stopped pulling away from him and moved toward him instead, burying her face against his neck. Still breathing hard, she whispered, "I thought you were Judd." He held her against him for a moment until she stopped shaking and her breathing slowed.

Reassuringly, he said, "You've been having bad dreams. I'm sorry. I didn't mean to scare you."

"Oh, Slade, he died." Her sad whisper against his skin gave him chills. He felt her breath on his bare chest and pulled her more firmly against him. Even this upset, she felt good here in his arms.

He held her as she cried again. It was much easier to hold her than just listening to her cry last night had been. That had killed him. She sniffled and through her tears said tiredly, "I'm sorry I'm being such a baby. It's just such a waste. What a waste of a young life." He stroked her hair. It wasn't pulled back and fastened for once and it was incredibly silky. He wished he could have seen it loose, but it was too dark and he wondered why she never let it down in the daytime.

Still stroking, he said, "I'm so sorry you had to see that, especially your first time." He whispered against her hair. "It's not usually like that, I promise."

He continued to hold her and stroke her hair until finally he was sure she was back to sleep. As gently as possible, he eased her back further onto her bed and went back to his.

Now he was wide awake, which was good because he needed to do some serious soul searching. He had finally found a girl who truly intrigued him, and it was actually frustrating. Because, first off, he'd promised her he would maintain a strictly professional relationship, and secondly, he'd found out she was ridiculously wealthy.

He had given his word, never dreaming that within a few days he would be more attracted to a woman than he'd ever been in his whole life. He should have known it would happen. He'd known there was something about her that first time he laid eyes on her. She'd felt so good in his arms just now. So right. She was warm and soft and smelled like wildflowers. She was so different from all the rodeo groupies who would have given him anything he asked, anytime, day or night.

But her world was obviously a far cry from a

ranch in Wyoming, although she didn't act it. The only thing that had even hinted at her wealth before their discovery was one day he had happened to notice her watch. He still felt foolish when he remembered those loads of jeans.

He turned over, telling himself it was just the novelty that intrigued him. He'd never really known a woman like her. In a few days, or weeks, when they got to know her better she wouldn't be so fascinating. Her perfume would stop haunting him and the magic of her laugh would fade. He didn't even try to tell himself he'd get used to the way her jeans fit. Even the most cynical part of him didn't really believe that.

The next morning Isabel slept late for the first time since she'd been with them. Slade hadn't pulled her curtain closed again after her bad dreams last night and he could hardly keep his eyes off her as she slept. He and Rossen poured cold cereal and went outside to eat. They were in the lawn chairs again when she stepped out of the trailer. Rossen was on his cell phone, and Slade looked up from his laptop as she sat in the chair beside him. Her hair was back in the twist again. She had little dark circles under her eyes, but other than that, she was as beautiful as ever.

She seemed a little hesitant to look him in the eye this morning and asked, "Did I, uhm, did I have bad dreams last night?" Her hands were fidgeting in her lap.

"I think you did. Yeah." He looked back at the

laptop.

"I wasn't sure if I dreamed it all or not. Thank you for waking me. Did I wake Rossen up too?"

He hesitated as well before admitting, "Yeah, I'm pretty sure you did."

"That bad, huh?" She began to massage her temple.

Trying to smile, he said, "You weren't too bad until the Judd part. That part was pretty loud."

They were silent for a minute or two while he worked at the laptop and Rossen talked in the background. Finally, Slade asked, "So, who is Dante?" He kept his eyes on the computer screen, but he held his breath for her answer. She'd mentioned him one other time and after her talking in her sleep, Slade wondered a lot.

"Dante is my tall, dark buddy from home. He's Eli's son. We basically grew up together. Why?"

He still tried to study the computer. "You were talking to him in your sleep last night. I just wondered."

"He's my best friend. He's like the brother I never had. He was six years older, and has always been my bodyguard." She laughed softly. "Anna and I used to try to get him to be the knight in shining armor. He would have none of it. I wish I had a way to contact him. I haven't called or emailed for fear Judd would somehow find me."

"I wouldn't try to call right now, but Email should be secure enough, if you don't say anything about where you are. He already knows you're

102

somewhere, he just doesn't know the location. An Email won't change that."

"If you really think it wouldn't hurt, maybe I'll try right now." She went back in the trailer and came out a minute later with her own laptop.

Grinning, Slade said, "No wonder that bag was so heavy. I've been meaning to ask you how you ever got to where we picked you up the other morning. Where did you come from?"

"I told you I came across the fields, remember? And you're right. That bag was heavy; I had a hard time getting it and me up on Ebony. He'd never carried anything other than a rider, and I'd never gotten up on him by myself. It was a bit of a trick in the dark."

Slade shook his head. "You rode that huge stallion bareback across fields in the dark, carrying that bag?"

"Oh, I wasn't bareback. I have his exercise saddle in the bag so it was a little lighter. And he's pretty bulletproof. The only time that horse acts up is if Judd gets near him. It's the weirdest thing."

She booted her laptop, logged on and typed away for a few minutes. At one point, she shook her head and muttered under her breath, "Twenty-four from Geoffrey," then made a dainty groaning sound that made Slade wonder who Geoffrey was, and if the groan was good or bad. Then to Slade, she said, "Dante left a message to take care and keep in touch."

Chapter 5

True to their word, the guys got through the next night's rodeo and then pulled out for their homes in Wyoming at daybreak the next morning. It was a fourteen hour drive straight through from where they were in Oregon, so they switched drivers several times, and got the horses out and exercised them at about the halfway point. That was a longer drive than they usually liked to make in one shot, but under the circumstances they thought it best.

They pulled off the highway onto a gravel road in southwestern Wyoming that night at a little after eleven p.m. They drove for several miles, turned off through a set of locked gates near a guard shack, and continued on for another twenty minutes before stopping in front of a cluster of outbuildings. The horses were unloaded immediately. Slade and Rossen turned theirs out into a large paddock together, where they could move around to loosen up after that long of a trip.

Rossen approached Isabel and asked, "Do you want him in a stall or a run?"

She looked around in the dark. "A run would be

great if you think it's safe."

"We're twelve miles from the nearest paved road, behind a locked gate that's monitored by video cameras, and the only people anywhere near are my family. They can be a little off the wall, but you can trust them with your life."

"Just like you, huh?" She put a friendly, tired arm around his waist. "A little off the wall, but absolutely trustworthy. Ebony is going to love it here, I can tell already." She breathed in a deep breath of cool mountain air. "What is that wonderful smell?"

"That would be horse manure. And you think I'm off the wall."

She laughed. "How could you still be silly when we're this tired? No. It's like a spice or a tree. Like Cedar only more . . . more . . . something."

Rossen walked over to a bush growing on the roadside, broke off a twig and crushed it between his calloused fingers. "More like this?"

She held the twig to her nose. "That's it. It's marvelous. What is it?" She breathed it in deeply again.

"It's sage. That's the sweet scent of Wyoming. Welcome home." As she tried to understand why he would say that to her, he unloaded the stallion and they led him into a run and turned him out still in his coverings. He trotted in a circle around the perimeter and began to buck like a weanling and Rossen said, "I'll bet that feels marvelous to be loose after more than a week of a stall and lounge line." They watched him play for a minute before Rossen turned away. "Come on,

Isabel. Come meet my family."

The Rockland family didn't appear to notice it was almost midnight. They were obviously glad to see the cowboys and didn't seem to love Slade any less than Rossen. Even Isabel felt loved among this large and happy family. Rossen's dad, Rob, and brothers Ruger, Sean, and Treyne were much alike in looks and mannerisms and the "little" sister Joey, who stood 5'10", was stunning as well as friendly.

Rossen's mother Naomi came straight up to Isabel and wrapped her in a motherly embrace. It was such a sweet moment that Isabel blinked back tears. This was what a mother was supposed to be like, fussing, and happy, and confident. Isabel couldn't help but wonder what her own mother would have turned out like, had she had a man like one of these for a husband.

Ruger introduced her to his wife Martina, who said cheerfully, "You can just call me Dr. Marti like everyone else does." Isabel later found out that Marti was a veterinarian who practiced locally as well as helping out on the Rockland Ranch.

Isabel was so tired she wasn't sure she would remember everyone in the morning. She was very much a morning person and felt like she would turn into a pumpkin at any moment. Naomi must have noticed, because she started to shush everyone and encouraged Rossen to send Isabel to bed.

Isabel assumed she would be staying in the trailer, but Rossen headed her off and said, "While we're here you can sleep in a real bed, with a real bedroom and bathroom for a change. C'mon, we'll grab a few things from your bag and I'll show you where."

He nodded to where Slade was headed into another room. "Slade will be here, too. He usually stays here unless we're home for awhile." Isabel's and Slade's eyes met as she walked past the door. They still hadn't established for sure whether she was going back on the road with them. She wondered what he was thinking behind those brilliant green eyes. It mattered to her a lot. Much more than was wise, probably.

As she lay down to sleep that night after her prayers, she placed the twig of sage on her pillow and drifted off to the sweet scent of Wyoming.

When she awoke, she was momentarily confused. Once she knew where she was, she quietly dressed and slipped out of the house to check on her horse. In the half-light of dawn, everything looked different. Last night she hadn't realized what a large and diverse operation this ranch was. She also hadn't been able to see that it was in an unbelievably majestic setting in this high mountain valley, completely surrounded by craggy mountains, their peaks and north faces still brilliantly white with snow. The mid slopes were deep green with conifer trees and lower down there was bright spring green where the fields and pastures lay below. It was a phenomenal view.

As she looked around in wonder on her way to Ebony, she noticed almost at once that the dirt road encircling the perimeter of the complex was, in fact, a small race track. It wasn't fancy and there were gated driveways that appeared to cross it intermittently, but it was definitely a track. She could see the starting gates in a straight-away off the south end. Why here? She didn't even care! Her heart raced as she ran to the trailer for her riding gear.

Five minutes later, dressed in riding breeches, soft, tight jockey boots, and a snug Under Armor shirt, she stood on a fence with Ebony pulled close so she could vault into the tiny exercise saddle on his back without a leg up. She hadn't brought her helmet and she no longer worried about someone recognizing her here, so she left her hair falling loose down her back. It had only been a few days since her race with the dawn, but she'd missed it so that this morning her heart felt like it would burst! Even the air seemed to want to run! Ebony must have felt the same way, and she had to hold him firmly as they trotted for one lap to warm up and become familiar with the track.

Finally, half way down the back side, she let him go.

It was glorious! The magic of the morning was hers once again and she reveled in it! There was an exhilaration that only came with this speed and this freedom—this greatness of steed. It was an incredible natural high!

On and on she let him run, just her, the horse, and the dawn. She felt this morning and this horse, even this track had been created for just such a race as this. She

109

felt the wind streaming his mane into her face, her body in perfect rhythm with his stride, and she felt rather than saw the sun starting to come up over the mountains to the east.

The scent of the sage was intoxicating as lap after lap the scenery seemed to float past the rail--that frail boundary between this mystical race in the dawn and the rest of creation. She was inside a sphere that held a seemingly magical power to halt any stresses and was pent with invigoration. For these few moments at least, girl and horse were more mythical than mortal.   It was a glorious lift--while it lasted.

All too soon, her run was ending. She felt Ebony start to ease up and the speed that was like a drug lessened. Gradually the world began to spin on its axis again, and she reined in the horse to begin cooling him down. Slowly she stood in the high jockey stirrups to stretch the taut muscles in her thighs, flexed her legs, and eased back down to his back.

****

Slade was up and dressing when he heard the unmistakable sound of a fast running horse. Several others must have heard it too, because he, Rossen, and Treyne collided in the hall on their way outside to find out what was amiss. They rounded the side of a barn just as Isabel and Ebony came around the corner into the home stretch. In unison the men halted in the shadow to watch the majesty of the girl and horse come flying

110

down the track.

Isabel and Ebony moved as one being, some mythical enchanted beast painted by the colors of the sunrise, almost iridescent on his glistening black hide. His mane, tangled with her long silvery-gold hair, streamed out behind them in the wind, the fine mist of early morning muting everything. Even with the rhythmic sound of each massive stride, the stallion's gait was so smooth the pair seemed to float, as the magnificent beast thundered past and started around the track again.

The three men were soon joined by the others, and they all watched in silent awe as horse and rider raced in the glory of the sunrise. The mystical pair circled the track three more times before the pace started to ease, but the spectators continued to watch quietly as she cooled the horse out, standing in her stirrups from time to time to flex her legs.

Someone breathed, "Now that's a horse!" Slade wasn't even sure who said it.

"Who's watching the horse?" Isabel had just gone past standing in her stirrups. That time he thought he recognized Treyne's voice.

"Hey, now, you all." There was no mistaking Joey's teasing voice. "You stop that this minute. She doesn't even know we're out here, and we're all going to quietly go back inside, and let her have this morning's ride to herself like she intended while you all go on and work on slowing your pulse rates." She herded them away and she was right. Isabel finished cooling her horse down, groomed him and turned him out, never having realized she hadn't been alone with him as she raced in the dawn.

A few minutes later, Slade and Rossen sat in wooden rockers on the expansive porch that ran the length of the house, enjoying the mountain morning as she came back from the paddock where she'd taken him.

Rossen commented dryly, "I guess she knows how to ride."

Almost to himself, Slade said, "And I thought she looked good in jeans." Isabel had stopped at the truck and leaned into the back seat to retrieve something, completely unaware she was being watched. Her form-fitting riding breeches and stretch shirt accentuated every curve and her shining hair hung all the way down her back.

Glancing sideways, Rossen asked, "You mean you're finally going to admit the attraction factor out loud? Easy there, Slade. I'm not sure you're having strictly professional thoughts right now." Rossen laughed. "You gave her your word, remember?"

Slade groaned and leaned forward in his chair. "I've been reminding myself on a regular basis, for what, a week now?"

Isabel left the truck and walked over to lean against the fence that surrounded the main pasture in front of the house. There were eight or ten mares with foals there, and the babies were bucking and playing in the morning sun.

They watched silently for a couple more minutes

until Rossen said, "I think this is the first time I've ever heard of the damsel in distress rescuing the knight in shining armor."

Slade frowned at him. "What the heck is that supposed to mean?"

Rossen didn't answer right away, then said, "I guess I just mean you're happier this week than you were last." Slade considered this in silence and Rossen went on, "Mellower. More at peace. I don't know."

Isabel leaned over and ducked through the rails of the fence and then knelt down. The foals near her slowly came to her in curiosity while their mothers looked on placidly and returned to grazing.

Slade finally answered, "I want to take her back with us." Isabel slowly stood amidst the babies and began scratching them and talking quietly to them.

"Why?" Rossen rocked slowly back. Out in the paddock, one of the babies near Isabel spooked off, and ran bucking to its momma.

"I honestly don't know." Slade leaned back in the rocker and left it at that. They sat in companionable silence, watching until Isabel ducked back through the fence and continued walking up to the house.

When she saw them, she skipped up onto the porch and said, "I went for a ride this morning! The first time in more than a week. It was wonderful!" Her eyes were shining and she was obviously happy as she chattered on for a minute, "Rossen, your home is great! If I'd known Wyoming was this beautiful, I'd have come here years ago. It's incredible! And it smells like heaven." She finally wound down a little and sat in a rocker beside them. She handed Slade a twig of sage she'd picked up somewhere. "Have you smelled this? I noticed it last night. It's marvelous! Rossen says it's sage. The sweet scent of Wyoming. I love it." She sat back in her rocker and took a deep breath.

Slade smiled at her exuberance. "Yes, I've smelled sage. And you're right, it does smell like heaven." He held the twig to his face. He was definitely more at peace.

****

Breakfast turned out to be a rowdy affair. The entire family was indeed there, including Cooper Rossen's youngest brother who'd been gone the night before with some friends. There were eleven of them, and the Rocklands, with the exception of Naomi, were all as nutty as Rossen, so the meal was pretty animated. Naomi was more serene. She joined in occasionally, but mostly she just smiled as she watched. Slade was obviously used to them, and they used to him. He was more reserved, but laughed along with them all when they teased Joey good naturedly. Isabel was comfortable in spite of being a newcomer to such a gregarious place. A few times when she glanced up, she caught Slade looking at her over his meal. She wished she could know a little of what went on behind those eyes.

Throughout the day, as she alternately worked and played alongside this family, she mulled over what she should do now. She'd arranged to have them care for Ebony Wind for her on an indefinite basis. He would be safe and hidden until she figured out how to handle Judd and the others. As it turned out, the bush track had been built to accommodate Ruger and his wife's small horse racing operation. They raised and raced Quarter horses. They race at smaller distances than her Thoroughbreds, although often they had a great deal of Thoroughbred blood in their pedigrees.

She'd decided she shouldn't stay here with Ebony for fear Judd would possibly find her, and then she would bring trouble to them, too. She hadn't told Slade and Rossen that yet, and in fact, didn't even know how to bring the subject up.

What she really wanted was to stay with them on the rodeo circuit, although, if she was honest, it was because of them, Slade in particular, and no longer because she was desperate. She knew she could safely find a way to hide from Judd, now that she was away and had the horse issue settled, so there was really no reason to tag along, but that's what she wanted to do. They did need her help on the road. There were problems though. First, she knew Slade was going to bring up the fact that she was somewhat wealthy. She could see it in his eyes. Secondly, if Judd ever found her, she'd be bringing the two of them serious trouble.

All that day and most of the next they spent there with Rossen's family. They worked around the ranch helping with various chores, and in the afternoons Rossen went into his home office to handle some business for the oil wells. Slade disappeared for several hours, in which she later learned he'd gone home to his own ranch further along the gravel road in the next valley over.

Isabel went with Rob, Naomi, and the others to move a herd of cows to another pasture. She'd never done anything like that before and it seemed like a great adventure. As they all saddled their horses, Treyne brought her a cowboy hat. It fit surprisingly well and she laughed as they mounted and he started to yodel a silly, old fashioned, cowboy song. She had a wonderful time and basked in the peace and camaraderie around her. Rob and Naomi rode side by side and on the other side of the herd, Ruger and his wife Marti did the same, working together to gather the cattle and move them across the hillside.

That night they roasted smoked sausages like hot dogs outside around a huge fire pit, and followed them up with s'mores. Isabel went to bed tired and happy. There was something about this family. She'd thought this kind of life was something from a 1950's TV show

The next morning she crept out of bed again to go for her race on Ebony. Their run was just as exhilarating, but as she stood to stretch her legs while he cooled down, she couldn't help but think this might be the last time she rode him like that for awhile. She would miss this. It had been a daily rush for her ever since her grandfather had felt she could handle a racehorse. As she unsaddled him and led him to his run, tears filled her eyes. She loved this horse. He had

116

been with her through so much. She stood with him for a moment then, heads together, silent, still, in an age-old ritual of rider and steed and devotion, as she tried to face leaving him.

****

Slade came to watch her ride in the dawn again. She was as magnificent this time as she'd been the day before. He quietly went off to saddle one of his own horses when he saw her there, silently telling her horse goodbye. As he rode into the outdoor arena, he decided that if she chose to stay with them, they'd better take another horse along. It wouldn't be the same as Ebony for her, but at least she would still have a horse with her. He knew they were a huge part of her life. That vision of their heads tenderly touching stayed on his mind all day.

****

Still tired, that evening Isabel offered to help Naomi in the kitchen while the others went somewhere nearby to fish. Joey invited a girl friend and the brothers all started to tease Slade about her. Apparently this friend had a thing for him, and he didn't seem very enthused about her coming. For some reason that made Isabel glad. She wasn't going to delve too deeply into why.

She had liked Naomi instantly and was enjoying

her company immensely while they cooked. Naomi was telling her stories of her children as they were growing up and she was keeping Isabel laughing. From time to time she asked Isabel questions about her own childhood and even though Isabel tried to be discreet, it was clear that her childhood had been very different from the Rockland kids'.

Isabel was making a huge green salad while Naomi made rolls when Naomi commented, "It sounds to me like what you're not saying is the way you were parented wasn't necessarily what you would have chosen. But your grandfather and his friend sound like wonderful people. What you need to remember, Isabel, is that all of that is in your past. You can and will leave it behind.

"What do you want your own family life to be like? That's what's important. The decisions you make, in the next few years especially, will be what determine how the rest of your life will turn out, as well as the lives of your children and their children."

Isabel paused in her slicing. "I realize that, and quite frankly, it scares me."

Isabel expected Naomi to ask why, but she seemed to understand when she said, "It's hard to know how to have a strong marriage and a happy stable home if you've never seen anything like that before, isn't it?" Isabel quit tearing lettuce and turned to look into Naomi's eyes.

Meeting her gaze, Naomi went back to making her rolls as she said, "My situation was different than yours obviously, but I know exactly what a violent father and fearful mother can do to a young child's life." She turned back to her rolls. "I just knew that the buck had to stop with me. I knew exactly what I wanted for a family life, I just wasn't sure I knew how to create it. I was three years into law school because I didn't think I should have a family, when I met Rob. In retrospect, without the gospel I don't know that I could have ever learned to overcome what I was taught as a child. Those were my secret weapons." She smiled. "The gospel and Rob." She laughed and patted Isabel's arm with a flour covered hand. "He was so cute when we were your age!"

She made Isabel smile. "I can imagine that he was. He's still very handsome now. And your boys all look just like him. I'll bet they give the girls around here fits."

Naomi nodded. "I think you're right, and Slade with them. I swear that boy has had to beat the women off with a stick since he was tiny. You'd be amazed the way some girls will behave these days! I swear there are times I want to blindfold my boys."

Isabel laughed. "Better not. Then they'd have to find their way around by feel." They giggled together like school girls and Isabel went on, "They've all turned out marvelously. I've only just met most of them, and I've only known Rossen for a week or so, but I can tell you in that time he's been the epitome of the perfect gentleman. They all seem like wonderful young men. If they can all handle questionable women as well as

Rossen and Slade can, they'll be fine." This time she patted Naomi's arm, and they laughed again when Isabel told about the phone number competition.

They were still working together when Isabel asked her, "What did you mean the gospel was your secret weapon?"

Naomi started to explain about how, as a young teenage girl, she had finally left the troubled home she'd grown up in. She struggled to find a way to go to college and had finally made it with the help of scholarships and grants. She'd met Rob. They'd fallen in love almost from the start and he'd introduced her to two young Mormon missionaries. They'd taught her about the true church of Jesus Christ and that by living its principles she'd learned how to have a happy life.

As she talked, Isabel had the strangest feeling. She wondered if this could possibly be the same gospel the two young missionaries had started to teach her own mother.

Her hands stilled, and her heart began to pound as Naomi finished talking. She asked, "Like what kind of principles?"

Naomi talked while she kneaded dough. "Like faith in God, repentance, the golden rule, service, honor, fidelity. Basics really. But they lead to a happy life. I would never have had the strong marriage and happy family I do without them. Through the gospel I learned all the stuff I missed growing up.

"I knew I wanted a family of my own, but I was afraid I'd fail like my parents. They've gone now, poor

120

souls. I've also learned that every family has their share of troubles, and that what we might think is failure at the time may all work out if we're patient and trust in the Lord." She finished a pan of rolls, covered it with plastic and started on another.

Wistfully, Isabel said, "You have a beautiful family. I've never been around anyone like them."

Casually, Naomi asked, "What about you? Do you want a family someday?"

"Yes, I've always wanted a family." Isabel stared unseeing out the window. "Sometimes it seems out of my reach, but that's what I want. I'm going to college. At least usually I am. But I really want an education more than a career. I've been studying sports medicine, mostly because we always seem to have a rider getting hurt. I heard jockeying was one of the most dangerous professions, but I'm sure it can't be as bad as that bull riding." She cringed, just thinking about it.

Naomi's voice held understanding. "Rossen told me you saw a bad wreck close up. I'm so sorry. I'm sure it was very troubling."

"It was. It still is. I had bad dreams over it. He probably told you how I screamed in the trailer." She smiled self-consciously. "I probably scared him right out of bed."

"How is that whole living in a small trailer with two men thing going?" Naomi hesitated, "If you don't mind my asking."

Isabel smiled warmly at her. "Not at all. If one of them was my son, I'd be a little concerned too. It's been wonderful. Surprisingly so. Actually, I know next to nothing about rodeoing. I'd never set foot in a trailer like that, and I didn't know either one of them. Honestly, I expected them to act like most of the men I know. They've been a very pleasant surprise.

"You'll think I'm silly, but I'm sure they were an answer to prayer. It sounds kind of weird, I know, but it's all worked out too well to have been coincidence. I don't know how much they've told you, but I was getting desperate. I was trying to trust in God, but I was also having this urgent feeling that I needed to go now. Like *right now*." She gave a shaky laugh.

"I must have been desperate to go off with two men I didn't know. Please trust me. I'm not that kind of girl." Smiling self-consciously, she said, "I made them promise they'd behave strictly on a professional level before I'd come with them."

Grinning back, Naomi said, "Good for you. I have to admit I was a little worried when they mentioned you. I feel much better after having met you." She patted Isabel again. "But they are good men. The best. Now I just wish they'd settle down and get married. I'm very impatiently waiting for grandchildren!"

Isabel grinned at that. "I have wondered why they're not attached. I don't think it's for lack of female interest. They create quite a stir, the two of them."

Naomi looked at her watch. "I wonder where they all are. They shouldn't be much longer. I'd better put the ribs on. Excuse me, I'll be right back." She went out, and turned on the grill on the deck as Isabel watched through the kitchen window. Behind Naomi she noticed a storm brewing. Great black and gray thunderheads piled up against the mountains to the west. Closer in, lighter gray mist flowed almost imperceptibly down into the canyons and draws.

Naomi stepped back into the kitchen, the door slamming in the wind behind her. "Whew! That breeze is really picking up. They'd better hurry or that's going to catch them, and they'll all be wet if it does." She waved at the gathering storm out the window.

As if on cue, two trucks appeared far down the valley, the dust in their wakes blowing quickly away by the gusting wind. They put the rolls in the oven and set the long table. Isabel felt butterflies start to flutter in her stomach. She knew Slade and Rossen would be leaving late this evening to go to another rodeo. Whether she would be with them would have to be decided soon.

****

Slade and Rossen were thinking the same thing as they drove up the valley. Rossen asked, "What's the plan, Marsh? How do you want to handle this?"

"I've been wondering about that all afternoon. What I've finally come up with is to just assume she's coming with. If she's decided she doesn't want to, we'll deal with it then. Who knows? The decision to come the first time was pretty hassle free. Maybe it'll be no big thing. She's been bullet-proof this far."

****

They all came piling in, laughing and talking. Naomi was given several big hugs and Cooper even came and gave Isabel one and said, "I didn't want you to feel left out!" He gave a great laugh that was very like Rossen's and added, "And I never pass up a chance to hug a pretty girl!"

Naomi swatted at him. "Bo Rockland, you behave yourself! You're gonna make her think I've raised a caveman."

With that, he gave his mother another bear hug and proceeded to tickle her. "Too late. I'm already a caveman, Momma! And I already hugged her and don't regret it a bit!" He gave Isabel an exaggerated wink.

They dumped a muddy and wet plastic bag that smelled like the ocean into the big sink by the back door. Isabel was amazed when Naomi went over and looked into the bag and remarked on what a great bunch of fish they'd brought. Isabel had expected her to be upset at what came into her kitchen, but apparently this was not uncommon. Everyone washed up and cleaned up and they sat down to dinner.

As they looked up from praying, Naomi noticed an empty chair and asked, "What happened to Kate? I thought she was fishing with you."

"She was. She had a little dip in the creek and decided she'd go home and dry out." Rossen was grinning at Slade as he spoke.

"Oh, really?" Naomi questioned sagely, passing the salad, "I'm assuming she had some help with her little dip. Which one of you did it this time?"

She was looking at Cooper who said, "Don't look at me, Momma! For once I'm an innocent babe. This time it was Slade himself. But I'm sure he didn't do it on purpose." They were all grinning at Slade who looked a little guilty.

Naomi looked around the table skeptically. "Yes, I'm sure not."

There was a story here. Isabel would have to ask about it later.

As they all helped clean up the meal and were loading the dishwasher afterward, Isabel was flabbergasted at how much food they'd just put away. They'd eaten six full racks of ribs! And they all appeared to be healthy and fit. Holy cow! Naomi must go through the groceries just feeding her own family!

When the last dish was neatly put away Ruger and Marti went home and the rest of the family went out onto the porch. The wind had died down, but it was raining and lightning was striking somewhere up the nearby canyon. Great racketing booms of thunder rumbled and rolled, echoing down the canyon walls. Isabel had never heard anything like it.

The Rocklands acted like it was a spectator sport. All the rockers had been pulled in under the overhanging roof, and they all sat in jackets and watched the show, listening as the thunder rolled. Night had begun to fall. It was an early evening because of the blackness of the storm. Lightning strikes lit the sky time and again in a glorious display of Mother Nature's force.

Isabel hadn't unpacked a jacket from the trailer and was hesitant to brave the rain to go get one. Naomi brought her a blanket and she snuggled up in it in her rocker and felt a sweet sense of belonging to this loveable and happy family.

At length, the lightning faded off down the canyon and the family started to move in different directions. Slade and Rossen came and claimed the chairs on either side of her.

This was it. She'd known it was coming and had fretted over it all afternoon. However, now that they were here to discuss it, it didn't seem like that big a deal. She was just going to assume she was going with and if they said differently, she would figure it out. She knew she'd been prompted to leave with them and she was going to stay with them if they'd let her.

They sat enjoying the peace of the quiet rain after the violence of the lightning and thunder. At length, she asked, "Is it that time then? Are we out of here?" Slade and Rossen exchanged a glance.

Rossen answered her, "We probably ought to be on the road within the hour."

She nodded. "I'll have my gear loaded."

They watched the night sky for several more minutes.

****

Apparently he really didn't know anything. Judd looked at the now unconscious body that lay in the hay. He'd been so sure Dante would know where she'd gone. After all, they'd been as close as brother and sister their whole lives.

Judd and a few of his friends had tried to find out something about her whereabouts, but Dante had quietly looked at them in disdain and let them hit him. Fool! He'd soon learn some respect one way or another.

Eight days now and not a trace of where she and that monster horse had gone.

****

When Eli found Dante beaten into unconsciousness in the hay barn, it made him sick. If they would do this, right in the midst of all the farm hands, they'd stop at nothing.

He called an ambulance and the County Sheriff this time, knowing help was not forthcoming from the local police. He'd have to triple security.

Chapter 6

They loaded the horses in the rain and had a sweet family prayer together before saying good-bye. Slade loaded a fifth horse, brought over from his place that afternoon, that Isabel wasn't familiar with, a tall bay mare with three high stockings and intelligent eyes.

Isabel was much sadder at leaving than she could have imagined. It wasn't just her horse, or that the couple of days there had been like living at a western resort. In the short time she'd been there, she'd come to love Naomi. For a little while she'd felt mothered again, and in a way she'd never experienced. As she hugged her goodbye, she knew she had made a true friend. All of Rossen's family had been wonderful to her. She felt more like the second little sister instead of a stranger who worked for their son and brother. As she climbed up into the cab she took a twig of sage with her.

Arrangements had been made to drop Ruger and Marti at the airport in Salt Lake City on the way out, so they sat in the back seat and Isabel was in the front between Slade and Rossen. She was close enough to smell the aftershave she hadn't been able to get out of her mind after Slade had lent her his pillow that first day. She didn't know how far it was to Salt Lake from here, but she hoped it was a long way.

Isabel listened to the conversation going on around her as they drove. Ruger and Marti were flying out to California for a veterinary seminar for her continuing education requirement. She'd be taking some classes that dealt with a disease they were experiencing in their herds at the time, and Slade and Rossen joined in the discussion. Isabel had no idea what they were talking about and her mind began to wander. She was tired, and the steady swipe of the windshield wipers was almost hypnotic.

****

Slade could feel Isabel begin to relax beside him. She was the most morning person he'd ever known, and she got positively loopy late at night. Soon her head drooped, and he reached over and gently pulled her over to lean on his shoulder. He didn't see Rossen's grin in the darkness, or Ruger and Marti exchange a look in the backseat.

Slowly Slade withdrew from the conversation too. He was having trouble concentrating and when Rossen had to ask him the same question over again, he admitted to himself that for the first time in he didn't even know how long, he really liked a girl. He could smell her shampoo and it got him started thinking about her hair. It was like a shining silvery-gold waterfall.

130

Blonde, but with silver highlights instead of brown, it caught the sun like spun gold. For a week she'd kept it twisted back tight. She'd admitted she was worried about being recognized, but since being at the Rockland's she'd worn it down. The first time he'd seen it down was that morning out on the track.

He had hardly even believed it when she'd come around that corner like an enchanted nymph on a mythical winged horse. The beauty of the girl on the magnificent horse in the sunrise had taken his breath away. It was the first time he believed that he'd truly seen the person she was. Alone and free from the expectations of society, she'd raced like a wild fairy in the dawn.

Just now she was soft and warm against his side and he wished he dared pull her closer. Why had he ever made that promise to keep it professional? But then he hadn't known how he would react to her nearness. Perhaps it was a good thing after all.

The drive to Salt Lake ended all too soon. Slade was wishing it had been longer as they pulled up in front of the terminal and let Ruger and Marti out. He was just about to get out and help when Rossen grinned and motioned him back. "Don't move. Let her sleep."

Even when they stopped for gas and switched drivers, somehow her head ended up on Slade's shoulder again on the driver's side of the car. Slade didn't have to see Rossen's face in the dark to know he was smiling.

Their next rodeo was in Idaho. They roped well, and stayed for the next go-round and won. Slade took second in the bulldoggin'. He hadn't even tried to draw a bull or bronc. He figured that would be a tender subject with Isabel and although he knew he'd have to deal with it soon if he wanted to continue to compete for all-around cowboy at the NFR, now wasn't the time.

He'd told Isabel the new horse was a spare in case one of theirs came up lame and then he'd asked her if she would mind riding it to keep it legged up while he and Rossen worked theirs. Her eyes had lit up and later that afternoon as they rode, he knew she was enjoying that part of her job.

They had three more rodeos back to back with long night drives in between and they came to appreciate having Isabel with them all the more. She could tie up all the loose ends and even drove sometimes when both men were tired.

She seemed to enjoy watching them perform in the rodeos, but she always left when they started the bull riding. If one or both of them wasn't helping one of their friends with their rides, they came and sat with her in the stands and walked her back to the trailer.

Isabel was getting to know some of the people on the rodeo circuit who were Slade and Rossen's friends. Most of them were men, but there were a few women who were friends and a few who weren't, but wished they were. Jesse had come to be a given, and Isabel and Rossen had become expert at protecting Slade from her affections. If they were in the stands, Slade would always sit in the middle or if they were in the trailer, he would sit at the table and then Isabel would slide in next to him so Jesse couldn't. One time Isabel said she even felt like she was guarding his horse's stall door while Slade was inside working on its feet.

Once after Jesse left Slade commented, "I almost wish we hadn't told her you were working for us. Maybe if she thought I was romantically involved, she'd leave me alone."

Rossen piped up, "Probly not, but I think it would work great with Angelique for me! Come 'mere and lay one on me, Isabel! We better practice!" His laugh was infectious and it appeared Isabel couldn't help but join in giggling.

She got an impish grin as she teased back, "I'm afraid you'll have to teach me. Where do we start?"

"Well, first ya have to learn to pucker up like this." Rossen proceeded to make the biggest lips he possibly could and then began chasing Isabel around the trailer. She ran with a squeal and tried to duck behind Slade, but Rossen tackled her and began to give her pretend kisses making big zerbit noises on her face and tickling her. She squirmed and squealed again for Slade to save her, but he was at a total loss for words as he looked on. He was absolutely unsure of how to deal with this. He didn't know whether to help her, or help Rossen, or slug Rossen. All of that must have been very apparent on his face when they finally quit giggling and Rossen helped her to her feet. They stood up, took one look at Slade, and burst into laughter again.

Slade just continued working with his rope. He wasn't sure what to think of Rossen and Isabel horsing around like this at all.

****

It was at this fourth rodeo in a row that Isabel met Leland Wilde. She'd been watering their horses and as she walked along the alleyway between the stalls she noticed a horse that just didn't seem right. She turned off the hose and came back to find that indeed there was a problem. The horse had been left in the stall with its halter on, and the halter had somehow caught on a piece of metal that had worked loose along the edge of the stall panel. The metal had dug into side of the horse's face and cut it deeply. Although obviously in a lot of pain, it was holding still with its head at a funny angle.

She looked around for help, but there was no one, so she quietly stepped into the stall and over to the horse, talking in a low gentle voice. She tried in vain to slip the halter off, but it was pulled too tightly. She stepped back out of the stall and hurried to the trailer, grabbed a utility knife out of the drawer and ran back.

It took her probably 20 minutes to saw through the webbing of the halter, being very careful not to get the blade anywhere near the horse's skin. It seemed to understand she was trying to help and was amazingly still through the entire ordeal. She'd finally released it from the metal and was standing next to it inspecting the wound with the shredded halter in her hand when she heard an angry voice behind her, "Hey, what are you doing? Get away from that horse!"

She calmly patted the horse and walked out of the stall as the man growled, "What are you doing in with my horse?" The angry face that went with the angry voice wasn't any happier when he saw what she'd done to his halter. He calmed down when she told him what had happened and what she'd done to help. The horse needed to be stitched up and the cowboy, who had introduced himself as Leland Wilde, changed gradually and became almost too friendly to Isabel as he readied the horse for transport.

They were in the alleyway of the barn and Isabel was just leaving when Slade walked in. He instantly tensed when he saw them and asked, "So . . . What's going on?" His voice was as angry as Leland's had been at first. "What are you up to, Wilde?" Isabel couldn't believe the tone she was hearing Slade use. He strode between them, grasped Isabel firmly by the elbow and started to walk her back out of the barn. Stunned, Isabel went with him, surprised even more when he turned back to Wilde and practically threatened, "She's with us. Stay away from her!" With that he continued almost marching her out of the barn. She didn't want to create a scene, so she went with him, but his dictatorial manner infuriated her.

Once out of hearing of Leland, she turned on Slade, jerked her arm out of his grip and snapped, "Don't you dare treat me like this! Who do you think you are? Don't you dare handle me like this!" She was furious! She had an abhorrence of physical domination after her childhood with Judd that left her angrier than she ever liked to be, and for Slade, of all people, to be one to try to push her around made her even madder. She'd trusted him implicitly. She wanted to completely tear into him, but thought better of it and spun on her heel and strode away.

****

Rossen came down the trailer steps just in time to hear Isabel's outburst and see her leave. He'd known Slade long enough that he must have known Slade was mad too. As Slade neared the trailer, Rossen asked, "What's going on?"

Slade shook his head. "I just found her in with the horses. Leland Wilde was standing there with her." He knew Rossen understood immediately as he continued, "I guess I didn't handle it too well. I thought I was protecting her, but I should have known better than to try to force her." Slade was still mad, but in retrospect, he understood that physical force was probably the worst tack he could have taken with Isabel. He hadn't stopped to think, before getting her away from the jerk.

****

Isabel walked for more than an hour around the rodeo grounds. She knew Slade and Rossen would've left to go warm up their horses by then and she didn't even care. As she walked she was calming down, but she was still angry with Slade.

There was a little voice in the back of her head that was saying he was right to want her away from the cowboy, and she'd felt that as soon as Leland walked up. He was too slick and too self-important. And the way he'd looked at her made her uncomfortable. She'd had a sense he shouldn't be trusted and had been in the process of excusing herself when Slade had walked up, but the fearful child in her, now turned adult, was still mad at the way Slade had treated her.

She steamed inwardly during the entire rodeo and was still ticked as she started back to the trailer alone when the bull rides started. She heard a step behind her and it automatically made her tense. It was a feeling she hadn't had in a couple of weeks, and it made her feel guilty for still being mad at Slade. She knew by now that he would never do anything that wasn't in her best interest and that he must have had a good reason for behaving the way he did. At the sound behind her, she turned around and was relieved to realize it was Rossen, obviously come to see her safely home.

He fell into step beside her. "Still mad?"

She smiled up at his candor. "Yes." At least she was honest. "I didn't realize I had such a short fuse. But I'm feeling penitent too. I know Slade was right. I knew I needed to leave before Slade even walked up. I just hate to be physically forced. A holdover from my father, I suppose."

They walked in silence toward the trailer. Finally Rossen said, "Isabel, I don't know how to put this delicately, but Slade had very good reason for being worried about your safety around Leland Wilde. We don't mean to be domineering, but you should stay away from him. You aren't safe alone with him. Slade just cares a lot about you. That's all. Try not to be mad."

They'd reached the trailer and she nodded. "I know. I'm not mad any more. You can tell him it's safe to come home. Thanks for walking me. I'll have something to eat when you get in." He went back to the arena and she went inside.

Thirty minutes later Slade came in the door. He closed it behind him, and she turned. Their eyes met and held and after a moment, he asked, "You still torqued?"

His wording made her grin as she shook her head. "No. But thanks for asking. Are you?"

"I wasn't mad at you."

She raised her eyebrows. "I'm the one you dragged off."

"I didn't mean to drag you. I'm sorry."

"Accepted. I'm sorry too. I don't deal well with being physically forced."

"I gathered that. I should have known. It was stupid of me. Wilde just lit me up—seeing him with you. We go back. He should have known better than to even talk to you when you're with us. Without sounding like I'm ordering you around, it would be a good thing to steer clear of him."

She nodded. "I will, and I'm grateful you were watching out for me." She started to set food on the table.

Taking a step closer, he said earnestly, "Isabel, you don't understand. But you need to. Leland Wilde is dangerous. I don't want to boss you, but you should stay away from him."

She nodded almost penitently. "I know."

"What do you mean, you know." His face held concern. "Has he hurt you?"

"No. I just knew." She met his eyes again. "I knew he was not to be trusted the same way I knew you could be. I'm not sure what it is. There's just this little voice in my heart that knows." She gave him a small smile, shrugged and put dishes on the table. "Women's intuition."

"Or the Spirit, giving you a prompting to keep you safe."

"It doesn't sound so nutty when you say it."

"Just so you follow it. Dinner smells wonderful. What can I do to help?"

Later that night Isabel checked her email. There was a message from Anna.

It said, "Judd and some others jumped Dante in one of the barns at the horse farm and beat him badly. He's still in the hospital, but will hopefully be home in the next few days. Be careful and stay safe. Love you, Anna"

The message was a couple of days old. Isabel felt

sick. She knew instantly why Judd had done it. He was trying to find her.

Slade and Rossen heard her rapid intake of breath and must have realized something was terribly wrong. She looked up and met their eyes and pushed the laptop around so they could see. She was quiet for several minutes, unshed tears in her eyes. Finally she said, "I need to go home. This is because of me. They did this to try to get him to tell them where I am. But he couldn't because he didn't know where I am."

She got up and started to pace the tiny space of the trailer and whispered, "I thought by leaving that I was protecting them." Incredible guilt washed over her and the tears overflowed.

Slade stepped in front of her and she stopped and looked up at him as he asked, "How is going home going to help? It seems to me that's the last thing you should do. Going back will only endanger them more. If Judd knows if he hurts somebody you'll cave, then he'll do it every time he wants something."

He was right. She knew it. He always was. She'd learned to respect his wisdom across the board. Still she felt terrible and said, "But I need to be there. I need to help take care of him. That's the least I can do since I caused it."

Slade watched her, then shook his head sadly and said, "The only ones who caused this are the men who did it, Isabel. If Dante really cares for you, and it sounds like he does, then what he needs is to know you're safe so he can focus on healing."

She sat back down at the little table. "I don't even dare call for fear that somehow they'll be listening in or find me." She knew she sounded discouraged and didn't even care.

Slade continued, "If who you're dealing with really is organized crime, then that's wise. And the simple fact that he's been so badly beaten means they aren't fooling around. Try emailing one of them. Just be sure you don't give any indication of where you are or that you're with us."

It was after nine p.m. back home, but she was hoping someone would check their email tonight anyway. Seconds later, she was thrilled to realize Eli was online and wrote her right back. She wished she could have talked to him on the phone so she could hear his voice. She was having a ball with Slade and Rossen, but sometimes she really missed Dante and Eli.

Eli told her what had happened in his typical level-headed way. He didn't get too flustered about much, but he didn't hesitate to tell her just how bad Dante was either. So she knew things were every bit as serious as they had seemed both before she had left and when she'd read the email.

As if to emphasize that, Eli wrote.

You be careful, girl. Judd's crazy and the men he's been hanging around with are as bad as they come. You were right to leave. You watch yourself and your horse.

She told him again that she was safe and doing well and though she missed them she wasn't coming back anytime soon. Slade was right, that would only make Judd bolder.

Eli wrote back and mentioned that they were trying to finalize the Bonner issue. Isabel knew immediately that what he was saying was they needed her notarized signature on some sales documents. She wrote back and asked if that was something they could work on there at the hospital. That was her way of telling them that somehow she'd try to have someone pick the paperwork up at the hospital and bring it to her, without making it obvious if someone else gained access to this email. She and the guys were going to be back near that area in the next day or two.

They stayed online for almost a half hour writing back and forth about what all was going on with the farm and those back home, and she explained in a rather bland and uninformative way that she was happy and watched over.

She still felt terrible for what Dante had gone through because of her, but when she ended the session online, she was much happier to know exactly how he was than when she'd first gotten the email. Turning to Slade and Rossen, she said, "He has broken ribs, a punctured lung and a brain concussion. He said he recognized Judd and his nephew, but there were several others with them he'd never seen before."

She paused. "He also has some legal documents, part of a sales contract on a horse, that have been

142

notarized by the buyer, but need my notarized signature." She looked from one to the other. "What do you think would be the best way to get them? They'll take them to the hospital. Now I just need to figure out how to get them from there. They've hired some off-duty policemen to guard his room, so hopefully someone can get in and out without Judd realizing we've been in contact."

Getting out the big calendar, the three of them pored over it for a minute and then Slade said, "We could drive that route on the way to Bakersfield without going much out of our way. We won't risk you being seen anywhere near the hospital. We'll drop the trailer somewhere and one of us could pick up the papers and bring them to you to sign. I'm just wondering, what did the police do? About what happened to Dante?"

"Eli said they are finally taking this seriously. Apparently, when Dante felt up to trying to identify some of the men who were with Judd and Deek, he actually identified a couple of men the police were very interested in for other things. They just haven't been able to find them. So far none of them have turned up, but at least now they're trying to bring them in. Before, they didn't even want to be bothered."

Sounding completely disgusted, Slade said, "It's about time they took it seriously."

****

Rossen came down with a cold the next day, and

took some decongestant that wiped him out, so he was sleeping in the back seat as Slade drove with Isabel keeping him company up in front. She had been waiting for an opportunity like this to ask Slade some questions. She wondered about the church Naomi had talked about the evening they'd cooked together, and she was finally going to get up the nerve to ask Slade about the saddle. When she started riding the bay mare he'd brought, that secretly she thought he'd brought just for her to ride, he'd simply walked into the tack room of the trailer and handed her the saddle she was using. She'd wondered about it ever since. It was much too small for either of the men, and it had the initials CM stamped into the leather at the back.

After worrying and hesitating, she asked, "Slade, may I ask you something?"

He glanced over at her and back to the road. She knew she'd been quieter than normal the last little while and he had probably been wondering where her thoughts had been.

Casually he said, "Shoot."

"Do you know anything about this Mormon Church Naomi belongs to?"

He smiled. "Some."

Isabel turned questioning eyes to him. "She seems to think it's the true church of Jesus Christ."

"It is." He answered matter-of-factly. She turned to stare at him.

"It is what?"

He laughed. "The true church of Jesus Christ."

144

She was confused. "What do you mean? Why do you say that?"

He checked his mirrors and said, "Because I believe it is the true church of Jesus Christ, headed up by Him, with the exact organization He used in biblical days. And incidentally, it's not just Naomi. The whole family belongs. Heck, half the population of Wyoming does. At least the part we live in."

"The whole family? Even Rossen?"

"Even Rossen." He indicated the zombie snoring in the back seat. "That sleeping beauty back there is actually a returned missionary. That's what they call them back home. The young men who are truly converted go on missions for two years when they're eighteen or nineteen or so. Sometimes the young women go, too."

Isabel turned to stare at the back seat. She was stunned. "Two years! Eighteen-year-old kids? Holy Moly!"

"All of them are returned missionaries except Cooper and he goes out next August. I assume Joey will leave when she turns nineteen here in a few months, too, although girls only go for eighteen months. They are a pretty devout family."

"I had no idea. Why hasn't he ever said anything?"

"Anything like what?" He slowed to avoid a big rig.

"Anything about religion, or if he spent two years being a missionary, why doesn't he ever talk about it?"

Slade checked his blind spot and changed lanes. "He doesn't need to. He lives it. Think about it. Think back over the last two weeks when you've spent practically 24/7 with him. Now compare him to the average Joe you knew in high school or college." The truck was silent for a few minutes except for Rossen's soft snoring.

Shaking her head, Isabel said, "Wow. You're right." *But then*, she thought, *you always are.*

Slade went on, "He's honest, he's clean living, he's hard working. He's the most upstanding guy you'll ever meet. He doesn't party or sleep around. He doesn't even swear--well, except when he sees Angelique coming." At this they both smiled. The more Isabel thought about it the more she realized he was right. He was also describing himself.

He went on, "He never passes up the chance to help someone, and if you think about it there are other things. He reads his scriptures every day, sometime. We never eat without first asking a blessing on the food. Last Sunday was about the only Sunday in forever that he hasn't gone to church in whatever town we happen to be in. You don't know that because you've only been with us this long, and last Sunday was the day we took your horse home. It was kind of an ox-in-the-mire deal. If you were going to describe someone who is trying to follow the Savior, he would be the poster child."

She looked up at him. "You're just like him in all those ways."

Slade chuckled. "Not even close. But he has been

the ultimate mentor for me. That's what I mean by saying he doesn't have to preach, he just lives it."

"So then, you belong to his church too."

Slade glanced over at her and then pulled at the collar of his shirt for a moment. "Well, yes and no. Yes, in that I do believe they're right. I do believe it is Christ's gospel, led by a prophet, but no in that I haven't actually been baptized yet."

She was confused again. "Why not?"

He hesitated with a frown. "That's a good question. One I've been asking myself a lot lately. Mostly because I'm stubborn, and bullheaded to a fault, and I've been a fool for way too long. When we first moved to Wyoming I'd never been around anyone very religious. Neither had my parents. The more we were around people like the Rocklands, the more we believed in what they did. I'm sure I would have been baptized a member when I was a teenager if I hadn't foolishly let two bad experiences color every aspect of my life. I was still a good kid, don't get me wrong, I just had a hard time understanding some things.

"For the most part, I've always lived the way they taught me, and they've always loved me no matter what a bone-head I've been. Rossen and Naomi ask me from time to time if I'm ready to be baptized yet. And I never felt I was 'til just lately. Strangely, you've had something to do with that somehow. Anyway, Rossen just hasn't asked me for a little while, and I decided to wait to tell him yes until he does."

Isabel considered what he'd said. In some ways

this was amazing, and in other ways it just made sense. After all, God would use good people like Rossen to answer prayers, wouldn't He?

Still thoughtful, she turned back to him. "What do you mean? I had something to do with it?"

He answered without looking at her, "I don't know, honestly. The last while before we met you, I'd been struggling. Things are going very well for me right now, but for some reason I've been, or had been, not very happy. There's been this deep feeling of unrest for a long time now. Something was missing. My spirit was tired. I'd lost my enthusiasm for everything. I knew I had, I just didn't know how to get it back."

He shrugged. "I'm not really sure how or why, but it's back." He looked directly at her this time. "The only thing different is you're here, so maybe it is you, or helping you. I don't understand it. I just know life is good for me right now. Since you've come, it's like I've been able to settle down and focus. The unrest is gone, and some really important things have become blatantly obvious to me. Like the fact that I should have been far more serious about the gospel a long time ago. I should never have put off something so important. Rossen thinks it's you."

They were quiet while they considered this. At length she asked, "And what do you think?"

There was just a moment before he answered, "I think it's you."

They rode in easy silence for several minutes. Finally she said, "I hadn't lost my enthusiasm. What I'd lost is peace. Or maybe I'd never even had it and was just now coming to realize it. At any rate there was none and I needed it desperately."

"And now?" He looked at her and their eyes met briefly before he had to look back at the road.

Softly, she said, "I have peace. I've come to know it's incredibly precious."

He thought about that for another minute and then said, "I noticed that you've put a Post-It on the photograph of the river in the trailer. That scripture from Isaiah about 'And I will send her peace like a river.' You're right. Peace is incredibly precious."

"It is." She was quiet for another several minutes, and then finally said, "May I ask you another question?"

He smiled at her, "Is it as deep as the last one?"

"Probably worse." She met his glance.

"Well, let me have it."

"Whose saddle is it?" She could tell instantly by the look on his face that she was right. It was worse.

She'd started to wonder if he would even answer when he finally said with an infinitely sad voice, "It was my sister's."

She softly asked, "Was?" She could feel the sadness clear across the truck.

"She was killed by a drunk driver a few years ago." He paused. "My dad was killed as well."

She had no idea what to say. Finally, she slid across the seat and laid her head on his shoulder. It was the closest thing she knew to giving him a hug, and she simply said, "I'm so sorry."

A long time later, Rossen raised his groggy head to see them sitting like that. He yawned and lay back down with a smile and Isabel knew he was wondering what he'd missed.

Chapter 7

As Slade walked into the hospital room the next afternoon to pick up the documents after being careful to make sure no one was watching, he was astounded to find that Dante was Black. His surprise must have shown on his face.

The very tall, very black man in the bed swathed in bandages looked him up and down and said casually, "You must be from Carrie."

"And I'm assuming you're Dante." For a second it was like two herd bulls sizing each other up. Finally, Slade shook his head and started to chuckle. "She's talked about you a lot. You're smart, you're funny, you're talented, you're tall, you're dark. That's what she told me. Dark." He laughed again. "Tall and dark. I never dreamed you were black and eight feet tall." He was still shaking his head laughing.

In a voice that was low and almost menacing, Dante asked, "Do you have a problem with that?"

Slade grinned at him. "Dude, since you are about twice my size, even if I did, which I certainly don't, I'd never admit it."

Dante smiled gingerly. "Good, because I'm too darned tired to argue. These nurses keep you up all night trying to make you well. Somebody ought to tell them that sleep would help." Just then the nurse came in and began to take his vital signs. "See what I mean."

The nurse teased him and said to Slade, "Try to ignore the whining. In a minute when his pain pill takes effect he'll completely forget whining and try to hug you. Watch out." She dropped her stethoscope back around her neck. "Everything's good!" She patted his foot as she bustled back out.

Without wasting time, Dante asked, "How's Carrie?"

"Well. Frustrated that she isn't here with you. She seems to like you quite a bit."

Dante smiled again and groaned. "She can be a bit feisty when she wants."

In a serious tone, Slade asked, "How are you? Really?"

"Better now. I wasn't so good a day or two ago. There were a bunch of them. These guys mean business. I hope wherever you have her they don't find her."

Their eyes met and Slade said evenly, "I think she's safe. If there's any sign of change, we'll do something else." There was no doubt they were on the same team.

Just then Eli walked into the room. He and Slade shook hands and introduced themselves. Slade had left his hat, belt and boots off and was wearing a plain white button down. Eli looked him up and down and seemed

152

to immediately decide to trust him.

They spoke for a few minutes both about keeping Carrie safe, and about the financial responsibility of the stallion. Slade had given it a lot of thought, and felt he should tell Eli who they were, and what they were doing. Having met the Johnsons, he knew they were as concerned about Isabel, or Carrie, as he and Rossen were. He explained and left both cell numbers and Rossen's parents' number in case they needed to contact them.

Receiving a file of documents, he shook both men's hands and left the hospital room. As he walked out of the door he was shaking his head again. "Tall and dark." He laughed all the way down the hall.

Back in the hospital room, Eli gave Dante a questioning look. "What was that all about?"

Dante cracked a smile that hurt his face. "She told him I was tall and dark."

****

Back at the trailer Slade handed her the papers and shook his head again, still laughing as he went outside.

Rossen came out to help him hook on and asked, "What's tickled your funny bone?" Slade chuckled again.

"You know her friend Dante, who she always talks about? The one who's tall and dark?"

"What about him?"

"He's gotta be 6'7, weighs about 290, and he's Black. Tall and dark." Laughing again, he finished securing the trailer and they got under way. Several times driving down the road on the way to have her signature notarized and mail the papers back he chuckled to himself.

When Isabel opened the folder they found that Eli had also sent three thousand dollars in cash with the paperwork. He must have realized she wasn't using any credit cards or bank accounts.

****

The fact that Isabel hated the bulls had actually turned out to be a convenient way for Slade to earn points in the rough stock without upsetting her. He and Rossen were careful to keep her from finding out he was drawing bulls, and by not being in the first few, so far she hadn't heard the announcer talk about him when he rode. Every time he rode he felt guilty for misleading her. Actually, every time he rode he felt guilty anyway. He wasn't nineteen anymore. He used to really enjoy riding bulls. The adrenaline rush was incredible. But lately he was questioning whether the risk was even worth it. He had nothing to prove like the younger guys did. He'd already earned his place among the top cowboys in the world at the last two National Finals.

He'd even bought a flack jacket, but had only worn it once because it felt stiff and awkward. Maybe if he used it more he'd be more comfortable in it. He resolved to try wearing it when he and Rossen were practice roping. For some reason, Isabel made him think a lot more about the future and being responsible—and not just to keep from offending her.

****

Slade and Rossen had been gearing up for something they called the Cowboy's Christmas. They'd told her it was about five weeks of as many rodeos as they could fit in, beginning in the last week of June. Their calendar was insane. There were times they were actually going to two rodeos in one day in nearby towns. This was the most important time of the year to accrue points to qualify for the NFR, which she'd learned was the championship in which only the top fifteen cowboys in the world in each event were allowed to compete. It really was a big deal. The National Finals Rodeo paid out over six million dollars in the week or so of competition, and it was at this rodeo that the year's world champions were determined. Slade and Rossen had set a goal to qualify again this year.

Isabel had never done this before and she had no idea what to expect. They tried to tie up all the loose ends of their non-rodeo business for the duration, and their agendas had been streamlined as much as possible. She stocked up on groceries and wanted to have the wash done and everything as ready as she could.

Not much had ever been said since they'd

discovered her real identity as far as who was working for whom, so they'd just continued the status quo as smoothly as possible. There was a jar of cash behind the sink in the trailer she sometimes used for groceries and the guys just always made sure it was full so the question of money hadn't come up much. She tried never to make a big deal of working for them because she knew the fact that she was relatively well off could become an issue. She'd been waiting for Slade to fuss about it and he finally did one morning when she went to leave the trailer with their dirty jeans again.

She carried them to the truck and he followed her and brought them back in. Rossen suddenly needed to check the horses, so she knew he'd been expecting this confrontation too.

She didn't want to argue with Slade but she wasn't going to let him win either, so she waited a minute until he was busy elsewhere, then headed for the truck with the laundry again.

He caught her at the cab and said, "Isabel, stop being juvenile. You aren't going to do our laundry. It's bad enough that we let you do everything else. Rossen and I will do it later. Just stop. This is silly." He picked up the bag, and headed back to the trailer. Isabel let him haul it inside only because she didn't want anyone else around to see them argue.

Inside she crowded him back against the wall. "Slade Marsh." She wished she knew his middle name, she'd have thrown that in for good measure. "Why are you doing this? What in the world is wrong with me simply doing the laundry? Do you think I don't do wash at home?" She folded her arms across her chest and prepared to stare him down. "What is any different with me now than before?"

Slade sounded frustrated. "We didn't know you had a net worth more valuable than both of us put together, times five. That's what. We thought we were hiring a college student, remember?"

She laughed. "I *am* a college student! Remember?" She took a deep breath. "Let me get this straight. First off, you're saying you should treat people differently based on how much money they have?" She smiled triumphantly. "That is definitely *not* what Jesus taught."

Actually, he smiled too. "That was good. But it's not going to work. Put the laundry down and stop. This is ridiculous."

"Slade, it's a load of jeans for heavens sake. Have you and I even once, since we've known each other, made a big deal of status? Until this particular moment I mean?"

She wasn't going to back down. "Slade, listen to me. You act like I am doing this great magnanimous service, when if you and I would just get really honest, we'd admit that I'm way more liability than I'm worth. We both know you two are basically acting as bodyguards or something while you're letting me enjoy this great adventure on the rodeo circuit. I told you I don't believe in coincidence. I know I was blessed to have the two of you need truck repairs next to Anna's diner at exactly the right time. Let's do be honest with each other, and actually come right out and say that if they find me, you and Rossen could be in the middle of an ugly, dangerous mess. How much is that worth to me, Slade Marsh?"

He opened his mouth to say something, and she put up a hand. "Look, how about if we look at it this way."

She took a step nearer. "How about if we say you'll throw me a bone, and let me feel like you really do need me, so I can rationalize that I should stay here, in spite of the fact I could be putting the two of you in possible danger."

Her voice took on a pleading tone. "'Cause I'm really enjoying myself, and I don't want to go. Could that work?" Not only had she backed him up to the wall, but as she was talking she'd moved closer and closer until she was only inches from him. He ran a hand through his hair and glanced down at her nervously and she hoped her perfume would cloud his judgment. It must have worked, because he looked at her for a minute in silence and gave in.

She laughed before he even said okay, and threw her arms around his waist in a hug and said, "Thanks, Slade. You're the best. Now give me the jeans." Hoisting the bag over her shoulder, she practically skipped out of the trailer, leaving Slade standing against the trailer wall with a slightly shaken look on his face.

The Cowboy's Christmas was every bit as busy as

they'd warned her it would be. After about a week, both humans and horses had begun to wear down and only the added excitement counteracted that. Isabel drove more than she ever had, and she definitely felt they needed her.

One evening as they pulled in, unloaded and immediately saddled the horses, Slade turned to her and asked, "Is, would you mind watching our horses for us? Rossen and I need to see the secretary first." She nodded as they hurried off. They were gone a long time and as rodeo time drew near she knew their horses were going to be stiff if they didn't get warmed up. Wondering what to do, she finally climbed on Slade's horse, tucked her boots between the leathers of his stirrups, grabbed Rossen's horse by the reins and began to pony him around the arena as she warmed them up with the rest of the cowboys and cowgirls who would be competing that evening.

As she loped the horses in slow circles, she felt like she was getting an unusual amount of attention. When the cowboys she'd been introduced to saw her, she saw surprise in their faces. She'd almost decided there must be a rule against someone who wasn't actually competing, being in the arena or something. It couldn't be helped. The horses needed to be warmed up.

Finally, as the riders left the arena and the announcer started up, she saw Slade and Rossen approaching. She rode toward them, slid to the ground and handed over their reins. Even Rossen seemed surprised that she was riding, but there was no time to talk. She went to unload the other horses and get their rope horses warmed up, and they went to the far end of the arena where they'd soon be bulldoggin'. She didn't think another thing about it until she was on her way back to the trailer after the barrel racers had finished and the bulls were about to start.

As she was skirting the concession stand, she heard Jesse's unmistakable voice. "They say she just works for them, but I don't believe it after seeing her on Slade's horse. He never lets anyone but Rossen even touch that horse, let alone ride it. And did you see him when she handed him over? He acted like it was nothing. Just nothing at all. I've thought there must be something going on. Since she's been around he hasn't come out dancing or anything even once . . ."

Isabel walked on out of earshot, although she'd been tempted to stay and listen. That must have been what all the surprised looks were about. That seemed funny because it hadn't seemed like a big deal to her or Slade. And had he changed his lifestyle when she came? It was something to think about.

****

One night in Texas, as she was walking back to the trailer by herself in the dark during the bull riding, she saw Leland Wilde standing near another trailer up ahead. Wishing Slade or Rossen had come to see her back, she hesitated to walk past him alone. It had been several rodeos since they had last walked her to the trailer during the bulls and she missed their reassuring presence.

Feeling a little sheepish for her lack of courage, she returned to near the arena and stayed where there were more people. She was standing there watching spectators come and go, when she heard Slade's name from the announcer.

No! Surely she was mistaken, but no, there it was again. The announcer was telling the crowd some stats on Slade's rodeo career while they waited for him to get ready in the chute. She flew up the ramp to the stands above her and was horrified to see Rossen helping Slade settle into a chute that held a huge, dark brown bull. She was close to that end of the arena and she could see it all perfectly.

Finally set, Slade leaned back, placed his free hand on the gate and nodded his head. The gate flew open to release the bull. The blood seemed to drain from her head and she couldn't catch her breath as the bull lunged out of the opening and spun violently to the left in a powerful rush. Even with her heart in her throat, she knew she was watching a master rider. His body seemed to sense what the bull would do next and adjusted for it with each raging plunge. The writhing animal was a thing possessed and it lunged and spun every which way to displace the rider stuck to its back. Slade rode with a rhythm and balance that were almost fascinating, as he and the beast careened across the arena in some kind of convoluted ballet.

At last the buzzer sounded and Slade timed the bull's lunges so he could jump off and away. With perfect balance, Slade sprung off the side of the bull to land gracefully on his feet in the torn up dirt like it was no big deal. Isabel felt like she'd been kicked in the stomach. He retrieved his hat and dusted it off as he crossed the arena to pick up his discarded bull rope. The bull made a lap around the end of the arena, and then came back after Slade and the official in the arena near him. Both men raced for the fence and literally ran up it to balance over the top rail as the bull roared past, missing them by inches.

Waiting for the bull to move off, Slade glanced up into the stands above him and, incidentally, right into Isabel's eyes. Time stood still for a moment, and then she looked away, turned abruptly and walked back down the ramp.

****

Rossen had watched Isabel exit the arena after the barrels, so he was dismayed to glance up from behind the chutes and recognize her standing just a short distance away. If he wasn't mistaken, all heck was going to break loose and soon.

Pulling his attention back to the chute in front of him, he finished helping Slade onto the bull's back. Now was a bad time to be distracted and he forced himself to focus.

He stood by as Slade signaled for the gate and then made a beautiful ride. Afterward, as the bull came back, Rossen was watching Isabel again, and after seeing her face as she turned, he made an executive decision to go to the cowboy dance that night. He'd rather face Angelique any day than be in that trailer when Slade faced Isabel.

****

Surprisingly, the trailer was empty when Slade tentatively opened the door and walked in. There were normal, square sandwiches made with bread on the counter in sandwich bags--something she hadn't ever made before. She usually did something more gourmet than that. He wasn't sure whether to be relieved or even more tense. The truck was here so he doubted she'd gone far.

He'd called Rossen a coward earlier when he'd nonchalantly mentioned he was going dancing. He must have seen Isabel too.

With a sigh of discouragement Slade wolfed down a sandwich, dumped his gear in the tack room, and headed for the little shower and the liniment. He tried to tell himself he didn't care, that Isabel was being silly, and that he was single and didn't have to bother with a woman. All his arguments sounded empty, however when he thought back to the night she'd watched her first bull ride.

He was standing at the table wearing only jeans

when she walked in. His hair was still damp and mussed and he was attempting to put liniment on his shoulders. She stepped over to him and unabashedly looked him up and down, then into his eyes and said, "You have a body like a young Greek god. I thought you would be more grateful for it than this." She turned her back on him and went to bed, pulling her curtain.

He shook his head. It wasn't quite a slamming door, but was definitely effective. With another long sigh he turned out the light and lay down. He'd expected anger, or tears, or anything other than the deep quiet sadness he'd seen. He wanted to talk to her, to explain, to tell her about the goal he'd set, and the hard work they'd invested, and the fame, and the money. It all sounded hollow here in the dark, with her ten feet away but ten million feet emotionally.

He was still awake when he heard Rossen come in and quietly undress. In the dark Rossen asked softly, "How'd it go?"

"Mmm. Okay."

"That bad?"

"Yeah, pretty much."

****

Isabel knew she was quieter. She tried to be herself and did all the things she normally did, but her smile was tired. She knew she had no right to expect Slade to change his lifestyle. After thinking it through, she had to accept the fact that she just didn't understand. He seemed more reliable than anyone she'd ever met. She knew he was the type to take risks, but calculated ones. Bulls seemed too foolish for him. And after all, it wasn't any of her business. It was his life. He'd been living like this for years quite nicely without her. He obviously didn't need her approval to make his own decisions. She resolutely decided she'd stand by him even in this. He had stood by her. What worried her as much as anything was that she'd been made abruptly and fully aware of how deeply she cared. She cared a lot.

****

Slade had to admire her depth. He knew his riding the bull troubled her deeply, but she managed to deal with it and still pull her weight without ever saying more than she had said that night.

He did a lot of soul searching and decided he'd still ride bulls, but only as many as he needed to get through the NFR. He could use points from the timed events, but he knew he'd have to ride both broncs and bulls too. After this year, he'd let the all-around title go.

Since the night she'd busted him they never tried to hide the fact that he was going to ride bucking stock, and she never left during the bulls anymore. Knowing he'd disappointed her stung, but knowing she had decided to support him in it anyway was priceless.

Two nights later, when he'd been thrown hard and was trying to reach his back with the liniment, she watched quietly for a minute and then offered her help saying, "You need to work the knots out first for it to help the most. The build up of lactic acid and loss of oxygen to the muscle inhibit the blood flow and increase inflammation. Turn around and I'll help." She sat behind him and smoothed her hands over the expanse of his back, identifying knots he didn't even realize he had and then worked over the muscles like an expert.

Amazed, he asked, "Where did you learn to do this?" Her fingers and hands were incredible. He was all but melting.

From behind him, she said, "I'm three years into a degree in sports medicine, remember? Most of it has been generals but some of it has been in my field. On top of that, the same principles hold true for the race horses. The science of it works the same in horses and humans. You just smell better and are much easier to reach." Her smile reached almost to her eyes.

She actually did end up using her expertise learned on the track in conditioning horses to help keep Slade's and Rossen's horses in top form, and occasionally, she worked on Rossen's strains and sprains too.

****

They were three weeks into the month of July and rodeo life was a whirlwind of roping, riding, bulldogging, and driving. Isabel had seen more of the country in the last month than she'd seen in the first

166

twenty years of her life combined. Much of their driving had been done at night, but still, she'd been places she'd never dreamed of six months ago. In all this time she had only been recognized once in the rodeo crowd. Apparently the blueblood race crowd and the rodeo types didn't have many people in common. The one guy who had known her didn't seem to realize she'd been missing from the race scene, so the encounter had actually been reassuring.

Dante had returned home from the hospital and was almost back to normal, and things in California were quiet, at least for now. Judd and Deek hadn't been seen and the police were still trying to find them. Several of the Wind Dance Farms racers had won significant races and news from home left her feeling she was right to stay where she was.

They were in Cheyenne, Wyoming for the Frontier Days Rodeo, one of the biggest in the country, and although they were only six hours from their homes in the western part of the state, there would be only a short time to visit enroute to their next stop.

She and Slade and Rossen had settled into a comfortable system of working and living together that made for success in the arena. Isabel's spare horse had come in very handy on two occasions, and Slade and Rossen were winning good money consistently.

Downtime lazing in the old lounge chairs had become a rarity, and they were making the most of it one warm July afternoon. Slade and Isabel were mildly surprised when Rossen quickly got up and headed into the trailer, saying, "I'm officially napping, and don't you dare let her into this trailer!" Isabel laughed out loud when she heard him lock the door from inside.

Within seconds they heard what had sent him packing. Isabel laughed again when she realized it was a double whammy. Not only could she hear the voice of Angelique headed their direction, but she heard Jesse with her.

Slade suddenly looked like a deer in the headlights, and when Isabel got up from her chair and quickly stepped across to sit on his lounger with him, his eyes widened even further and she laughed once more. The reaction of both of these grown, responsible, adult men to these two floozy cowgirls had entertained her from the start, but boy did they make these guys uncomfortable.

Isabel was enjoying her role immensely as she leaned into Slade just as the two girls rounded the corner of the trailer.

Jesse pulled up short. "Isabel! What are you doing?" Isabel looked around innocently at Jesse's demanding question.

"Just having an ice cream." She smiled as she teasingly reached up to wipe a little off Slade's upper lip, and then turned and leaned back against him comfortably. "What are you two up to?" Thinking that Slade had incredibly nice lips, Isabel nonchalantly laid her hand on his thigh next to her hip and added, "I'd offer you one, but Rossen ate them all before he went in to nap."

Angelique, her clothes scanty, as opposed to Jesse's tight ones, had been looking around and said, "I was wondering where he was." Jesse hadn't been looking around. She was looking straight at Slade and Isabel. The jealousy on her face almost made Isabel feel guilty until she remembered how this woman had tormented them.

"He's just tired. We're out here so we don't disturb him." Isabel got goose bumps as Slade wrapped his arm loosely around her waist. She slid her small hand into his larger one and entwined their fingers.

The conversation slowed right down. The two cowgirls were speechless and Isabel lost all coherent thought. Slade saved them by offering some mindless small talk and eventually they walked back the way they'd come.

Once they were good and gone, Rossen popped right back out of the trailer with a huge grin on his face as Isabel laughingly switched back to her own chair and proceeded to finish her ice cream. Slade smiled at her and said, "Dang, for once I wish the girls had stayed longer."

Isabel licked her Popsicle stick and laughed. "It seemed to work." Not to mention the fact that it had been heavenly to snuggle against Slade—even if it did make her heart rate increase markedly.

Later that afternoon her heart rate went even higher. Slade was grooming his horses when Isabel saw Jesse headed their way through the trailer kitchen window. She slipped out the door and hurried to the horse barn, came down the row and slipped into the stall with Slade. Walking right up to him, she put her hand on his waist, looked up into his face and whispered, "Kiss me. Hurry."

Her request seemed to surprise the heck out of him, but she didn't have to ask twice. His back was to the stall door, but he hugged her and whispered back right against her lips, "I assume this sudden need for affection is the result of the imminent arrival of Jesse again. Right?"

She didn't have time to answer before he began kissing her. Her mouth was busy anyway. His suspicions were confirmed a minute or two later. Surprisingly, he seemed to be enjoying that minute immensely. His mouth was firm and warm, and at the moment remarkably willing. Not that she would complain. She'd dreamed about this.

She'd tried not to, but from that first meeting, he was just so marvelously attractive that she hadn't been able to help it. Plus, she knew she wasn't the only one who felt the attraction between them. He'd noticed it. At times it had been like electricity sparking across the trailer. Still, she hadn't really expected him to be this cooperative about kissing her.

They had both completely forgotten about anyone else when Jesse's voice brought them back to reality. "Slade, I . . . Slade! What are you doing?"

He hesitated and then sighing reluctantly, raised his head and swore under his breath. Isabel felt like doing the same exact thing. She knew Jesse was none too bright, but really.

With a disgusted tone, Slade said, "I'm kissing a girl, Jesse. What does it look like? Or I was."

Isabel didn't even have the strength left in her bones to act her part. She was a little dazed. She'd forgotten about Jesse. Actually, she'd forgotten about everything. If she'd known kissing him would be like that she'd have taken up their charade when he'd first mentioned it.

Jesse's voice was eminently accusing. "I thought you said she was your cook, or your secretary or something."

With one arm still around Isabel, Slade said, "She is or something, why? Have you got a problem with it?"

Jesse stuck out her bottom lip in a pout. "Yes, of course I do. You're not supposed to kiss your secretary. It's, it's . . . it's unethical."

Pulling Isabel more snuggly against him, Slade looked down at her and said in a velvet voice that made her stomach do a somersault, "Well, I like it. A lot. So would you go away, so I can do it some more? Please." With that he turned his back on Jesse and went back to kissing Isabel. Neither one of them heard her leave.

A few minutes later Isabel tentatively pushed him away and said somewhat breathlessly, "I . . . I'm sure we convinced her you're romantically involved." She looked up at him with a smile that was a little shy.

He smiled back and said softly, "We certainly convinced me."

Isabel laughed softly and said, "That was a terrible line."

"Sorry, your mouth short-circuited my brain. That's all it could come up with with you this close. And it fits."

He still held her shoulders and she asked hesitantly, "What do you mean?"

Moving a hand from her shoulder to her cheek, he looked at her mouth as he said, "Mmm, I mean that I *am* romantically involved." Her eyes flew to his and he softly admitted, "Man, I've wanted to do that for the longest time, Isabel. I've wanted to see if I'd enjoy kissing you as much as I thought I would." He bent and kissed her again and then pulled away.

She gave him a small hesitant smile. "And?"

He put a finger tenderly on her lower lip. It made her knees weak as he gave a lazy smile and said in that same velvet voice, "I'm not entirely sure. I need to continue my research." He bent his head to kiss her again, this time more softly, his touch infinitely gentle. He was slow to pull away and then hugged her and leaned his cheek on her hair and said, "It was even better than I'd hoped."

Completely unsure of herself, she couldn't think of anything to say, and finally, simply said, "That's good. Isn't it?"

He chuckled, kissed her once more, hugged her close, and said huskily. "Better than good, girl." They stood there like that for a long moment while his horse went on eating, completely unaware that Isabel's world had miniature fireworks going off in it.

Finally, Slade broke the silence. "Um . . . Isabel. This is not exactly that professional relationship I promised. My only excuse is you walked in here and asked. I'm weak, I know. But I am only human. So, do you think you could release me from that promise soon? 'Cause I'd really like to do it again sometime."

She hid her face against his chest and he said, "Hey." His voice was gentle as he lifted her chin. "Are you okay?" She nodded. "With this, I mean?"

She gave him a shy smile. "I don't know what I am. I mean. I didn't really do this to put you on the spot. I mean it's great! It's what I've wanted. I just didn't know you did, too."

He looked into her eyes and quietly said, "You did too."

Nodding tentatively, she said, "Okay. You're right, but . . . This is probably not very well thought out, but I loved it anyway."

"So can I be released from my promise?" His brilliant green eyes searched hers.

Her heart was pounding so hard she thought he could see it. She asked, "We're living so closely. Do you think that's wise?"

He nodded and said without hesitating, "Absolutely."

She swallowed hard and said, "I'll, uh, I'll just trust your judgment."

As his head slowly came back down to hers, he mumbled, "We're gonna need more research."

Sometime later, from what seemed like a distance, she heard, "Hey, why do I get the impression I've missed something?" Rossen's cheerful face appeared outside the stall.

Isabel reluctantly pulled away from Slade's mouth and laughed softly and said, "We were just trying to convince Jesse that Slade is romantically involved."

"I see." Rossen looked up and down the empty alleyway and laughed as well. "Well, yeah. Not a sign of Jesse anywhere. It must have worked, huh?"

Slade opened the stall door for Isabel, smiled at her and said, "Like a charm." He took her hand and they stepped out into the alleyway of the barn.

Seeing their linked hands, Rossen said, "So. . . About that promise that we'd keep it completely professional."

Slade elbowed him and said, "Already dealt with. I'm officially exempt from that promise."

Rossen grinned. "What about me?"

Isabel laughed and Slade elbowed Rossen again and said, "You're still under oath, dude. Permanently. And you're still in the dog house for horsing around with her that day with the zerbits. So don't get any ideas."

As the three of them fell into step beside each other on the way out of the barn, Rossen said, "Hey, as I recall, you were the hesitant one about bringing her that day we met. I had to kind of nudge you along. I should

174

have some kind of clout here."

"You have tons of clout. Just keep away from my girl or I breaka you head."

Rossen grinned again and said, "I could take you."

Slade only shook his head, and chuckled and Rossen went on. "However, I am far too much of a gentleman. I'll concede. But I get the next bored college student we adopt. Deal?"

Slade high-fived him and Isabel added her hand as well and the two of them said in unison, "Deal."

As they headed back to the trailer to dress for the night's rodeo, Rossen asked, "So, was Jesse really around? Or were you two just saying that?"

Chapter 8

Slade and Rossen cleaned up in Cheyenne. After that big rodeo they were ranked 5th in the world in team roping, and Slade was in the top 6 for all-around. After kissing in the stall Isabel started to ride in the front seat of the truck regularly. Although their itinerary hadn't changed, their relationship had.

They all three realized that living so closely in the trailer and being more involved would require a delicate balance, and Slade voiced concern about Isabel's reputation. Even though Slade and Isabel definitely acted romantically involved, they were careful to go easy and be completely beyond reproach. It was heavenly to not have to pretend anymore that theirs was only a professional relationship.

It was nice just to be able to hold his hand if she wanted. When he occasionally held her, she wanted to be thinking much more long term than about the next rodeo. Much more long term than was wise, considering their situation.

Rossen and Slade had indeed attended church every Sunday wherever they were, and they'd taken

Isabel with them. She didn't really have a clue what was going on at first, but she'd left every time feeling happy and spiritually fed. The principles she was learning in Rossen's church exactly dovetailed with what little her mother had taught her and although it was very different than the church she'd attended with Eli and Dante, she felt good about going. Rossen still hadn't said anything as far as trying to preach to her or Slade, and she knew Slade was impatient to break the news that he wanted to be baptized. He'd thought Rossen would have asked him again by now.

Their next stop was the rodeo in Salt Lake City, Utah, and Isabel looked forward to it. She'd never been there other than the night at the airport, but she knew it was the closest big city to their homes. It was also where Rossen's church was headquartered, and the rodeo celebration was all a part of the commemoration of the first settlers of the area which had been the earliest members of the church. They'd been telling her some of the history of the region, and she was fascinated.

Stories of a boy prophet, gold plates, wagons trains, extermination orders, handcarts and all kinds of interesting trivia about the area had her wishing they would be spending more time there than they could spare. She was sure they would be back in the area several times. It was obviously a place they loved.

She had had no idea before coming here with them that Salt Lake City was such a cultured metropolitan area. It had not only one of the top ballet companies in the country, but a full symphony as well

178

and an opera company. Apparently the church leaders had believed the arts to be important from the earliest time here.

They stopped at the Rockland Ranch for a few hours' visit on the way through from Cheyenne to Salt Lake City. Isabel was thrilled to see Naomi again and she was gratified to realize how well Ebony Wind was doing. Marti herself was riding him occasionally and he was as sleek and shiny as ever.

Isabel mentioned to Naomi that she'd been attending church with Rossen and Slade and that she had begun to understand what Naomi had meant about the gospel principles. They shared a sweet moment that Isabel felt only they two could understand.

Later, Naomi asked, "Has Rossen given you a Book of Mormon of your own yet?" They were walking out to the truck together as the rodeo threesome prepared to leave.

Isabel shook her head. "Not yet. They told me they would get me one on this trip though."

"They?" Naomi perked right up at the use of the plural.

"They." Isabel smiled at her. She could imagine how this good woman felt. She knew she loved Slade like a son and wanted him to have the same happy life her own family enjoyed.

As Isabel climbed into the truck to leave, Naomi held Isabel's hand in both of hers and said, "Take care of my boys and hurry home."

The rodeo in Salt Lake City was actually held in a huge arena in the crush of the city. There was nowhere to stall the horses. In fact, they had to park the trailer in the middle of a parking lot cordoned off for that purpose.

On the way into the arena they had driven past the Salt Lake Temple, a glorious cathedral-type building with multiple spires. As they drove past and she commented on how beautiful it was, they told her it was one of the many temples that belonged to their church. They would just mention things in passing, and she'd begun to wonder if she would ever understand all the aspects of this gospel. Sometimes she felt they were speaking a different language.

They arrived in mid-afternoon and would compete that night, then planned to leave immediately afterward so they could bed down their horses somewhere other than tied to the trailer on the pavement. They would head straight up I-15 to southern Idaho.

Before the rodeo, Isabel was working in the trailer when she found what looked to her like one of the flack jackets the bull riders wore in a storage compartment under one of the beds. Slade and Rossen were outside tacking up and she carried it to Slade and asked, "What's this?"

He glanced up at it and then met her eyes. "You know exactly what it is, Isabel. It's too stiff and constricting. I can't ride with it." He finished saddling his horse, untied it and stood waiting for Rossen. He

180

looked at her again for a long steady moment that didn't hold any attitude, but it didn't hold any backing down either. Finally, she turned and went back into the trailer.

Through the trailer window, Isabel saw that Rossen finished tightening his cinch, stepped into the saddle, grinned down at Slade and said, "If you get hurt you'd better just go ahead and die rather than face her."

Inside the trailer Isabel was torn. In a way she was disgusted with Slade for making a stupid decision on top of a stupid decision, and she was hurt that he hadn't even bothered to try to accommodate what she'd obviously been trying to get him to do. But, in a way, she also respected the fact that he didn't always give in to her will the way other guys sometimes did. It ticked her off, but if he'd have let her call all the shots, she wouldn't have been attracted to him. Somehow, her strong will and spirit needed a man whose will and spirit were even stronger.

It was frustrating at times like this, but she never doubted he was strong enough for her to lean on when she needed it. That was invaluable to her.

For most of her teen and adult life she had found that because she was smart and decisive, many of the men she came in contact with always deferred to her will or judgment. Not only did it get old quickly, but there were times she really just needed someone else to make the tough calls and let her lean on their strength.

It wasn't a men are superior or not thing, it was just that sometimes she needed to know the guy had it all under control. Before Slade she'd never been able to be sure of that. She just hoped and prayed that his strong will wouldn't come back to hurt him.

Later, Isabel was unusually nervous for some reason. The rodeo wouldn't even start for another forty minutes, but she was already in the building. After asking Slade about the flack jacket and Rossen's comment about getting hurt, she'd been unable to focus on anything. Finally, she had given up and decided to come over early and watch the cowboys warm up. She didn't remember being this tense even at her first rodeo. Maybe it was just that this one was so different from what she was used to because it was in such an unusual venue. She decided to try walking the concourses to release some of her emotions.

Bo, Joey, and Treyne came, but didn't get there until just before it started. By the time they showed up and climbed over all the others on their row, Isabel was a mess. Her nerves were shot. She absent-mindedly stood for the National Anthem, usually one of her favorite parts of the whole night, and even the fact that the queens rode into the arena in a convertible and evening gowns didn't catch her attention. *What was wrong with her tonight?* Finally, she just mentally shook herself and managed to calm down by sheer force of will.

The show was good, the clowns were excellent, and Slade and Rossen placed first or second in each of their earlier events. She'd finally mellowed and was beginning to enjoy herself when she realized they were

182

through with the barrels and were setting up for the bulls. All of her hard won self-control went out the window, and she excused herself from her seat.

She wandered for a few minutes during the first few bulls, and found herself just above the alleyway the cowgirls used to race into the arena from outside. She heard the announcer call Slade's name and begin to go into his spiel about Slade's record, standing, and what not. From where she was at the end of the arena she had a bird's eye view of the chutes and area behind them. She could clearly see Rossen helping Slade as he settled onto the back of a black bull.

The entire world seemed to move into slow motion as he leaned back and nodded his head. Everything was strikingly clear and in sharp focus as the bull exploded from the gate and began his violent attempt to unseat the cowboy on his back. Bucking and spinning left and then right, it would kick high into the air and then whip its massive head back only to plunge forward and whip the other way. Slade was the ultimate picture of grace under fire and rode with a precision and balance that were both terrifying and fascinating at once. She wanted to look away and at the same time couldn't bring herself to move.

Finally, the buzzer sounded. Slade brought his free hand down to his rope and prepared to dismount. At the last second as he leaned forward, the bull gave another huge lunge, and flung him violently up and to the left. Slade landed in front and to the side of the bull on his shoulder, and was lost to sight for a split second somewhere under the animal.

In the melee and dust, it was impossible to tell if he was being stepped on as the bull went over the top of him. Almost instantly he came to his feet and lunged for the fence as the bull spun and charged. Motion seemed to slow even further as she saw the bull slam into his side and smash him into the rail. In what could only have been a split second, but felt like hours, both bullfighters were there slapping the bull in the face. It turned on them and spun away from Slade.

Miraculously, he stood and pulled himself up the fence and hung there by one arm until the bull was run out of the arena. Isabel finally breathed as he slid back to the ground and stood leaning on the bullfighters at his side. One arm hung at an awkward angle and he couldn't seem to stand up straight.

Rossen was there instantly as a group of cowboys tried to help him out of the arena and to the attending physician at the gate. Without even knowing how she got there, Isabel found herself on the arena floor, and watched as they loaded him on the stretcher and into the ambulance. Rossen pushed her in the door before they closed it and the ambulance pulled away.

She stayed out of the way of the medics as they tried to check his vitals. She wasn't even sure where it was safe to touch him, and was amazed when his good arm reached out to her. As she moved to his side as best she could, their eyes met and locked.

His skin was ashen and beads of sweat stood out on his brow, but his grip was strong enough to hurt her

184

and she was reassured, even as she heard them say he was bleeding internally. He had a dislocated shoulder, but it couldn't be immediately put back in because they believed he also had a broken collar bone. They were still assessing him as the ambulance pulled into the emergency entrance of the hospital a mere six minutes later.

Doctors were waiting as they wheeled him in, and instantly went to work to try to determine where the internal injury was. They knew he was bleeding badly and prepped him for surgery on the spot. Rossen and Treyne came flying in the door just as they started to wheel him out.

Isabel finally cried when she saw these two friends reunite. Rossen gripped Slade's good hand and the look that passed between them was unfathomable.

Slade spoke for the first time, "Can I have a blessing before they operate?"

An attending doctor interrupted, "Make it fast." Isabel had no idea what was going on, but the hospital staff seemed to. They wheeled him back into the cubicle and quickly pulled the curtains closed. Treyne placed a drop of something out of a tiny vial on the top of Slade's head and then placed his hands there. He said a short prayer and then Rossen put his hands on top of Treyne's and said another slightly longer one.

He said that Slade would be made whole and well again and that his Father in Heaven loved him and was mindful of his needs.

Isabel didn't understand it all, but she didn't need

to. The warm sweet peace that filled her was enough.

They started to wheel him away almost before Rossen finished his prayer, and Isabel buried herself in Rossen's embrace. He just held her, his head resting against hers as they prayed silently for the safety of their friend.

He was in surgery for less than two hours, but it seemed like forever. She and Rossen had finally gone to a waiting room near the OR and recovery room, and tried to settle in to wait. Treyne and Cooper brought them a change of clothing, then took Joey and the horses and trailer and went home to the ranch. Isabel felt like she'd aged years by the time the surgeon finally came back.

What he had to tell them scared her worse than ever. Slade had suffered a ruptured liver and had narrowly missed bleeding to death tonight. Only the fact that he'd been so close to a hospital had saved him. Multiple other organs were badly bruised, and internally and externally he was a mess.

He had several other injuries, but none were life threatening. They'd set his shoulder and collarbone and he would be wearing a brace for awhile, but all in all he'd been lucky. He had a long road ahead but he would be fine, just as Rossen had promised.

The longest night of her life passed and morning had come and gone. Slade had been taken to the ICU for four hours in the night until they'd been able to stabilize him with several units of blood. He was now in a regular room hooked up to what seemed a myriad of machines and tubes. He was scarcely darker than the white sheets and was heavily sedated. She and Rossen had struggled through the night together, and now dozed intermittently in chairs in his room. She felt like she had sand in her eyes.

Mid-afternoon Naomi showed up and was like a breath of hope. Her calm reassurances and tranquil faith soothed Isabel's troubled heart, and she was finally able to really fall asleep. Rossen left Slade in his mom's capable hands and went to the cafeteria for a quick bite.

****

Slade knew there was someone in the room, but he was much too tired to open his eyes to see them. Whoever it was, he knew that everything was okay from their peaceful calm. He realized someone was holding his hand and went back to sleep.

Sometime later when he finally did open his eyes, he saw Naomi Rockland sitting beside his bed. She held his hand and patted it gently as he woke up.

"Good morning." Her voice was low and gentle as she smiled at him. "Sleep well?" *Only the Rocklands could tease him at a time like this.*

"Actually, no. Whatever they've given me gives me strange dreams." He gave her a tired smile

He noticed Isabel asleep in the chair. "Has she been there all night?"

"And all day. She's been beside your bed whenever they'd let her. In the ICU she could only come in every half hour, so she waited in the waiting room between."

Tiredly, he admitted, "She tried to get me to wear my flack jacket last night." There was infinite regret in his voice.

Naomi winced. "You might be in a lot of trouble once you're better."

"No." He barely shook his head. "She loves me unconditionally." Somehow as he said it, he knew it was true.

"Is that a good thing?" He could hear the hope and love in Naomi's voice

His voice was husky as he answered, "Yeah, it's a good thing. A really good thing." She squeezed his hand and he closed his eyes and drifted off again.

****

When Isabel awoke in the early evening, all was quiet. She felt much better. She sat up, running her fingers through the tangles in her hair. Looking at Slade, she realized his eyes were open and following her every move.

He slowly reached across for her with his good arm and she moved to his side. They just sat for a moment looking at each other. Finally, she spoke, "If you had died on me, I'd have been really ticked." He gave her a tired smile and she gently kissed it.

She said, "They think it might take awhile, but you're going to be okay." She cupped his face with her hand. After a minute, she lowered her forehead to his good shoulder and whispered, "I was scared."

He awkwardly stroked her hair. "I was, too. I'd finally figured out what I really wanted and almost messed it up. I love you, Isabel." She raised her head again, searching his eyes.

"You'd better be careful what you say when you're on narcotics." She smiled and sat up, brushing the hair back from his forehead. "How do you feel?"

"Like I've been crushed by an angry bull and then drugged."

She studied his face and scanned his bandaged body and grinned. "That's about how you look."

His abdomen was bandaged all the way around, and his left shoulder and lower neck were tightly taped. He wore a brace that looped around the front of both shoulders and under his arms and behind his neck and back. There was heavy bruising visible in multiple places, and she could only imagine what was under the tape and on his back and side, where the bull had hit him. Just thinking about it made her shudder.

She wished there were something she could do to help. "Tell me what I can do for you. What do you need?" She could tell he was in pain and still needed to sleep.

He gave her a weak smile. "Time to heal. The nurse just gave me pain medication, and other than to see your pretty face, there's not a thing I need." She sat beside him, and he drifted back to sleep. She leaned her head against his bed and was dozing again when Rossen and Naomi returned.

****

Bo and Joey had told Naomi how nervous Isabel had been at the rodeo. She wondered if Isabel was that way every time.

Rossen seemed to read her mind and said, "She's held up well considering what she saw that first night. These last several rodeos she's been a trooper as far as I know. We're never with her when he rides bulls because I'm helping at the chute, but I think she's been okay.

"I can't imagine what went through her head last night."

Naomi stayed overnight and when Slade seemed to be out of the woods the next day, she and Rossen started to plan out the next few days and weeks. The doctors wanted him to stay hospitalized for another three or four days and then he needed to recuperate for at least several weeks. For the first little while he would need a lot of care. He had a six inch incision in his stomach and internally he was still terribly fragile and was not to do anything but lie around for at least ten days. Then it would be weeks before he could do anything even mildly strenuous.

With Slade's input, they decided to take him home to the Rockland Ranch, and Isabel and Naomi

190

would help him as long as he needed them. When he was a little stronger, Rossen would take Sean, who had offered to take a college semester off, and head back out on the road to try to salvage their run at the NFR. They would play it by ear as to whether Slade would really be up to that, even though it was still more than four months away.

Slade was incredibly weak and tired. Everything he owned hurt when he tried to move. So far about all he had been up to was occasionally raising and lowering the head of his hospital bed.

Isabel was always there beside his bed when he awoke, always attentive to his needs. He wondered if she ever ate or slept

Even though it'd been more than two days since his surgery, they hadn't let him eat and he hadn't even missed it. He was used to being so physically strong and independent, and it was proof of what rough shape he was in that he was willing to just rest and let the people around him fuss. Now he was stiff, not only from his injuries but also from just laying there. He knew it, but was unable to move much to ease the stiffness because of the pain. Even the physical therapist hadn't helped much. Slade felt like one big bruise. The medication helped the pain, but often left him in such a haze that the only thing he really knew for sure was that Isabel was always at his side. It was incredibly sweet to have her near.

****

Isabel was still there. She watched over him and prayed, and he knew it was hard for her to see him so badly hurt. Slowly and gradually he improved, and on the morning of the fifth day he felt like he had turned a corner. He was finally hungry and wanted to stand up and try walking around.

With the help of the physical therapist he moved to the edge of his bed. He was light-headed and they had him just sit there for several minutes, then lie back down.

It was the first time Isabel saw his back and he heard her gasp. When he looked around, there were tears in her eyes and he tiredly asked, "What?"

She shook her head and then whispered, "Almost your whole back is bruised."

With a weak smile, he said, "I know, honey. But don't worry. My heart's strong as ever."

All she did was close her eyes and swallow hard.

The next day they removed some of the taping from his dislocated shoulder and he was backing off on the pain pills, so he was much more alert. Sometimes she caught him quietly watching her and he knew she wondered what he was thinking. He hoped she trusted the things he'd said when he was sedated.

That afternoon he finally stood up and, although he felt ridiculously weak, he was elated. He wanted out of this hospital in the worst way. He wanted real food and more than two hours of uninterrupted sleep at a time. There were a lot of things he wanted.

For days he'd watched Isabel near his bed and it was incredibly frustrating to be so incapacitated. Sometimes late at night when he was awake, they talked into the early morning hours. He'd told her things he never told anyone, not even Rossen, and felt that she'd done the same with him. Their backgrounds were in some ways opposites, but in many ways they had a lot in common.

She'd asked him about the two bad experiences he'd let keep him from getting baptized and he'd finally told her about his mother. He knew that somehow she understood how hurt he'd been over the years. He'd told her more about his father and Chante and she'd cried there in the semi-darkness holding his hand.

His heart had been full when she haltingly admitted she wanted a home and family more than anything else, but was afraid she wouldn't know how to have one successfully. He'd come to realize that she'd had more mothering in the couple of times she'd been around Naomi than she'd experienced in most of her life, and she worried she would fail as a mother herself because of that lack.

She was sweet and smart and beautiful, and he'd fallen hopelessly in love with her.

What to do about that was entirely another question. She was still living in fear of her father, and even though Slade was comfortably well off, his assets paled in comparison to her wealth. Moreover, he'd never thought about settling down anywhere but home in Wyoming, but her home was far away and very different from his. Although he'd uproot even from his beloved Wyoming if he had to for her—something he never dreamed he'd consider.

On top of everything else, she was only twenty years old and he wondered if she was even ready to think about the same big decisions he needed to make in his life. He knew she loved him even though she hadn't told him so. She'd proven it over and over, especially in the last few days. She never put limitations on him and accepted him exactly as he was. He just wondered how much of that was the fact that she'd needed help so desperately when they came along. And would she marry him even when she knew she was in love with him, or would she refuse out of some warped sense of protecting him from Judd and his friends?

He thought about all these as he rested on and off. The pain medicine was still making him have bizarre dreams, and that mixed with his deep thoughts made an awful combination. He awoke in the night drenched in sweat from dreaming of a hellish bull ride, all tangled with Isabel, the mafia, Judd, and the FBI. Even Dante and Rossen's brothers were in there somewhere.

She woke him with a gentle hand there in the dark, dried his brow, and helped him back to sleep by massaging the part of his shoulder that didn't hurt.

****

Naomi came back and was as much comfort to

Isabel as she was to Slade. Isabel was tired to the bone. It'd been days since she'd slept through the night in a bed. Even when she went to a nearby hotel to rest, she slept poorly and felt she should be with him.

The nightmares from the first bull ride had come back with a vengeance and between visions of it, and Slade's wreck, she hardly dared close her eyes. Naomi came in and her tranquil, sweet calm filled the room. She must have known what was going on, because she had the hospital bring in a chair that made into a bed for Isabel. She literally sat between Isabel and Slade, helping them both to rest in peace. The next morning Isabel felt like a new woman.

That afternoon Rossen stayed with Slade while Naomi and Isabel went to run some errands. They ended up at a place called Temple Square. Naomi took her into the Visitor's Center. They needed to get back, but Naomi took her on a short tour and to a huge statue of Christ which was incredibly touching.

Isabel had never felt like this in her life. She and Naomi didn't say anything. There was no need. The tears filled Isabel's eyes, and flowed down her cheeks as she stood and looked at His face and hands with the infinitude of the universe spread out behind Him.

She'd come to know He was the Savior as a child from her mother and Eli, but her experiences of late had taught her with a surety that He and the Father knew her personally and of her troubles, hopes and needs. This beautiful statue was such a tangible image of His love and sacrifice that it filled her whole soul. Its beauty and magnificence were almost overwhelming. She stood and looked up and could feel her spirit being strengthened and renewed. At length they quietly left, neither speaking for fear of losing the Spirit they'd just experienced.

Isabel walked back into Slade's room feeling strong enough to face the days and weeks she knew were to come. She was still too emotional to even speak when Rossen asked where they had been. She started to try to tell them but Naomi had to explain. Rossen put his arm around her shoulders and gave her a big squeeze as she tried to smile through her tears. As she sat down beside Slade, he reached for her hand and gripped it hard.

That night, late in the dim and quiet of the hospital, she and Naomi talked into the wee hours as Naomi answered Isabel's questions about the Church. One of the things that had puzzled Isabel most was what had happened when Slade had asked for a blessing before his surgery.

At her questions, Naomi taught her the concept of worthy men being ordained to the priesthood by one having authority. They then could use the priesthood's power to do Christ's work much the same as the Savior Himself had done when He walked the earth. These same priesthood holders could also perform other priesthood ordinances like baptism and more.

Trying to understand, Isabel asked, "So Rob and Rossen and the other guys have this priesthood, and can use it to serve others?" Naomi nodded and Isabel asked further, "After Slade gets baptized, can he be a priesthood holder and baptize me?"

Naomi took Isabel's hand in hers and tears filled her eyes. She was too weepy to answer right away. Finally, she said, "Yes, I'm sure he'll be able to baptize you. Have I missed something? Rossen hasn't even told me Slade is getting baptized. When did he decide this?"

"Rossen doesn't know yet. Slade's waiting for him to ask him again. He wants to surprise him, so don't tell him."

Naomi answered dryly, "Oh, I'm sure he'll be surprised all right."

She continued to answer Isabel's questions until they were both too tired to think. Naomi finally asked, "Would you like to pray together?" Isabel nodded and Naomi prayed, and they each drifted off in their respective chairs. Naomi smiled, even in her sleep.

Chapter 9

As the car finally pulled into the driveway of the Rockland's main house, Isabel had a sweet sense of coming home. This place brought a sense of safety and peace and she felt such love here.

Opening Slade's door, they carefully helped him sit up, then get out and stand up. It was an amazingly long process. Sweat beaded on his forehead and he gratefully sat down in one of the chairs on the porch when he made it to the top of the steps. They left him sitting there as they unloaded the car and tried to get things settled in the house.

Earlier Rossen had rented a hospital bed, and set it up in the great room in front of the picture window. Slade would be able to watch what went on outside around the ranch and still be near a bathroom and the kitchen, where Isabel and Naomi could work and be close by. It was bright and cheerful, and they hoped it would make staying down a little easier for Slade.

Bo brought Isabel's duffle bag in and put it in the guest room where she'd stayed before.

Once they were unloaded, Isabel went back

outside and sat in a chair beside Slade. He was tired after the long drive and was content to sit quietly in the early August sunshine. Despite trying to build up his blood in the hospital, he was still pale and chilled easily, and she brought him a small blanket.

It was the same one she'd used here when they watched the thunderstorm and it brought back memories. He must have been thinking along the same lines because he said, "It seems longer than just six weeks ago that we first brought you here."

"It's only been seven weeks since I first met you."

Their eyes met and he reached over with his right arm and took her hand. "Looking back, I think I was actually in worse shape then than I am now. A lot has changed in seven weeks." He rubbed his thumb across the back of her hand.

Feeling tingly from his touch, she asked, "What things have changed for you?" She waited for his answer, wondering if it would be good or bad.

"My life is more organized and well thought out now than it was then, and more importantly, I've found my enthusiasm. It's hard to tell in this condition, but the spirit really is happy even though the flesh is a little trashed.

"And I'm not nearly so cynical. I'm actually looking forward to the future and settling down." He looked from their entwined fingers to her face. "For the first time in my life, I'm thinking about forever."

Her eyes searched his. At length, she asked, "What, did you meet a girl?"

"I did. She's beautiful and smart and kind, and I fell for her like a ton of bricks. She's kind of rich though, and I'm not sure what her thoughts are about all this."

"Have you asked her what her thoughts are?"

"No. I'm actually a little afraid to."

"I don't really believe you're afraid of anything, Slade Marsh."

He was quiet for a few minutes, then finally, he asked, "What things have changed for you in the last seven weeks?"

She considered this and softly said, "God sent me peace like a river. It's hard to explain. This rodeo lifestyle is exciting and busy, and a couple of times I've had years scared off my life, but my constant fear is gone. It's a happy excitement, not anxious.

"And I've seen a lot of new things and places.

"I've discovered I like kissing." She smiled self-consciously. "A lot.

"I've answered some deep questions about the meaning of life.

"I've met wonderful people I've come to love. Especially one in particular." She looked up at him.

"And I've decided I don't want to live in California anymore."

He turned to look at her so fast it made him wince. "Why not?"

"I'm much happier away than I was there. I've found places I'd rather be, both physically and emotionally."

"Where?"

She gazed out at the mountains in the distance. "I'm a little hesitant to tell you."

"Why?"

"I don't know. Makes me vulnerable to rejection I guess." She looked down at their entwined fingers.

He seemed to consider this as his thumb continued to stroke her hand. "What exactly is it that makes you prefer these other places?"

Shrugging, she said, "Beauty, peace, security, sage, biceps. Lots of things." She gave him a grin.

He laughed right out loud, and then groaned from the pain.

She said, "You asked."

"But what about your horse farm? You love it."

"I do. It's pretty, and racehorses can be addictive. I have some dear friends there and some very good memories. But there are many more bad than good. I don't know that I ever want to go back. I'm not sure I will, even if things here don't work out." She gently pushed the rocker with her foot.

"What would it take to make you choose to stay in Wyoming?"

"To be invited."

She looked up at him hesitantly. He looked back at her intensely and asked, "Could you wait to be invited until I think I can get down on one knee and be able to get back up?" His smile a little self-conscious.

She couldn't help the smile or the moisture in her eyes as she looked into his and said, "I love you, Slade. I can wait forever if you need me to, but I'd never want you down on your knee. You're the strongest man I know. I love that strength. I would never want you to do something to deny it or humble it." The teasing grin came back. "But we could wait until you have a little more stamina."

It was probably a good thing Naomi came out just then to call them to lunch. Afterward Slade went back to bed and slept until dinner.

Isabel worked in the kitchen all afternoon so she could be near in case he needed help. As she worked she thought about the conversation on the porch. She was sure he was talking about becoming engaged, which she wanted more than anything in the world. But when she really thought about it, she needed to deal with the Judd issue before she could become that definite a part of his life.

Slade's first night at home was a rough one. He'd gotten a little behind the pain and then struggled to rest. Isabel didn't even try to go to bed until after two, and then was back out there to help him settle down and rest again at four-thirty. When he finally went soundly to sleep an hour later, she put on her riding breeches and went out to ride.

The dawn was glorious as always, but honestly, she was too tired to even enjoy it, and returned to the house sooner than she normally would have.

****

It was pure chance that Judd got a break in the whereabouts of Carrie. When Slade got hurt so badly Isabel had told Dante when he had called Slade's cell from a pay phone across town. That afternoon Dante was talking to Eli in the race barn, unaware that they weren't alone.

There was actually a stable hand two stalls over. One of the few who weren't fiercely loyal to Carrie and the Johnsons. He was supposed to have been mucking out the stall, but spent most of his time leaning on his pitchfork sending text messages to his girl. Because he wasn't working when they came in, they didn't know he was there and he heard Dante report, "Carrie's friend was hurt bad in a bull riding wreck. About died, I guess. If the hospital had been a little longer drive, they'd a lost him."

Eli and Dante had gone on to talk about other things and the stable hand had gone on to Judd with the information. He figured it would be worth something to her old man and he was right.

Judd didn't know which rodeo it was and, in fact, had the day of the wreck three days late because of the delay in Dante calling Carrie, but he finally knew how she'd gotten away so slick. She was with a cowboy. He tried to think back and remember if she'd known any cowboys, but there were none he was aware of.

He and Deek got on the internet and it wasn't long before they knew where there were rodeos going on and who had ridden bulls in them. From there it was simply a matter of finding out who had crashed and burned on a bull. There were nineteen rodeos being held that week across the country, but only twelve bad wrecks on bulls. So they narrowed the field quickly, and began to check rodeos to try and figure out where they would go next.

****

Isabel loved Naomi and all the Rockland family dearly, but she was a little uncomfortable just hanging out there, even though she was there to help Slade. She tried to pitch in wherever she could around the ranch, and although it was fun and interesting, she didn't feel nearly as needed as she had on the road.

After Slade had been home for five days, he and Rossen made a big joke out of arm wrestling to see who got to keep Isabel with them when Rossen and Sean headed back out on the road to rodeo. She knew it was their way of asking her what she wanted to do.

What she wanted was to stay with Slade, but because of Naomi's care for him, where she was needed the most was probably on the road. Where she was safest from Judd was anybody's guess, and where she ought to be to keep this wonderful family safe was far away from them all.

She was at a loss about what to do, so she took it to her Father in Heaven, then had a heart-to-heart talk with Slade and Rossen. What they came up with was that she would stay in Wyoming, but she would do most of the scheduling of the rodeos over the internet and email the information to Rossen's laptop. She and Slade would stay with Naomi for a while longer until they thought they could be okay on their own, and then Isabel and Slade would move over to Slade's house in the next valley with the couple who took care of the ranch and house when he was away. This way they wouldn't feel like a burden and Rossen's family would be protected from Judd as much as possible.

The fact that Sean liked to cook would help him and Rossen on the road. Sean and Isabel planned menus for the first little while and she made sure the trailer was stocked beforehand.

It was the third week in August and Rossen and Sean were headed first to Caldwell, Idaho which was a long day's drive from home. They decided to leave early in the morning. That way their horses would have the night before the drive to rest, and the night before the rodeo to rest again.

The evening before they were going to leave they had a big family dinner. The atmosphere was festive, but there was an undercurrent that was subdued. Slade and Rossen had been rodeoing for years as a team and as best friends, and even though they would both be with family, in a manner, they'd be apart. Isabel was sad to tell Rossen goodbye, as well. She would truly miss him. And it was heart-breaking to watch Slade be left behind in such bad shape.

One thing saved Isabel from being totally depressed. Part way through the dinner, Naomi asked

Slade if Rossen had asked him recently if he was ready to be baptized.

Slade replied, "No, he hasn't for a long, long time." All eyes at the table looked at Rossen, who looked around puzzled.

"What?" He spoke around a bite of spaghetti. "What are you all looking at me for?" Slade smiled and looked from Isabel to Naomi.

Joey piped in cheerily, "Why haven't you asked him?"

"I guess I've just been kind of busy. Why?" Rossen looked around the table suspiciously.

Joey looked markedly at her plate. "No reason. Just wondered."

Rossen still looked around, then said, "For crying out loud. What is up with you people?" He turned to Slade. "All right, Marsh, are you ready to get baptized yet? There now, I've asked him. Satisfied?" He went back to his spaghetti. At first he didn't even hear Slade say yes. After a second or two of silence around the table, it sunk in.

He turned to Slade again. "What? What did you say?"

Slade smiled at him across the table. "I said yes."

"Really?"

"Really." Rossen tipped his chair over backward trying to get around the table to Slade. Isabel almost tipped hers over trying to get to Slade to protect him from Rossen's enthusiasm.

"No!" She stepped in front of Rossen just in time.

"Rossen, no you'll hurt him! Just shake his hand or something. You can't be too rough right now!"

Slade struggled to stand up and tease him, "C'mere, you big teddy bear. Just hug me very softly."

Rossen took his hand, and the look they shared was of the deepest brotherhood, then Rossen very slowly leaned and embraced Slade gently.

Pulling away, he asked, "When?"

"As soon as I feel good enough to do it."

A huge smile lit Rossen's face. "Aw, that is so great! Why didn't you tell me?"

He went to grab Slade again, but Isabel stopped him with a hand on his chest. "Careful."

"Sorry, sorry." Rossen went back around the table and sat back in his seat and dinner resumed normally for a few minutes.

Finally, Isabel asked in a timid voice, "Do I have to wait to be asked, too?" Every person at the table except Naomi stared at her, open-mouthed. Forks were poised and it was utterly silent.

Finally, Naomi clapped her hands laughing. "Of course you don't, dear. You can be baptized as soon as you're ready." Everyone at the table began to laugh and cheer except Slade and Rossen. They were still staring at her.

****

The next morning, as they were getting ready to go, Isabel asked, "Is there any way I can get a copy of the photograph that hangs in the trailer?" It had meant a great deal to her while they traveled and she wanted that same image of peace to keep with her while she was here. They all looked at her almost strangely, and then turned to Slade.

He just smiled at her. "I think I have a copy around somewhere. I'll find it for you."

Finally Rossen and Sean loaded up and the big truck and trailer pulled away. Isabel tried to brush at her tears unseen. Slade carefully put one arm around her and said gently, "Don't be sad. This isn't the end, I promise."

For the next few days, Slade continued to rest and stay down. Slowly he began to have his color and energy return. The bruising had all but faded the day he turned to Isabel and said, "Let's go home to my house." Isabel had been helping around the ranch as much as possible and had enjoyed every minute of her stay, but she too felt like she didn't want to wear out her welcome. She'd been glad to find that Slade's home was only five minutes away, further up the gravel road and that she would, in fact, drive right past the Rocklands' homes whenever she needed to go anywhere.

In all this time she'd never seen Slade's property, and she was curious about what his home would be like. She wondered if it would be her own home too someday and was excited to finally see it.

She had come to love Naomi more than ever and was grateful she would be so close. These weeks

209

together had been the perfect opportunity for Isabel to continue to learn from her. She taught both gospel principles as well as everyday practical things that Isabel needed to know to live and work in this rural place.

The only thing similar to her life back home was the fact that there were horses around. Here there was also work to do for the cattle operation, and maintenance of farming equipment and of the homestead itself. Most of the operation was handled by members of the family.

The oil part of the operation was run almost exclusively by employees on a distant part of the ranch. It was separate, although still behind the locked gates out on the gravel road. It was the reason for the tight security.

When it was finally time to move, Cooper helped to load up Naomi's car he'd brought around. It was the only vehicle on the place that wasn't a truck, and it was easier for Slade to get in and out of. Between the two of them, she and Slade only had two duffle bags of clothes and a few odds and ends. Cooper volunteered to take the rented hospital bed back the next time he went to town.

After assuring them all that they could get settled into the house alone fine, Slade and Isabel hugged Naomi and said goodbye.

Isabel was trying to miss the potholes in the gravel road to keep from jarring Slade and look around her at the same time. The scenery was glorious. Both homesteads were in the lowlands of two valleys and the

210

mountains that surrounded them were magnificent. They drove along the road for a few minutes before it started to climb slightly in elevation. As they topped the ridgeline and entered the next valley, Isabel let the car drift to a stop. She couldn't believe it! Before her was the actual river valley from the photo in the trailer. The scripture from Isaiah softly escaped from her lips unbidden, "And I will extend peace to her like a river." All she could do was stare at the scene before her

At length, she turned to Slade. "Why didn't you tell me?"

"Actually, until a couple days ago I didn't know it was a big deal. I mean, I'd seen your Post-It on the photo, but I didn't realize it really meant anything to you." He smiled, and carefully leaned to kiss her. "Welcome home."

They continued down the road until they rounded a bend, and the house and barn appeared, tucked into the trees in a fold in the hill.

They were built of wood and stone with a cedar shake roof and looked like they were a part of the mountain. Massive logs held up the roof over the drive in front, and vaulted windows rose to the ceiling to take in the view across the valley. It looked like it would stand against that hillside for a thousand years and yet the architecture was magnificent. This house exactly matched this man.

"That's a house." She started the car moving again.

Softly, Slade admitted, "Today it feels like home."

Their eyes met. "It hasn't always felt that way. That's why I stay with the Rocklands a lot. Sometimes it's been lonely."

She drove in and parked under the porte-cochere and stood by as he climbed from the car and walked to the front door. Once there, he punched some numbers on the keypad and turned the knob. Inside the foyer she stood on a stone floor and looked around. It was timber framed with massive logs holding up the walls and spanning the ceiling. An imposing river rock fireplace climbed to the second story in the center of the house, and the whole west end of the great room was glass that brought the view across the valley inside. The furniture she could see was covered with canvas dust covers.

He walked inside and crossed the great room to the other side. She helped pull the dust cover off a leather recliner and he gratefully sank into it and said, "I should have asked Hank and Ruby to get things ready for us. Do you mind if I let you give yourself the tour. Just here is about as far as I want to go right now."

She unloaded bags from the car and brought them in. "Which way to your room?"

He pointed. "Just toss it on the foot of the bed and I'll put it away later." He caught her hand as she went past. When she looked down at him, he gently kissed her hand and said, "Thank you for helping me to survive an injury I wouldn't even have if I'd listened to you in the first place."

It was the first time he'd broached the subject of either bull riding or the flack jacket. She set the bag down, pulled an ottoman over and sat on it beside his chair and said kindly, "Slade, I'm not your mother. I really had no right to even intimate what you should be doing. I'm sorry I said what I did in the trailer that night."

Leaning his head back, he said, "Actually, it was almost worth disappointing you to have you tell me I have body like a young Greek God." He gave a sad smile. "Almost." He took her hand again.

She shook her head sadly. "I'm trying not to question your wisdom, Slade. You've proven time and again to have wonderful judgment, and you're obviously very good at what you do." She lowered her eyes. "I'm trying to understand the bulls. Really I am. But I'm afraid I'll never get it. We're just going to have to agree to disagree on this." She looked up into his face. "I'll respect your decisions. I owe you at least that because of how you haven't questioned my actions."

Rubbing her hand with his thumb, he asked, "Can I explain my decisions?" She nodded. "At first it was the adrenaline. I was a hotshot kid with a chip on my shoulder. Fortunately, or maybe unfortunately, I had a knack for it, and ended up competing at higher and higher levels. For the last two years I've competed at the National Finals and done well. Rossen and I set a goal to go to the National Finals again this year as ropers, and at the time it just seemed to make sense to go all-around, too. It's not that much bigger deal to go for all-around when I'm already at the rodeo. At least it hasn't been in the past."

He leaned carefully back in his chair again. "If it helps, I'd already decided to only ride enough to make it to the NFR this year and then let the bulls and the all-around go. Actually, I may quit rodeoing full time after this season anyway. It's been a fun ride, but we're both getting a little burned out. I think Rossen would've quit at the end of last year if it weren't for me." He ran his fingers through his hair with his good hand. "It's kind of intoxicating to strive to be one of the best in the world at what you do. That sounds egotistical I know, but it's been a rush."

When she saw it from his perspective it made a little more sense. Not enough in her mind, but a little.

He continued, "I need to be honest with you, Isabel. There's a chance I can heal fast enough to still reach our goal." He met her eyes. "If I can, I'm going to try. I owe that to Rossen."

She nodded. "I can respect that."

His look was penetrating. "Even if it means I have to ride another bull?" In her heart she was horrified. She tried not to let him see that.

She couldn't look him in the eye as she said, "Do what you have to do." She turned away and went into his room. The thought of another bull made her sick. The only way she could deal with this was to try to put it out of her mind and pretend it was far away in the future.

His room was a masterpiece. It was obviously the master suite with an oversized rock fireplace and flat screen TV on one wall. One whole other wall was windows that looked out over the river valley with French doors out to a private deck.

A massive four-poster bed was covered in brown and tan brocade bedding with wild horses running across the pillow shams. Leather fringed pillows with saddle conchas were piled around them. The drapes matched the throw pillows and even the walls were a leathered faux finish with nail heads.

He'd said he'd put his stuff away, but she knew he was still too sore to do much so she unpacked his clothing and sorted it in piles on the dresser top, hoping he wouldn't have to bend to open drawers. She took his shaving kit into his bathroom and left it on the top of the stone counter.

He had a huge Jacuzzi tub that would probably really help his injuries if he could safely get in and out. The shower next to it would prove easier for the time being. There were no towels out, so she pulled some from below the counter and left bath towels near the shower and hung a hand towel above the sink.

Going back out to get her own bag, she carried it into the great room and asked, "Where do you want me?"

At her question he flashed a teasing grin. "Here in this chair beside me."

"I meant to sleep." She instantly knew she'd made a mistake, as he gave an even bigger smile. She put her hands on her hips. "Slade Marsh. Which bedroom, other than yours, should I put my stuff in?"

"Oh, all right." He pretended to pout. "Take the

one across the hall."

Her room was similar to his with its tans and browns, but instead of wild horses it had an old-fashioned patchwork quilt with burgundy and gold and old farm antiques. The fireplace was much smaller and her bathroom had only a large shower with a built-in seat.

Returning to the car, she brought in several bags of groceries and took them into the kitchen on the far side of the great room. Slade watched her opening and shutting cupboards and drawers as she tried to find where to put things. There were a few staples but mostly the cupboards were empty. The huge fridge was also empty and had been turned off and propped open. She turned it on, wiped it out and wiped off the stone countertop. His home was incredible, but had obviously been lived in very little. Turning on the radio under the counter, she dug for garbage bags for the trash compactor and opened the window over the sink to let in the breeze.

She went back into the great room with Slade, and sang along with the radio as she started to pull dust covers off the rest of the furniture. She took each one out the French doors to the deck to shake out the dust and then folded them into a pile. "Where do these live?" She indicated the covers.

"Just put them in one of the cupboards there in the laundry room." He pointed toward two doors next to the kitchen. She opened one and found an almost empty pantry and tried the next door. It was a laundry

216

room with a stacked washer and dryer and large utility sink between cupboards and counters. Stowing the dust covers she walked back out.

"You know that guy who was hassling me about my net worth? He has a house about five times nicer than mine."

He shrugged his one shoulder. "I bought Microsoft stock at the right time. It's just a house." Sadly, he added, "The ground I inherited from my dad. I'd rather have him than the ranch, but I didn't get a choice."

Wishing she knew what to do to lessen the sadness, she came back in and sat beside him again and gently took his hand. She could tell he had a headache from the slight grimace between his eyes and how he kept changing positions to try to get comfortable and she asked, "How long has it been since you've had something for pain?"

She stood and stepped behind his chair and started to massage his head. She loved doing this for him and his hair between her fingers was incredible.

"I quit taking anything."

"You're taking nothing at all? Not even Ibuprofen?"

His eyes were closed. "Nothing."

"Nothing isn't working very well, is it?"

"No, but your hands are." He paused, seeming to enjoy her touch, then continued, "Do you want to know something funny? One day Rossen and I were joking about how we needed someone to cook for us, organize

217

us, run errands for us, and was a masseuse too. We thought it was a fantasy too good to be true." He pulled her hand down to his lips and kissed her palm. "Two days later we met you."

Smiling, she answered, "And now look what kind of shape you're in." She gently turned his head to work on the other side.

"Only because I didn't listen to you." He closed his eyes and continued, "Rossen thought we needed a large Swedish woman with sweet rolls on her head."

She leaned around to look at his face. "Sweet rolls on her head?" She laughed.

"Like Princess Leia. Didn't you see that Pink Panther movie with Helga, the masseuse, that Clouseau stuck the vacuum on, just before he sucked up the parrot?"

She laughed again. "I must have missed that one."

"You should see it. It's very funny." After a moment he qualified that. "You're not like Helga at all, by the way." He shifted still trying to get comfortable.

"What else still hurts?"

"The tape on my collar bone is driving me nuts and keeps catching on the seam of my shirt. And I feel like I'm in a straightjacket in this brace."

"Take your shirt off." He opened his eyes to look up at her. "Come on, the doctor is going to take the tape off tomorrow anyway. We'll loosen it where it's pulling and you can go shirtless. Or at least leave it unbuttoned. Hank and Ruby won't mind."

"I take it you won't mind either."

She laughed softly and shook her head. "No. I definitely won't mind."

He smiled tiredly as she helped him off with his shirt and carefully peeled back the tape where it was pulling.

"Better?"

"Much. Thanks."

Squeezing the top of his shoulder, she said, "Okay, my beautifully-sculpted friend, what can I do around here to keep busy? Help me find something to do so I don't get into mischief."

He smiled. "Mischief, huh?" He considered for a moment. "Are we talking scrap-booking here, or finding a cure for cancer?"

"No scrapbooking, but nothing that requires laboratory chemicals either. Something in between. Something close, so I can help you if you need me, but will keep me from driving you crazy."

"Do you like to read? You could cook, play chess, swim. You could . . . "

"Swim? You're kidding me! You have a pool here? This high in the mountains? I would have thought it would be way too cold here for a pool."

He struggled out of his chair and held out his hand. "Come with me." He led off through an archway at the back of the great room and around a corner.

Through double glass doors she could see a large pool cover. It was indoors!

"It really is too cold here for an outdoor pool.

You'd only be able to use it a few months of the year."

The pool house was timber framed the same as the house and barn with huge logs spanning the ceiling above. On the stone deck there was an elliptical trainer and a universal gym with a TV and DVD player on the wall. Several lounge chairs lined up on the edge of the pool and there was a basketball hoop on the other side.

He walked inside a small room to the side, flipped some switches and the pool cover began to retract. "The main computer can be accessed remotely so they can be up to temperature when I arrive." At the word "they" she looked around and saw a hot tub outside the pool house on the deck.

"There's a shower and dressing room through there." He indicated a door.

"This will be great! When your doctor recommended pool therapy, I assumed we'd have to drive into town to the high school or something."

"It will be nice to be able to do it here. Honestly, Cooper and his friends use it more than I do, but I enjoy it sometimes. It's great in here in January when there's about two feet of snow outside."

"I can imagine! Two feet! That's a lot of snow! How do you feed the cattle?"

"We keep the snow pushed off near the barns, and use an old Snow Cat to load hay."

She looked out a window. "How many barns?" She'd only seen one out there.

"There are three more around in the hills. Rocklands push all their cows up here in the winter.

This valley is more sheltered and we feed together."

"Do you have to maintain that whole road in that much snow?" That seemed like a daunting task.

"Actually, there's an elk wintering station further up the road, so in winter the fish and game people split it with us."

They headed out of the pool house and back to his chair.

As she fixed a late lunch, she asked him again, "I'll love using the pool, but isn't there something you need done? I'd like to do something useful too."

She brought him a hot beef sandwich and he smiled and said, "I'd say you're pretty useful."

After lunch as he rested, she explored the rest of the house. There was a home theater and game room in the basement, as well as another bedroom suite, a large storage area and what looked like some type of wine cellar or vault with beautiful backlit glass.

The theater room actually seemed lived in and there was an impressive movie collection. A throw was tossed over a recliner and there was a bowl with a few unpopped kernels of popcorn still in it on a table. *Probably Cooper and his friends again.* She took the bowl back upstairs.

There was a gorgeous office off the front entry and a library on the other side, as well as one more bedroom suite at the end of the hall.

The upstairs held four more bedroom suites, all of which stood empty with plain walls.

Back downstairs, as she went past him to go

explore outside, she commented, "This place is huge. Why did you build so big?"

He innocently answered without opening his eyes, "I want seven children." She gave a small scream and he said, "Just kidding." She heard him chuckling as she let herself into the garage.

There were stalls for three vehicles, one of which held a large steel blue truck, a workshop/storage area that held a deep freezer, and some ski gear and fishing poles. Above the garage was the self-contained apartment accessed by a set of stone stairs on the south end that she knew Hank and Ruby lived in, and she found a cement storage room underneath.

Through the other side of the garage was the barnyard. There was a six stall horse barn with a tack room and an open area in the back. The alleyway between the stalls had barn doors at the front and back and there was an open hay loft above.

Outside the house there was no formal landscaping. The woods and pastures came right up almost to the house. Between the driveway and the walks were beds of bare dirt.

It was an incredibly beautiful home and setting that was obviously not much lived in. She made a mental note to make the flower beds loved before she left here in a few weeks.

Slade was gone from his chair when she went back inside. She found him standing on the deck overlooking the river to the west.

Coming to stand beside him, they watched the

sun go down behind the mountains. Its last rays pushed through the lavender clouds to shine silver on the surface of the water in a glorious display and she gazed almost in wonder.

Beside her, Slade spoke without turning his head. "It's the Salt."

"I beg your pardon?" She turned to look at his profile in the dusk.

"It's not really the Peace River. It's actually the Smith's Fork of the Salt River." He nodded toward the shining current below.

She leaned back against him and he wrapped his good arm around her as she said, "It'll always be the Peace River to me."

Chapter 10

The next morning in the half light of dawn, she was up and about. She didn't have a horse here to ride yet so she put on her bathing suit and quietly moved through the house to the pool. In the cool of the early morning the windows of the pool house were fogged and the room was steamy and dim. The only sound was the riffling of the water as she stepped in.

The warm water was like silk against her skin as she slid in. She turned quietly on her back and spent the next while in slow laps, considering her life and the amazing turn of events of the last few months. The massive logs on the ceiling above her seemed a tangible proof of the power of God and His hand in her existence.

Before, she'd felt set on a course over which she had little control. She felt she was to continue her life the way it had always gone. For years she'd thought she should "Bloom where you're planted" and had done her best to do so, and hers had been a good life. In retrospect, she had so many blessings that few had been given. She was grateful for her own struggles over someone else's, but after the experiences of the last months, she knew her life would never be the same. The thought of going home to the farm just because that's where she had been raised was out of the question. The pace and the priorities there were things of the past.

The sweet gift of the gospel, knowing what her Father in Heaven wanted for her, and the blessing Slade had been in her life made her old existence just that, existing. She'd never felt this burgeoning hope and excitement to get started on the future like she did now. So much of life seemed pointless when the bigger picture of Slade and forever and all that entailed, as far as marriage, family, and eternity came into view.

She had always assumed she would someday settle down and be married. But it had always been "out there" somewhere, a long time away, with a faceless being who had no particularly outstanding characteristics. Having now been around Slade, her thoughts of a husband would never again be ordinary.

She'd never known someone, other than Rossen maybe, who was as rock solid as Slade was as a person. The scripture she'd read in the Book of Mormon last night fit him exactly. It began, "Therefore, I would that ye be steadfast and immoveable, always abounding in good works".

That was him, steadfast and immoveable, and abounding in good works. He was so steady and level headed. In all the time she'd known him, even living so closely in the trailer and traveling, she'd never seen him really get upset. The angriest she'd ever seen him was

226

that day with Leland Wilde. To her, with the experiences she'd had in her life with anger, that was the most reassuring feeling she could know.

It wasn't just that he was mellow. He was always so in control. His natural competence and confidence was a foundation she'd known she could rely on from their first meeting with Anna. He knew he could handle whatever he needed to, no matter what came along, and the people around him picked right up on that. It was eminently satisfying to work and walk beside him, knowing that together they were capable of whatever they put their minds to.

Even the day-to-day grind of a life's work was no big deal to him. The horse farm, though very valuable, had been a huge daily process involving large numbers of people, with a myriad of aspects to be dealt with every day. Here with Slade, even though many of the responsibilities of animal care and business were the same, it had largely been reduced to an hour or two in the office everyday, and minimal management of a few key people who helped. The emphasis had moved from making a living to living a life. She knew that would change again when he felt better and was more up to hard work, but she still knew that what he chose to do would not become a big deal. She was honored and grateful he had included her along for the ride this far.

As she swam she thought about their friendship and relationship, where they were and where they were headed. He had talked a couple of times in a round about way concerning marriage, and true to his personality it had been a comfortable topic from the start. Their reciprocated trust had been uncanny. She was unsure of exactly where they stood as far as the future, and Judd, the rodeo and commitment and all of it, but the peace that had indeed come to her with this man left her with a complete inner calm that it would all work out.

The only thing that troubled her from time to time was the unbelievable physical attraction she felt toward him. Never in her life had a man affected her this way, and there had been times it almost scared her. Although, even in that, he had always handled those feelings in such a way that they'd been able to enjoy their attraction, and look forward to the future with respect for each other. She smiled as she floated. His kiss had become her new best thing.

Thinking of him now, here in the silky, warm water had her keyed up. She turned over and swam laps to get his lips off her mind before she had to face him at breakfast.

When he walked into the kitchen a short while later, wearing only jeans and his brace, with his hair still damp from the shower, she wondered how in the world she had imagined she could control her thoughts about him when she'd been thinking in the pool. Even injured he was incredible, and she had a hard time not staring. He came to her and his soft spoken, "Good morning," and long kiss made her completely forget what she was doing. He looked into her eyes, laughed that low, warm laugh and took her pancake turner to rescue the hot cakes and said, "I invited Hank and Ruby to eat with us, but they ate early."

It took all of her concentration to focus on breakfast and what he was asking as he said, "So what are you going to do today?"

She pulled her thoughts away from the muscles of his shoulders and tried to remember what she'd planned. "I'm going to load you in the car and take you to the doctor, where he's going to rip off your surgical tape and take your stitches out. Then I am going to explore the booming metropolis of Evanston, Wyoming, where I'll buy a new dress and matching shoes for church Sunday. And then, if you're up to all this, you're going to take me to lunch at some folksy little place. When we come home, I'm going to dig in the dirt of your front flower bed." She smiled up at him. "Any more questions?"

He considered this for a moment. "Do we have to drive the car?"

For a second she was confused. "You want to walk all the way to Evanston? I thought it was like sixty miles." She looked at him incredulously. "Wait, you're not telling me you have a helicopter?" After this house, she wouldn't be surprised.

He laughed and groaned. "No, but that's a great idea. I just want to take the truck. I feel like such a sissy in the car." Isabel looked him over. *Sissy? Not in a million years.*

He was watching her eyes, gave a hint of a smile and she was sure he knew exactly what she was thinking.

Trying to focus on the conversation, she said, "We can drive whatever you want, but the car might be a smoother ride."

Still with that smile, he said, "I'd rather take the truck. Why do you want to dig in the dirt?" Him sitting across from her at the breakfast table had slowed her brain and it took her a moment to change subjects.

"That flower bed in front just seems a little forlorn. Even if it's only for a couple of weeks, I'm going to give it some attention. Do you have any favorite flowers?"

At that, he looked away for a second and she wondered if she'd offended him. After a moment, he said, "I've thought about someday putting wildflowers in there. I've had a sprinkling system installed, but I've never been here much to maintain a yard." He looked sad as he continued, "Chante loved to garden. She would have loved those beds."

She placed her hand over his on the table. "Did she have any favorites?"

He shook his head, still looking out the window. "No. Just wildflowers."

He stood and straightened up carefully, taking his plate to the sink. She could almost see him try to shake off the memories as he changed the subject again. "It may be a trick to find matching shoes in Evanston. Maybe if you went with black or something."

She drove the truck. It appeared as little used as

the house, but he did seem more at home in it than the car.

She shouldn't have joked about ripping the tape off. It had been hyper industrial strength to keep his shoulder in place and his collarbone aligned, so it was terrible to remove, even with the solvent they used. When they were finished his skin was red and irritated. He wore his shirt, but only buttoned it when they were in public.

When they left the doctor's office, he really didn't look up to much, so they ate Subway in the truck on the way home and skipped the shopping and sightseeing.

As they drove down the gravel road to his house he sighed and said, "We should have driven the car."

****

Back home he laid on the couch and fell asleep while she sat on the floor next to him scrolling through the music on his MP3 player. When he awoke, she was sleeping on the floor beside him with her arm under her cheek, and soft country music playing on the sound system around them.

She was so not what he would have expected from her background, and she was so unlike any other woman he'd known. Every day he thanked God that they had had to have truck repairs that day in California. Hanging his arm over the side of the couch so he could softly touch her silvery-gold hair, he whispered, "I love you, Isabel." and then went back to sleep.

When he awoke again, she was nowhere to be seen, but the smell of whatever she was baking filled his home. He was still lying there thinking about her when she came back in wearing an old pair of cut offs. She opened the front door and paused, brushing dirt off her knees, then came on into the kitchen where she washed her hands at the sink and bent to take their dinner out of the oven. Seeing his eyes on her, she came around and watched him struggle to sit upright.

She put a throw between his bare back and the leather couch and said honestly, "You don't look so good."

That's not what he'd been thinking about her. Trying to shrug his one shoulder, he said, "I look better than I feel." He sighed. "I can't believe it's taking me this long to get back on my feet. The shoulder and collarbone are okay, but whatever I did inside is still a mess." He glanced down at his stomach and then laid his head back against the top of the couch. The bandage on his abdomen had been removed and there was just a strip of clear tape over the long red scar that lay neatly between rows of muscles on his belly.

She went around behind him and started to massage his head. Moving in small circles she rubbed away the tension. Her smooth, warm hands felt like heaven. He leaned his head forward and she slowly worked her way down his neck and carefully rubbed his shoulders around his collarbone brace, focusing on pressure points.

After several minutes, she asked, "Do you feel

232

like eating?"   He didn't feel like doing anything but sitting here with her hands on his skin, but he didn't think he should tell her that.

Instead, he said, "In a minute. I'm a little busy right now."

They ate on the deck with Hank and Ruby as the sun set, and then went downstairs to watch a movie while Hank and Ruby went to visit their daughter. He stretched out on a double recliner and she curled up next to him. The movie was good, but he couldn't focus on it for anything. She was warm and soft beside him, and her perfume was clouding his brain. He pulled her against him with his good arm and her breath on his bare skin was intoxicating.   He finally quit even pretending to watch, and turned on his side to begin kissing her neck in the hollow at the base of her ear. He looked into her eyes and saw the same things he was feeling. Slowly he lowered his head to her mouth. For a moment or two he basked in the sweet passion of her kiss.

Reluctantly, he pulled back with a groan that had nothing to do with his injuries and said, "Help me up, Is. I should go upstairs. Now." His voice was almost a little harsh, and he could see the uncertainty in her eyes.

Standing, he held her to him and kissed her again gently and admitted, "I'm a mere mortal, Isabel. You are far too tempting." Their eyes held and then he turned and walked up the stairs.

He was on the deck, looking at the night sky,

letting the canyon breeze cool his body and mind, when he heard her go to her room and close the door. He was twenty-seven years old for Pete's sake. He'd thought he was past this.

The next morning when he walked into the kitchen from the garage he had a shirt on, buttoned part way up. She turned to him from the orange juice she was stirring. He could see in her eyes she was still a little uncertain of him, and he pulled her to him in a gentle hug and gave her a long kiss good morning, and then said, "We either have to get married like tomorrow, or spend a lot more time with Hank and Ruby." He stated it absolutely matter-of-factly and she looked up at him with wide eyes.

At length, she dropped her head to his chest and softly said, "You know I can't marry you until I get this Judd mess handled."

He rubbed across her back once more, then pulled back from her and started to set the table. "I knew that's what you'd say, so I already asked Hank and Ruby to move into the room at the end of the hall. They'll be in to eat with us in a few minutes, but said not to wait."

She nodded hesitantly. "Oh, good."

He smiled. "Oh, good that we don't have to wait to eat? Or that they'll be living right here in the house with us?"

Looking thoroughly self-conscious, she admitted, "That they'll be living here."

He chuckled at her obvious relief, and pulled her

chair out to seat her and said calmly, "Waiting until the Judd thing is settled is a stupid argument, by the way. Wouldn't marriage solve the Judd problem? And aren't I already in this up to my neck? Or at least my heart?" He put a hand on her shoulder and she reached up to cover it with hers.

Softly, she asked, "Would it solve the problem, or put a big bull's eye on your head?"

He sat across from her and asked her to pray over their breakfast. When she finished he continued, "Couldn't you do something legally with your holdings to get him off your back? Put everything into a trust or something that has to have both yours and Eli's okay on every decision and put in a provision about if something happened to incapacitate either one or both of you, another designated trustee would step in. If you had a long enough list of people who would take over to make certain he could never have control, wouldn't Judd give up this wild goose chase? This is crazy."

She poured blackberry syrup over her waffle. "That's the whole problem. Judd is crazy. He's totally unstable. He would have to be to have tried to do any of this anyway. If you could reason with insanity, this would have been over at the time of my grandfather's death."

She was quiet for a few minutes and then said, "That is a really good idea. I wonder how it could all be worked out, and how could word be gotten to Judd and Deek about legal changes in my estate? Last week when I got an email from Dante, the police were still trying to find them." She ate another bite and swallowed.

"Dante thinks they come back to the house sometimes in the night. Apparently someone is staying there. Said they rented it from Judd, but won't tell the police where he is, just showed them a rental contract that states he'll come by and pick up the rent.

"Dante says they're every bit as questionable as the others. He thinks they're there to watch for any sign of me." They ate in silence for a few minutes.

At length Slade asked, "Couldn't you leave a legal letter with the tenants? If you sent something to his last known mailing address and his house and to the private investigator he first hired, I'd think he'd get the message."

She put down her orange juice. "How would we know for sure that he'll leave me and Ebony alone? And how would we know what the others, the bookie and his men, have in mind?"

They'd finished eating and pushed their plates back. He hesitated, considering. Finally, he said, "I don't know if you'd really know for sure. Probably just time. I don't know how you'd see if he would leave you alone without going home and putting yourself at possible risk." He looked across the table at her.

She shook her head. "I have no intention of going home. It doesn't even feel like home anymore." She got up to clear the table, and he followed her to the dishwasher with his plate.

After loading it in, he pulled her to him and said, "Good, because I need you in Wyoming."

236

Several minutes later she stepped reluctantly away from him. He sighed and ran a hand through his hair as she went back to clearing the breakfast, and he leaned against the counter to watch her work. Finally she turned to him with a sheepish smile and said, "I'm dying to ask exactly what you told Hank."

He grinned. "You don't even want to know."

Hank and Ruby came in just then to eat. Slade knew this was a good idea. He felt strongly about saving intimacy for marriage, and Isabel felt the same, but the physical attraction in this house was a tangible thing. She seemed a little embarrassed as she helped them reheat the waffles, but the older woman just smiled a bashful smile and said, "We were young once too, sis. And it just looks better to have us living right in the house with you. Avoids that darned appearance of evil thing. Your reputations are invaluable, you know. We're just glad to help."

****

The next day was Sunday, so they loaded into Naomi's car and went to pick up some of the Rocklands for church. Isabel had gone to church with them enough now that she was starting to get the hang of how their meetings went. She'd been pleasantly surprised to find that the topic the men studied in their Priesthood meeting correlated with what the women were learning in Relief Society. This made so much sense to her. She

237

believed that men and women had different roles, but it was a wonderful plan to have them learn the same principle at the same time, just from different perspectives. It made for some great discussions afterward that helped to reinforce the principles in her heart.

She and Slade were taking a class during Sunday School that was more of a gospel basics than the others were studying. She was sure he was in that class to accompany her because he seemed to already know almost everything they discussed. It was the most amazing feeling to finally know that what she was being taught was the correct interpretation of Christ's word because of His prophet on the earth. The more she learned the more sense it made.

She sometimes couldn't understand why Slade had waited so long to become a member of something that felt so good and so right. It was hard to imagine the man she knew to be hesitant about anything, especially not something so important.

The taking of the sacrament had come to mean a great deal to her. Naomi had first taught her that this was the most sacred part of their meetings, and the idea of taking upon herself the name of Christ was both wonderful and intimidating to her at the same time. She wanted to be numbered among Christ's true followers and was so looking forward to being baptized, but sometimes she worried she wasn't good enough.

She tried to explain that to Slade on the way home from the Rockland's. She pulled into his garage

238

and shut off the car as he turned to look at her and said, "Isabel, I don't mean to downplay how you feel, but I have to tell you, I'm not worried that you're not good enough to become a member. You're the best person I know. I'm just hoping to be able to keep up with you. Have you ever thought about how you've lived most of these principles before you were formally taught them and knew them to be God's plan?"

He reached across and took her hand and said honestly, "From the first moment I've known you, you've always tried to do what you think is best, often with someone else in mind. You're right up there with Rossen, and you know how I feel about him. C'mon, honey, Jesus doesn't want perfection yet. He just wants your heart. Well, and your hands too. He's kind of big on being actively engaged in good works, but mostly He just wants your heart." Slade smiled. "Same as me." He hugged her as she climbed out of the truck and she fairly basked in the encouraging things he'd said about her.

She had found a book on wildflowers on Slade's book shelf, and set out the next afternoon with buckets and a shovel to find some of the varieties he'd told her grew abundantly around the hills. She had one of the front beds prepared and ready to go.

By nightfall she'd transplanted fifteen bunches of Columbines, Indian Paintbrush, Wild Geranium, Asters and some other low-growing purple flower she hadn't found in the book. Maybe she could find some more varieties in a nursery the next time she went into town.

Ruby and Isabel worked out a deal to take turns cooking and on the other household chores, but Isabel still had far too much time on her hands.

Slade had Ruger bring her a new horse to ride. It was a young race filly that was broke but needed more riding, so she spent an hour or so with it every morning after breakfast. She had it going well under a western saddle in the arena, so she switched to a jockey saddle and started taking it on an improvised race course around the pasture west of the house.

While working it the third day on the course, a bird flew up and the filly shied violently. Isabel went out of her stirrups and over the horse's shoulder in a somersault and landed unceremoniously on her backside in the grass. Catching up the filly, she led her to the nearby fence, and after several attempts to get her to stand still long enough, she climbed back aboard and continued her ride. She had no idea Slade and Hank were watching until Ruby asked her that night at dinner if she'd been hurt in the fall.

"You saw that?" She was a little embarrassed.

Ruby waved a hand. "No, I missed the whole thing. It was these two saw it."

Then Isabel was really embarrassed. She shook her head and said, "No, I wasn't hurt. Just my pride, and it wasn't hurt until now because I thought I was the only one except the horse who knew about it."

Hank commented, "No need to be embarrassed. You're a right good little rider. I can't imagine how you

240

ride with that crazy little saddle anyhow."

Slade only smiled as he passed the creamed peas and said, "Watching you ride with that insane little saddle has become my new favorite spectator sport. I can't even imagine being able to handle a spunky horse with only that thing."

The next day she talked Slade and Hank into letting her halter-break the foals she had been watching with their mothers in the pasture closest to the house. She dug through Slade's tack room for a foal halter and a long soft cotton lead, then went out with her leather gloves and a bucket of grain. Catching the broodmares two at a time she brought them and their babies into the arena.

Some of the babies would walk right up to her to be caught, but with some of them she had to crouch down nearby until they were curious enough to come close. Once she caught them around the neck, she slowly talked to them and scratched them before she slipped the halter over their heads and clipped the buckle. The ones that walked right up to her usually stood still as she did this and the others would raise a ruckus.

In California she'd halter-broken the foals at just a few days old and they were much smaller and easier to control.

After talking to them some more, and brushing them as they stood in the halter, she slipped the soft cotton rope over the foal's back and around its hind end

241

and back up under its chin. Then she'd turn and face away and make a clicking sound as she gently pulled its head and rump forward at the same time. After a few pulls most of the babies would figure out what she wanted and start to walk forward when she clicked, before she even had to pull on the lead. A couple of them took a little more work than the others.

She worked with each baby going forward, and then taught it to back up by standing in front of it and saying, "back" and pushing on its nose and chest at the same time. She spent only ten or fifteen minutes at a time with each foal. After the lead lesson, she would carefully pick up each hoof and handle it for a moment, then gently set it back down and go to the next one, all the while talking to the little horse.

Some of them had no problem with this, but some of them didn't want her anywhere near their feet. Either way, she just kept quietly trying, talking and scratching and stroking all the while.

Before she turned the babies loose she fed them a handful or two of grain and crouched down again with her head close to the foal's.

****

Slade had been watching from the deck and presently Hank came to stand beside him and said, "She looks like she knows what she's doin', I'd say.

Slade nodded his head. "She's gonna be sore though. That stout little bay stud colt just turned and nailed her right in the thigh."

"I noticed she had to tie his momma up. That's the rankest mare on the place. Baby acts just like her." Hank sounded disgusted, and Slade laughed.

"I'd sell her, but those muscley colts of hers sell every time."

Isabel worked with eight mares and foals before coming in to start dinner. Slade was right. She limped all the way in.

****

That evening she called her attorney about setting up the trust as Slade had suggested.

She'd been reading her Book of Mormon every evening before bed, and Slade answered questions she had. For not being an actual member yet, he usually knew the answers.

Everyday but Sundays she swam in the mornings before she made breakfast. It had become her ritual of renewal the way her race with the dawn had been. In the steamy pool room by herself in the quiet, she swam and pondered and prayed and was then ready to face the day.

In the afternoons she'd begun to take long walks around the ranch in the hills.

She finished planting the flower beds, and worked with the babies, but within two weeks they were all broke to lead and she was again in need of a project.

Slade spent time everyday in his office, and she worked with him there, off and on, arranging Rossen's and Sean's rodeo schedule, but she was still at a loose end for something else to do. Never much of a TV watcher, she worried she'd drive him crazy just hanging out. She spent three days fixing worn spots in the pasture fence, and then went into town for paint and learned to faux finish in the upstairs bedrooms where the paint had been just a stark white. Slade struggled up the stairs to see what she was doing and laughed at the paint in her hair.

She brought a flat of raspberries home from the market one day and she and Ruby made freezer jam, something she'd never done before. It was a great feeling when she loaded all those little red containers into the freezer.

Slade was up and around more and more. He was able to finally take the brace off. He still couldn't lift anything heavier than 15 pounds or ride, but he started to work out on the elliptical trainer and swim laps in the afternoon while she lay on the deck with a book. She seldom read when he was there, but watching him exercise was incredible.

Lately, he'd begun to accompany her on her walk. Sometimes they would even drive to somewhere new to her on the ranch and start walking from there.

Hiking through these glorious hills holding his hand had become the highlight of her day. She had never spent time in the mountains like this. They seemed worlds away from the hustle and bustle of California and its crowds. Even life on the rural horse farm seemed hectic compared to this.

244

This man exactly matched these mountains. He was rugged and tough, sometimes tranquil, always beautiful, always standing strong and immoveable.

Once they barely made it back to the truck before a wild lightning storm crashed down the canyon. They hurried through the first blown drops of rain, and then sat together in the truck, marveling at the grandeur and later listening to the rain on the roof.

Another time they took a picnic to the river and sat near a series of short falls that made the water white and emerald green. She was leaning against a tree watching the falls when Slade came to her and kissed her. It was a good day.

****

On Labor Day, during the first week of September, Slade told her in the morning he had a surprise for her. He loaded her in his truck and they set off down the gravel road. It was the first time he had driven off the ranch since his accident, and Isabel was grateful that everyday he was stronger.

His surprise was a trip to the local horse track, Wyoming Downs, for the last races of the season. Compared to what she was used to, it was a miniature operation, but the spirit of the race was the same and she thoroughly enjoyed herself. The first time she heard the bugle again, her heart leapt.

She had never seen Quarter Horses race and was amazed that their races were completed from start to finish within eighteen seconds and said to Slade, "Holy smokes! What if you got a bad start out of the gates? You'd never have time to overcome it! Half of this sport is luck!"

They had a friendly competition to see who could pick the most winners. She beat him consistently until he finally insisted she clue him in to how she could tell which horse would win when she knew nothing about them.

"Watch them in the paddock. Some are sleepy looking, some are alert, and some are out of control. Look for the ones that are almost a little wild, but are alert and focused. Then watch them as they load in the gates, same thing, energetic but focused."

"What do you mean in the paddock?"

She pointed, "There, where they saddle them and put the jockey up."

They talked and laughed and ate concession food as they watched the beautiful, sleek horses until she could tell he was starting to tire. They were on their way out of the park when she had the uncomfortable feeling that she was being watched. She began to walk faster and was looking all around, not even sure what she was looking for. She knew Slade could tell something was up and they were all but jogging as they approached the truck and heard someone near the park entry call toward them, "Carrie! Carrie, wait! It's me, Geoffrey."

She grumbled under her breath as he pushed the keyless remote and they hopped in and literally squealed out of the parking lot. As they passed by the caller she ducked against Slade, hiding her face as he drove.

For a moment he concentrated on driving to make sure they weren't followed. Finally, he questioned, "Who was it?"

Letting her breath out in a rush, she said almost disgustedly, "Stupid Geoffrey." She said it as if that was all that needed to be said.

He laughed out loud, breaking the tension that had built and asked, "Stupid Geoffrey? That can't really be his name."

She looked up sheepishly. "Well no, but that's what Dante's called him for years now. It's rude, I know, but trust me. It fits." She furrowed her brow. "I wonder why in the world he's at a place like Wyoming Downs."

"Who exactly is Stupid Geoffrey?"

She flashed him a teasing grin. "He's a member of the stupid hat club."

"Oh, well that explains everything then." He chuckled. "Isabel, come on. You're not saying anything."

"When Dante and I were young, we'd pretty much decided that some of the bigger races were fixed so that whoever's horse won was the person who wore the dumbest looking hat on race day." She laughed at herself. "For awhile there I was convinced! A couple of times completely unknown horses won and the owner's wife had this unbelievable thing on her head!" She laughed out loud.

Slade shook his head. "What are you talking

about?"

She nudged his arm. "You've seen them on TV. I'm sure you have. You know, like at the Kentucky Derby. After the race, all the bigwigs line up for the win picture and to accept the trophy and flowers and stuff." She was still giggling. "And the owner's wife is wearing some outlandish hat!

"When I first had to stand there, I rebelled, but now Dante and I get into the spirit of the thing. We both wear the stupidest hats we can find. We're only honorary members of the club, but we're working on it.

"Stupid Geoffrey's father owns Thoroughbreds, and he truly is one of the stupid hat club. You should see some of the dumb stuff he wears on TV!"

Her face sobered. "I shouldn't be laughing. This really is a problem. He's had a thing for me for years. I'm certain he's the reason for the TNN spot you and Rossen saw when I first left California. He's convinced he and I were meant for each other, and he used to practically live at Wind Dance Farms. No amount of *'Geoffrey, I will never marry you. Leave me alone!'* would deter him.

"I can't imagine why he would be here. Do you suppose he got your license plate number?" She didn't wait for his answer. "This could be bad. If he did, we'll have media parked at the gate or some other asinine thing. A lot of money and no brain is a deadly combination."

He chuckled and put a hand on her knee. "I'm going to assume that my license plate is at least partially
248

covered with mud. We haven't washed the truck since we drove home the other day after the rain."

She worriedly looked all around again. "I hope you're right. At the very least he'll blab around that he saw me."

They were both right. The license number had been illegible, but Judd knew within just a few days where she'd been spotted with a cowboy getting into a truck with Wyoming plates.

Talking about Dante made her more homesick than she had been. Not homesick really—she didn't miss home, she just missed Dante, Eli, and Anna. Dante called the number Slade had left them every couple of weeks when he was away from the farm at random pay phones, but Isabel knew in her heart that she truly wasn't ever going back to live on Wind Dance Farms. Even if things didn't work out between her and Slade, she wasn't going back. Being away had shown her that she wanted her life away from where she had grown up. She knew it was the right decision, but sometimes the thought of being away from Dante and Eli made her sad. Slade seemed to read her mind because that evening he suggested she invite them to visit her there at his house. When Dante called that night, she invited them.

Chapter 11

Rossen called one day and said he was coming home for over a week and they arranged for Slade and Isabel to be baptized that weekend. Isabel had decided to not wait until Slade could baptize her. She would have Rossen do it at the same time he baptized Slade. It had been more than six weeks since that awful bull ride.

Slade was finally feeling like whatever he had torn internally was beginning to truly heal and he'd started riding again. He was taking it slow, but at least he was back in the saddle. He and Isabel had begun to take rides out into the hills everyday instead of walking, and his color had finally returned.

One morning, as she went out after her swim to feed, she saw that the leaves had started to turn on some of the highest hillsides. It was only mid-September and she was surprised. At Wind Dance Farms the leaves wouldn't change for weeks. Even then they would turn more gray and brown than these brilliant reds and golds. The September morning was cool and the scent of the sage was indescribable.

She and Slade went down to the Rocklands, and

she watched as they separated calves. She helped Naomi harvest her garden, and they brought the mares and foals into the paddock with the wood fence and began to wean the babies. The Friday before Rossen would return, she and Slade drove into a far valley and picked wild apples by the bushel and stored them in the cement room under his garage. She saw two of the outlying barns with huge piles of hay stacked nearby ready for winter feeding. The wild asters in her flower beds were a riot of color, and where they grew wild; they made whole hillsides glow purple.

Rossen and Sean returned late in the night and Rossen's and Slade's reunion the next morning warmed her heart. These two friends were closer even than the brothers were, and Rossen actually ended up staying at Slade's instead of his mom's. They stayed up into the wee hours talking about every thing imaginable. She and Slade were to be baptized the next day and the three of them felt a closeness about this that was hard to put into words. She was so excited to finally be a member of Christ's church, and to know she would be washed completely clean and start with a new slate spiritually.

She sat on the leather couch next to Slade as they talked, and eventually fell asleep on his shoulder as the evening drew on. She completely slept through Slade's revelation to Rossen that he planned to marry her as soon as she would consent. They both knew she felt she had to have the threat from Judd reconciled before she could become permanently involved in Slade's life. They both also knew the Judd situation didn't matter because

252

Slade was already committed to her forever.

When they finally quit talking, Slade gently woke her enough to help her up and steer her to her bedroom door, where she was loathe to end his hug. He bent to kiss her goodnight and walked across the hall to his room.

Sunday morning Isabel awakened while it was still fully dark. She took the quilt off her bed and sat wrapped in it in a rocker on the deck listening to the river and the wind in the trees, and looking at the myriad diamond stars in the black velvet sky. She thought back to the morning she had left home on her horse in the dark, and the time Naomi had taken her to the statue of Christ at Temple Square. She wondered when she had become so conscious of her Father in Heaven watching over her. She couldn't really pinpoint a time, but she knew now that He was there in this heaven somewhere and was absolutely aware of her.

Today she would be baptized, and as big of a deal as that was, it was also so much the obvious next step that it almost seemed like just the natural progression of living. Naomi was right--knowing the principles of the gospel and living them did make a happy life.

Slade found her there at sunrise. She knew he could see the peace and happiness in her smile. He sat in a rocker beside her and they watched in silence as the first bright rays colored the eastern sky lavender and pink, then orange and gold.

That afternoon, after their meetings were over, Naomi and another couple from their ward, took her,

Slade, and Rossen and gave them white clothing to change into to be baptized. They all went into a room in the church building she wasn't familiar with and Isabel sat and watched as some folding doors were opened to reveal the baptismal font. She was surprised to see the room fill to overflowing as neighbors and friends came in and spoke quietly to them and sat down. By the time the font was filled they were bringing in extra chairs to find seats for everyone.

Isabel whispered to Naomi, "I didn't realize there would be so many people."

Naomi just smiled and patted her hand. "Most of these people have watched Slade grow up. They feel like he's one of their own family. We've all been waiting a long time for this day. We've also waited a long time for him to find you. This is a good day."

There was a prayer and a song and the bishop spoke briefly, then Slade and Rossen stepped down into the font. Isabel wiped at the tears that filled her eyes as she watched. Never had there been better friends, and love and mutual respect shown in their faces as these two strong men performed this sacred act of obedience.

After Slade was baptized and had come up out of the water, the look on his face was something she'd never forget. Then he exited the font and sat to the side and watched as Rossen took her own hand to help her down into the font. When he baptized her, the Spirit that filled her heart was the sweetest peace she'd ever known.

It was such a simple thing, so quickly done, but of

such lasting importance. She'd never felt so grateful, or so humbly willing to do as her Father in Heaven asked. A few minutes later, as Naomi was helping her change out of her wet clothing and do her hair, her heart was filled with wonder at what had just taken place.

They quickly dressed and went back in to be confirmed. They'd been studying baptism and she'd come to more fully understand what a blessing this gift of the Holy Ghost would be. As honorable priesthood holders placed their hands on their heads in turn, she marveled at the great love God had for his children.

While Rossen was home, he and Slade started roping together again. Slade went easy in the beginning and at first was sore, but within just a few days he was encouraged enough about how much stronger he was feeling to commit to getting back on the road in time to still make it to the NFR. While Slade had been out, their rankings had dropped from 4th in the world to 9th and 13th in roping, and 11th in all-around. Still, they felt they had a realistic chance to pick it back up and compete.

The night they decided Slade truly was going to rodeo again was a momentous night, but Isabel had mixed feelings. She had missed Rossen and the rodeo life they'd been living, and she dearly wanted Slade to feel healthy and whole again, but the thought of another bull scared her more than she could even admit. The only thing stronger than her fear was her need for Slade to feel strong and successful.

Two nights later, Hank and Ruby were out and she and Slade had been watching a movie together with Rossen and Joey and some of her friends. As the movie ended, Joey and her friends got up to leave and Rossen went upstairs with them to see them out. As the credits started to roll, Slade tugged Isabel to her feet, and there in the soft light of the theater room, took her in his arms to gently sway to the theme song of the movie. They slow danced close through three songs until the movie quietly shut itself off. The only sounds left were the fan cooling the projector and their hearts beating steadily against one another.

Their feet slowed and time stood still as he kissed her there in the dark. Slowly and gently at first, his warm, firm mouth teased her senses until his kiss slowly made her forget everything. Her hands moved over the muscles of his back, pulling him closer and his fingers tangled in her hair. Tugging it back, his lips left her mouth to kiss the hollow at the base of her ear and trail kisses down to her shoulder.

Rossen, whistling as he came back down the stairs and went into his room, brought them back to the present.

With a groan Slade raised his head, holding her to him almost painfully close, and whispered, "Isabel, I need you." His breathing was ragged as he rested his chin on her shining hair. "I need to ask you to marry me, but I'm afraid you'll say no because of Judd." He pulled a hand through his hair, and pushed the dimmer switch beside them until there was enough light to look into her eyes. "I love you, Isabel. I need you in my life forever. I could no more be without you than I could live without oxygen. With you here, my life has meaning and hope, but without you there's nothing. Is there any way we can at least make plans to move on?" His eyes were searching hers, and she had no doubt he could see the passion she was feeling. His lips touched her forehead and he whispered, "It's the hardest thing I've ever done to kiss you goodnight at your room and go into mine alone." He sighed against her skin into the silence of the room.

After a minute he continued, "I know you think you're protecting me, but that only proves that I need you more than you know. We'll continue to be careful of Judd. We'll go away if we need to. Hire bodyguards. Whatever. Just, let's move on. Not getting married isn't doing anything but frustrating us. It's not like anything he does is going to change how we feel. Nothing could ever make me choose to be without you. You know that by now, don't you?"

She looked into his sparking green eyes and could see clear to his soul. Softly, she said, "Yes, I know that. And since you're the wisest man I know and I can't bear the thought of being without you. Ask." She hid her face on his chest.

He put his hand under her chin, and tipped her face up to his. "Isabel, will you marry me?"

She searched his eyes and knew she could see forever when he looked at her like that. Without hesitating, she answered, "Yes, I would be honored."

Several minutes later when he raised his head, she asked, "Can I ask a couple of favors?"

His voice was husky as he answered between kisses to her neck again, "Anything in my power."

"Can I officially change my name to Isabel?"

He still held her close and said, "Absolutely. And the second?"

She had to push him away from nuzzling her ear so she could remember what she was asking. "Can we get back out on the road soon so we can get you to the National Finals?" His look was questioning as he searched her eyes and she explained, "I love you, Slade. I'll do whatever it takes to make you happy and feel successful. Don't you know that by now?"

****

The next day they drove into Evanston to pick out rings. He wanted a chunky diamond solitaire, but she insisted on a simple wide gold band. The diamond was beautiful, but she said the band was what she really wanted. She said it was solid and steady and unpretentious, just like their friendship, and would be much easier to wear with her lifestyle. They decided she'd wear it immediately as an engagement ring, and as he slipped it on her finger with a lingering kiss, he had never imagined his heart could be so full. He smiled at her as she laughed and cried at the same time as they walked back to the truck hand in hand.

He kissed her tears away as he helped her up

onto the seat. He'd never even wanted to date another girl a second time, and had all but given up hope that he would someday fall deeply in love. Years ago he'd decided that soul mates along the lines of Rob and Naomi only happened once a century and he wasn't meant to find his. Now, as happy as he could ever imagine being, he recognized that in giving up hope, he had lost faith that his Heavenly Father truly had a plan for him. As he slid behind the wheel, and leaned to kiss her again, he realized he was looking forward to discovering the rest of the plan with a passion for his life that was almost overwhelming.

She finally got the intimate lunch date and the matching dress and shoes that she'd planned for weeks ago when they had come into Evanston the first time. He'd been right about finding the matching shoes, so she went with a slim fitting, little black dress and as she came out of the dressing room and twirled for him, he found it hard to breathe for a moment. Never in his wildest dreams had he imagined finding a girl like this. She was beautiful and sweet, smart and funny, and he loved her incredible talent for smoothing the wrinkles out of his life. Nothing was a hassle with her. She took things in stride with a calm confidence that made everyone and everything around her more comfortable. To him it was a priceless gift.

They hadn't told anyone at home what they were doing and when they showed up at the Rockland's home that afternoon, they made quite a stir.

Naomi was the first to notice Isabel's ring and she

swept Isabel into her arms in an emotional embrace. Pulling back, as they looked into each others' glistening eyes, each woman seemed to know the other would be an integral part of her life forever now. They embraced again and Naomi said, "Isabel, I've prayed so long that he would find you." She could hardly speak.

Isabel drew back and wiped at the older woman's tears. "At least you knew I was out there. I had no idea I would come across a sweet angel mother somewhere. I've never known anyone like you, Naomi. I couldn't have dreamed up a more wonderful unexpected blessing." They hugged and wept as Slade looked on, emotional himself.

When Rossen came in and realized that they were really engaged, the handshake that became a huge bear hug made the women tear up again. There was never a more faithful friend.

Isabel truly was one of the family at dinner that evening. Everyone had welcomed her always, but tonight, realizing she would be with Slade forever, she had fully become their sister and daughter.

Bo offered some comic relief. "Dang it all, Isabel! I was hoping you would finally come to your senses and throw him over for me! Now you've gone and busted my heart all to pieces!" His hang-dog face over his taco salad was hilarious.

As Isabel, Slade, and Rossen left the Rockland's to return to Slade's home in her Peace River Valley, the scent of the sage was poignant. Rossen had been right on that first night when he'd said, "Welcome home."

260

****

Rossen and Sean left to rodeo again with the promise to return in ten days for Slade and Isabel.

Dante flew in the next week and brought Anna with him. When Slade saw Anna in the airport, he tried to tell her how grateful he was for her introducing him to Isabel. He supposed when Isabel broke the news that they were getting married Anna would understand the depth of his gratitude.

Dante had never seen anything like the Rockland's ranch, and most of Wyoming had never seen anything like him. He had been mistaken in the airport for a pro basketball player again. It happened almost every time he flew. Some little old lady would ask for his autograph. For awhile he had tried to explain that he didn't play basketball, but now he just signed whatever it was they handed him, smiled and excused himself. When he did this outside the Delta terminal in Salt Lake, Slade doubled over, and laughed until he hurt.

Slade, Anna, and Dante talked and laughed in the truck on the way home like old friends. Isabel had stayed home in case there was a chance that any of Judd's group had found out Dante or Anna were traveling, so they had open season to tell funny stories on Isabel in her childhood.

When they finally made it to Slade's house, Dante literally picked Isabel up and swung her around in a circle. Their joy at being back together was obvious. She and Anna hugged and laughed as they greeted each other, and Anna actually squealed out loud when Isabel told her of her wedding plans. Dante beamed his big white smile at the news. They didn't have to ask if Isabel was happy. She had always been beautiful, but getting away from the immediate threat of Judd, joining the Church, and falling in love had made her lovelier than ever.

They stayed and played for four days and Isabel enjoyed every minute of it. She tried to share all of the wonderful aspects of her life in Wyoming, and the gospel in that short time. When they left to go back to California she was tired but happy.

Anna walked back onto the plane finally completely satisfied that she had done the right thing that day to encourage Isabel to go.

Dante left with mixed feelings. He knew Isabel was happy and in good hands, but he could also see in her eyes that she would never be coming home to California to live. He was happy for her, but he would miss her.

****

They had come and gone without any of them realizing that Judd had, in fact, found out Dante was traveling to Utah and had had him followed. The black sedan lost Slade's truck in traffic in the city but got his license number. Before Dante boarded the plane back, they finally knew who she was with and approximately where she was. However, the only address they had for Slade was a post office box, and because the ranch was owned by the ranch company, they hadn't yet found its exact location. The post office was in town and no one in rural Wyoming was answering questions from the slick strangers in the rental car.

Judd was furious that they had hit another roadblock. They'd come so close to finding her after the talk of the bull riding incident, but somehow they had never figured out the right cowboy. It had been more than four months and Tony had already roughed him up a couple of times. If it hadn't been for a really lucky gambling win at the track one day, he knew he'd probably be dead by now.

Judd was scared. More scared than he'd ever been in his life. He finally realized just how tenuous his position was. At first it hadn't occurred to him that they could put him out of the way far easier even than Carrie. Then he realized how simple it would be for him to disappear. Nobody would come looking for him if he failed to show up someday. And he knew now how hard these people would be to hide from.

He and Deek had fallen in with their schemes from time to time without really thinking that knowing too much could be dangerous. They had started to think about it a lot the other day when they had been present as some "loose ends" had been summarily shot and dumped in the river. He had to find Carrie and fast! It wasn't even just about the money now. It had become a vendetta. She would pay for all the trouble she had

caused him. He wouldn't even pay someone. He would
see   to   her   himself!

Chapter 12

Rossen and Sean came back and as the first snow storm of the year threatened, they packed up, and with Slade and Isabel along, hit the road for Waco, Texas. They left Slade's ranch in Hank and Ruby care, and then stopped at the Rockland's on the way out to say goodbye.

There were four of them now in the trailer and organization had become even more paramount. The rodeos were much fewer at this time of year and they had time to pull in, settle the horses and spend time site-seeing for usually at least a couple of days between.

Slade completely missed the first steer out, but got back in his game almost immediately after that. They competed in three rodeos in Texas and then went to two in Oklahoma.

They had been back on the road for more than two weeks when Rob called Slade to report suspicious activity at the ranches. There had been a small plane hanging around for most of a day, flying low over the whole region, then two days later the security guards at the oil wells had seen someone on the security cameras sneaking around. They hadn't seen anything else yet, but everyone was alert and the brothers were actually carrying guns on their saddles as they moved the cows out of the summer pastures.

As much as Slade hated to do it, he knew he needed to pass this news on to Isabel. It may have just been coincidence, but there was a chance Judd had found out where she had been staying in Wyoming.

They were engaged but not a lot had been said about when they would marry. He knew marrying before the NFR posed a number of problems. Their schedules and their trailer were jam packed until then, and although they hadn't talked much about it, he assumed she would need some time to plan a nice wedding.

He had been hoping the Judd issues would work themselves out with the new trust in place and with the passage of time, and hated to bring back the fear he'd seen in Isabel's eyes when they first met. He decided to tell Rossen and Sean first and see if they could just be vigilant about security on the road, and not have to tell her right off, but she busted them in earnest conversation from the first time they talked.

From their sudden silence and serious faces she instantly realized something was up and asked, "What's going on?" She looked questioningly from one to the next to the next. She looked at Slade last and he couldn't face the complete trust in her eyes with less than the truth.

She handled it well and he resolved to be

completely forthright with her always in the future. They started to be more careful as they traveled, and made it a point to ask the rodeo secretaries not to post their names anywhere on the schedules or online where the public could find them. Someone tried to be with Isabel at all times and they kept an eye out for anything that seemed the slightest bit out of place or unusual.

****

They were almost militant with their care for her as they competed in rodeos in Louisiana and Texas again before heading back out west to Hobbs, New Mexico. It was by the merest fluke that Isabel ended up alone in the horse stalls one evening at dusk. The three men had been tied up trying to iron out a mix up with the rodeo secretary before the rodeo was to start that evening. Isabel went back to water the one horse that wasn't being used that night and found herself alone in the alleyway when a half drunk Leland Wilde showed up. At first she'd been relieved that it wasn't Judd or one of his cronies, but as Wilde approached her, and she realized how inebriated he was, she became afraid fast.

He walked right up to her and put his arm around her shoulders without even hesitating. She could smell the alcohol on his breath and the look in his eye was predatory. Slipping out from under his arm, she retreated quickly to the hose spigot to turn off the water and leave when he grasped her arm from behind and asked, "Where are you headed, doll? Not so fast.

267

Come and talk to old Leland for awhile. You remember me. We're friends from way back."

He was slurring his words and she realized he was much more than half drunk. Knowing she was definitely not in a good situation, she shrugged out of his grip and tried to run away from him in hopes he was too far gone to be able to catch her. All she succeeded in doing was making him instantly violently angry and as he caught her again, he literally threw her into an empty stall nearby.

She started to scream, but he put his hand over her mouth and slammed her back against the side of the stall repeatedly with enough force to knock every drop of wind out of her body. As she doubled over to gasp for air he knocked her to the ground and drove the air out of her lungs even further when he landed hard on top of her body on the stall floor.

"You little . . ." He grunted and began to curse as she tried to wrestle away from him. She still had no air and her chest hurt desperately as she continued to gasp. She almost got away from him, only to feel him grasp the back of her shirt and rip it half off as he hauled her back. She focused every bit of energy on trying to inhale and got enough air in to let out a split second scream before he slugged her in the stomach, knocking her back against the stall wall yet again.

She started to feel faint and lightheaded and wondered if this is what blacking out felt like, when she heard the sound of someone running down the alleyway of the barn. She saw Slade look into the stall and realize what was going on a split second before she heard him roar like a mad bull. He shoved into the stall to literally pick Leland up by the shirt. Throwing Leland back against the partition, Slade went berserk. Rossen and Sean were just a second behind him. Sean tried to pull Slade off as Rossen dropped to the stall floor to help Isabel.

She was unable to breathe and something was wrong with her vision. She could see, but there was a jagged line like someone had ripped a photo in half in the middle of her horizon and there were sparkling lights in her periphery. Rossen was holding her and talking to her gently, but she was still panicking because she could not get a breath. Finally, with a great, painful gasp she was able to take in oxygen and the relief she felt was overpowering. She began to cry against Rossen's shoulder. On some level she realized her sobbing made breathing harder, but she couldn't seem to stop.

Rossen was still talking to her and his gentle voice was helping to calm her, but she clung to him, afraid to let go. She realized Slade was kneeling next to her, and his voice and touch for some reason made her cry all the harder. He backed up to sit against the stall wall and gently pulled her onto his lap. Slowly, with his tender encouragement, she got control of herself although she was still shaking. She looked up to realize there were a number of cowboys in the alleyway. A uniformed police officer pushed his way into the stall followed closely by a paramedic.

The policeman began to ask Rossen and Sean discreet questions, and the paramedic crouched down in front of Isabel and was carefully trying to check for injuries. Through the haze in her brain she understood that the police in the barn alleyway, with the help of the cowboys, had handcuffed Leland and were having to practically carry him through the barn to remove him.

The paramedic was saying something about a concussion, and Slade helped her up and into a waiting ambulance. Once inside they helped her lay down on the gurney, but almost immediately she had to sit up to be violently sick. She was still shaking and couldn't help the tears that kept overwhelming her. They helped her to a seat on the side of the gurney instead and she felt the ambulance pull away from the barn.

Twice more on the way to the hospital she was sick and her head throbbed. Every time she took a breath a sharp pain would shoot through her chest. The pain brought back the fear and the fear made her sad. It all made her control feel so fragile. Kenny was watching her and kept hugging her and she knew he could see what she was feeling.

By the time she was unloaded at the hospital emergency entrance she was doing better. She kept telling herself she was safe and Slade helped that, but she still felt positively miserable. They helped her in and she lay in a cubicle with Slade standing beside her holding her hand. They were trying to give her something for pain, but every time they gave her a pill, she threw it up, so they ultimately gave her a shot.

Finally, after what seemed hours, she felt herself growing relaxed, the pain receded and she slept.

Waking sometime later, the pain was better. So was the fear, but she was horribly disoriented. Even just trying to turn her head made her sickeningly dizzy. Slade was there beside her, holding her hand and encouraging her to talk to the nurse. They adjusted the head of her bed and eventually, if she held her head perfectly still, she could keep the world from spinning. She was still incredibly sick to her stomach and the nurse laid a cool cloth on her forehead and placed a cold pack on the back of her neck.

The next twenty-four hours were a mixed up dream of nausea, nightmares, and fading in and out of a spinning world. Rossen and Sean came and gave her a blessing, and ultimately Slade sat right on her bed and put his arm around her. She leaned against the strength of his chest and was finally able to relax and rest.

When she next awoke again, she could finally open her eyes and turn her head without making everything spin out of control. Slade was still there beside her, looking a little tired but handsome as ever. He took her hand in his, smiled sadly and said, "I don't know which is worse, being the injured, or watching."

She considered this for a minute and had to agree. "I'm not sure either, but I'm grateful you're here." Her voice sounded as weak as she felt. "Thank you for holding me and helping me rest." He kissed the palm of her hand and she closed her eyes again just for a moment and awoke again hours later.

This time she felt markedly better. She wanted to sit up, albeit slowly, and order a pizza. Slade laughed at her and said he had a surprise. He walked to the door and disappeared into the hallway and returned with Naomi in tow. Isabel basked in the hug she received. She couldn't have loved her anymore had she known Naomi all her life.

Naomi sat on the other side of her and asked, "Rough couple of days huh?" There was sympathy in her eyes.

Isabel nodded carefully. "Actually, I've felt ridiculously lousy. However, I've had a very handsome and attentive caregiver." She squeezed Slade's hand. "I feel so much better this afternoon and now I just want to go home to the trailer with the guys."

Naomi patted her other hand and said, "Actually its two-twenty in the morning and the trailer is two states away at a rodeo in California."

Isabel's eyes flew to Slade. "Did I make you miss two whole rodeos?"

"No, just one, but you're worth it. Heck, I'd rather sit at the bedside of a seriously delusional, hot woman than rodeo any day. It's very enlightening. I can now say I've seen you completely out of your head and I still adore you." He smiled at her, but it didn't reach his eyes.

Naomi looked from one to the other and said to Isabel, "I just now got in and I'm starving. Would you mind if I run grab a bite down at the hospital coffee shop?" Isabel only shook her head and then wished that she hadn't as Naomi patted her hand once more and slipped out.

After she left, Isabel studied Slade's profile trying to figure out what was bothering him. Even Naomi had seemed to sense it. Finally, Isabel decided she was still too out of it to understand and she asked him outright, "Are you upset with me?"

He shook his head. "No. Of course not, why would I be?" He looked up at her, but she still sensed that there was something he wasn't saying.

She grimaced in confusion. "I'm trying to figure that out, only my brain is still a little fuzzy for much deductive logic." She paused. "I'm assuming I've had a brain concussion."

He blinked and nodded sadly. "A bad one."

Yeah, he was upset with her, but why? She asked, "Slade, what's going on?" She didn't understand at all.

"Nothing. What do you mean?" She was suddenly very tired—too tired to try to read his mind. The only time they had really been angry with each other had been her first experience with Leland Wilde. Now Slade wouldn't communicate with her over him again. Did he think she had sought Leland out after he had warned her? Is that what was going on?

She didn't want to irritate him, but she couldn't just ignore the problem either. Tiredly, she said, "Saying nothing is going on, when something is going on, isn't honest. Are you sure you don't want to tell me about it?"

"Is, hon, I don't have anything to tell. Honest."

Still confused, she asked, "Do you think I sought him out? Is that it?"

He turned in his chair to look at her. "No, of course not. Why would I think something like that?"

She rubbed her forehead. "I don't know. It's just the only reason I can think of for you to be angry with me right now." She knew she sounded close to tears and she was.

Softly, he asked, "Why do you think I'm angry with you?"

"Aren't you?" Her question was gently put and she added, "You seem like you are. I feel like you wish I hadn't done this."

He leaned forward. "Done this? Isabel, you didn't do this. Honey . . ." He pulled his chair closer to her bed and took her hand in his again. His voice was eminently gentle. "Isabel... The last thing I would be at you right now is mad. I'm sad that you're hurt. I'm afraid it's more than physical hurt. I'm unable to forgive him—yet. I'm unsure of what to do about this. But mostly, I'm just so, so very sorry that I didn't protect you. Oh, honey, I'm not mad at you. I'm just bitterly disappointed in myself for letting you down. You didn't do this."

He looked down at their hands. "The doctors didn't think he raped you . . ." He closed his eyes and shook his head before continuing, "But I'm sure that's what he had in mind, and I'm sure you understood that at the time. He's done it before."

274

Slade sighed and looked at her and asked huskily, "How do I apologize for not preventing that? How can I ever take back broken bones, or a brain concussion and a black eye from a beautiful, sweet daughter of God? I was supposed to be protecting you. And I blew it. All for a stupid rodeo. I'm not mad at you. I just don't know how to fix this. I'm so sorry. This certainly wasn't your fault. It was mine. We shouldn't have left you alone." He met her blue eyes with his own sad emerald ones.

She carefully shook her head. "This was not your fault, Slade. Or mine. The blame is his and his only." She started to cry again and whispered, "I don't know how to fix this either, Slade, but I'll be okay if we're trying to be strong together." The tears came faster because if they couldn't pull together, she'd be more hurt than ever.

He sat on her bed again, leaned back against the raised head and gathered her back into his arms. "Go back to sleep, honey." He smoothed her hair back from her face. "I'll be here when you wake up and we'll be strong together."

Snuggling against him, she closed her eyes. His solid chest was unbelievably comforting. He was wrong. He knew exactly how to fix this.

They released her the next day and Slade took her and Naomi to a nearby hotel. She really did have a black eye. She couldn't even remember getting it in the ordeal. Her head felt better and her ribs were healing.

When the police finally came to take a report from her she was adamant full charges be filed. The police were surprised she was so sure about it and Slade wasn't thrilled about her having to testify against Wilde face to face, but they both understood when she explained that she had to do this so Leland Wilde could never hurt another woman this way again.

Because she was from out of town the local law enforcement was going to try to speed everything up. They asked if she could actually stay in town for the proceedings. She finally persuaded Slade to catch a flight to meet up with Rossen and Sean so he didn't miss any more rodeos. He only agreed to go if he hired a local security service to stay with her. When they arrived, she thanked Naomi and sent her home as well.

It actually worked out okay even though sometimes Isabel still felt completely lousy from the slowly healing brain concussion. One of Isabel's bodyguards was a tough but dynamic young woman named Megan who was working her way through the local police academy. The other was a former marine, now PI, named Beverly. Isabel felt strangely protected and befriended at the same time. When she felt up to it, they shopped and she bought them all some beautiful new clothes while she was hanging out. In the wee hours of the morning when the nightmares would hit, they would order pizza and sit with her and talk. Slade called at least once everyday and they had long conversations. He eventually flew back to be with her for the trial where Wilde was convicted.

****

Unbeknownst to any of them, the wait for the trial was actually a blessing in disguise. The strangers spotted at the ranches had been working with Judd, but they'd never caught sight of either Carrie, Slade, or Rossen so they'd given up looking in Wyoming. By using information he found on-line from the different rodeos, Judd himself had finally caught up to Slade, but after watching him for several days without catching a glimpse of Carrie, Judd decided he had the wrong cowboy again and went back home to California to restart at square one. He lost more than a month before he realized from more checking that Slade had, in fact, been the cowboy with Carrie.

Chapter 13

When the trial was finally over and they flew to meet up with Rossen and Sean, they were only three weeks out from the National Finals Rodeo in Las Vegas. Slade and Rossen had all but clinched a spot among the top fifteen in the world and though Slade was only ranked 16th in the all-around standings, things had turned out remarkably well.

They were back in Texas for a round of four rodeos before their final trip of the year out west. After leaving Texas they'd have one more rodeo in California and then head for Las Vegas and their goal of the National Finals.

They had just checked into a hotel in New Braunfels which was going to be their home base between three of the last rodeos, and Isabel was dressing for that night's competition, when Slade knocked on her door. As she opened it, she was amazed to admit not just Slade, but Dante and another man and woman she had never met, as well.

She squealed when she saw Dante and ran into his arms for just a moment. All four of them had relatively serious faces so she cut her greetings short and went to Slade and took his hand, waiting to hear his explanation. She was again amazed when he said, "Isabel, I'd like to introduce you to Special Agent Douglas Gray and Special Agent Natasha Keary of the United State's Federal Bureau of Investigation." Isabel looked back at Slade wide-eyed and hesitantly shook their hands politely.

Slade began an explanation. "It would seem that Judd is into even more questionable stuff than we thought." He nodded at Dante. "Tell her what you told me."

"They finally caught Deek, Carrie. Actually, it sounds to me like he turned himself in, hoping the police would protect him from the others. He came forward with enough evidence to put a number of criminals behind bars. He also gave the police some info about Judd. He said Judd knows who you're with and knows you're going to be at the National Finals Rodeo. Deek thinks Judd is mentally unstable and is after you now even more for revenge than money. He intends to nab you at the National Finals."

She broke in. "Revenge for what?"

He shrugged his shoulders. Special Agent Gray took over. "Deek says Judd thinks you cheated him out of money from Hugh's estate. And he blames you for all the trouble with Tony Delvechio, his bookie. Apparently, they've come to collect his gambling debts a couple of times, and when he didn't have the money, they made him pay in other ways. He's slowly become

280

involved in their operation. Whether by choice or coercion is anybody's guess.

"Deek says he and Judd know enough about their dealings to pose a threat to their organization, but he has also witnessed firsthand how they handled situations like that. Deek said he and Judd actually saw them execute some men and dispose of their bodies in the river.

"Judd has disappeared. Deek thinks he's trying to hide from Tony and the others, but he'll still come after you at the NFR. Apparently, Tony thinks so too and is planning to come after Judd when Judd comes after you. When Deek realized they planned to go after Judd, he figured his own number would come up pretty quick. That's when he went to the police for protection. Some of the people involved, and what they're into, prompted the local boys to call us in. We've been trying to nail Tony Delvechio forever. Thanks to Deek, we finally have enough evidence to put him away. Now we just need to find Judd and arrest him. That's where we're hoping you'll come in."

At this point Slade interrupted, "Isabel, could I speak to you in private for a moment?" She followed him to the bedroom and he closed the door behind them.

Taking both of her hands, he looked down at her and admitted, "What he hasn't said yet, Isabel, is that they would like to use you as bait. My first reaction is to say absolutely no, but there are some things to consider. If they can catch Judd, they'll put him away for life and we'll finally be free of him forever.

"Secondly, whether or not you agree to help, Judd is stalking you. If you agree, we'll have a slew of law enforcement and federal agents to help keep you safe.

"And I guess thirdly, you'd be helping the good guys catch the bad guys. However, that being said, you're the one who will be in harm's way, out in the open." He wrapped her in an embrace. "It could be very dangerous. You're the one who has to make this call."

He stepped back and took her by the shoulders, looking into her eyes. "You don't have to do this. Don't feel pressured to say yes. If you decide not to, just say the word. We'll keep you hidden and won't let you anywhere near the Nationals."

She gazed earnestly up into his face and asked, "Are you going to ride bulls?"

He looked puzzled. "What?"

"Are you going to ride bulls at the NFR?"

He let go of her shoulders to run a hand through his hair, frustrated. "Isabel, what does that have to do with any of this?"

She looked him square in the eye. "Slade, I need to know in order to make the most informed decision."

He was still puzzled. "How can my riding bulls or not, matter either way?"

She folded her arms across her chest. "If you are, I have to be there. Are you or not?"

His green eyes flashed. "Isabel. Don't base a decision concerning your life on a bull ride!" Their eyes

282

met and held. Finally, he looked away. "I don't know."

"What do you mean?"

He looked back at her. "It will all depend on what happens in the next two weeks. There's a chance I won't even qualify all-around or for the bulls. If not, then I won't get on another bull in my life. If I do, I'll need to ride." He didn't tell her he would need to ride one everyday until the end of the rodeo.

She gave him a half smile. "You make it hard to decide if I want you to qualify or not." Coming close, she wrapped her arms around his waist. "Would you pray with me?"

He hugged her back, letting out a deep breath. "Excellent idea."

They knelt beside the bed with hands intertwined. He was just about to ask her who she wanted to say it, when she began, "Dear Father, we're so grateful for our blessings, especially for each other. We're planning to help the FBI catch these criminals. Please help us to know if this is the right decision." After closing her prayer, they stayed on their knees for a few moments.

Finally, he helped her up, wishing he could tell what she was thinking, and followed her back into the other room.

She calmly walked up to the agents and said, "I'll help you. What do you want me to do?"

****

It seemed like the next three weeks flew by. Rossen and Slade were furiously competing in any rodeos, big or small, they could find to clinch their spots in the top fifteen while still trying to stay on top of plans the FBI shared with them. The FBI committed to helping protect her in exchange for her willingness to be the bait for their sting, and they began to put an elaborate operation together.

The National Finals are held in an arena which holds over 16,000 fans and law enforcement had to walk a thin line between apprehending dangerous criminals and endangering that size of a crowd. They had determined to try to keep Isabel as close to the chutes as possible when she was in the arena, thinking there would be fewer people and more room for various personnel. They would have seats near the bottom of the arena and had arranged for a hidden gate from the stadium seats down into the stock area in case of an emergency. They had also made provisions for a safe room called a bolt hole, under the tunnel near the stock pens, to be set aside where she could be safely kept if something went seriously wrong.

They were hoping to actually make arrests in the relative seclusion of the hotel but were making preparations for all contingencies. Isabel had assumed the FBI would insist she stay in certain areas or do things at certain times, but apparently they were okay with her being out in the open in order for her to be seen by Judd and the thugs they were after. When she thought about it, the idea that they wanted her seen was a little unnerving, but at the same time she knew they were taking steps to keep her safe.

A whole block of rooms had been reserved in the hotel and her room had been wired for surveillance. The hallways and elevators already had security cameras, and the FBI had been patched into the hotel security system. They had a specially equipped van that would be wherever Isabel was for the duration of the ten day event. The security system of the arena was patched in to the FBI as well, and any other areas the FBI deemed necessary that didn't have existing security cameras had been retrofitted. Arrangements were also made to have agents in several venues from security to the food concessions. Also, Isabel and Slade would have earpieces so they would be aware of what was taking place, and so agents would always have a handle on what was happening with them.

Isabel had been moved into the hotel more than a week early for her protection. She was thoroughly sick of room service and TV long before the rodeo even began. Special Agent Keary was rooming with her in a two-bedroom suite, and she had been around about half the time, so at least Isabel wasn't alone. They went out occasionally, but the casinos held no appeal, and Isabel was hesitant to be seen. For the most part she stayed in and read or worked out in the hotel exercise room.

Slade and Rossen called everyday, but the day they announced they had made the rankings and were for sure going to compete in the National Finals was bittersweet for Isabel. They both qualified to team rope and Slade had indeed qualified for all-around in bulldogging, saddle broncs, and bulls as well. She was glad they had achieved the goal they had worked so hard for, but that old fear of the bulls reared its ugly head.

Two days before the official start of the rodeo, Slade, Rossen, and Sean pulled into Las Vegas. A set of portable stalls had been brought in by the FBI and put somewhat aside from the other competitors, so the area could more easily be secured as they cared for their horses.

Isabel was surprised to find that, one by one, all the Rockland men showed up—a fact the agents weren't very pleased with. She never went anywhere without a veritable entourage. Slade came to her room the morning before the rodeo was to begin with a bullet-proof vest and a tentative smile. He was so hesitant to even step into her room that she couldn't help but laugh as she pulled him through the doorway.

He didn't know it, but she'd already talked to Special Agent Keary about getting one to wear, and she had arranged for vests for him and all the Rocklands to wear under their shirts as well. Without mentioning it to anyone, she'd also loaded her little pistol and kept it with her all the time. She had no idea what the gun laws were in Nevada, but she decided if she ever got desperate enough to use it, she'd worry about self-defense and not legalities. It was probably silly, but it did make her feel more secure.

Even Dante reappeared early the next morning.

He was wearing a set of official LA Lakers warm-ups, and his tales of the people he had met in the airport were hilarious. Even though she knew he was just trying to keep her spirits up, she enjoyed his quirky sense of humor. And he fit in perfectly with the Rocklands' particular brand of practical jokes. She definitely felt loved and cared for with everyone around, but in truth, she didn't know whether to feel safer because everyone had shown up, or more uptight that someone might be hurt because of her. At least Eli was safely back at the Wind Dance Farms because he hadn't felt that both he and Dante could be gone so long at the same time, And Naomi and Joey had stayed in Wyoming to watch over the ranch.

After worrying for more than two weeks since she had decided to go through with this sting operation, she finally gave herself a lecture on faith and let it go. She'd felt this was the right decision when she and Slade had prayed, and she was going to trust that peaceful reassurance.

Of course she would be careful. They all would, but God was over all and she decided to let Him do the worrying from here on out. After all, these were the rodeo championships of the world! Slade and Rossen were some of the finest on the planet, and she was going to do all she could to see that they enjoyed the journey, especially if they were thinking about quitting rodeoing fulltime after this. They probably wouldn't be back and she was going to make the most of the opportunity to be here at this time and place.

Slade questioned her sudden change in attitude and when she explained, he considered it for a moment, then smiled his heart-stopping smile. "You're absolutely right. I'd lost sight of why we do this, and it probably will be my last time here. I fully intend to go home, marry a beautiful girl, and live happily ever after. Let's enjoy the ride!" He pulled her to him and hugging her tightly, kissed her like he hadn't since the night they got engaged.

Looking back, the crazy pace of the last couple of months had helped her and Slade keep their relationship on a happy and even keel. Being on the road and under the time and space constraints they'd had, even the time spent apart had helped them not to dwell on their frustrations but rather to look forward with anticipation to the future.

On the opening night of the rodeo, in spite of the risks, they went out to the arena early. Leaving their horses tied to the rail, they browsed through some of the booths and shops that had been set up. Isabel and Slade had their earpieces in and knew surveillance was up and running, so they listened to the bands, shopped and walked, holding hands and laughing with the others. They truly were glad to be part of it all. The only thing to mar her experience was the number of females who tried to gain Slade's attention.

The show started as only Las Vegas could do a rodeo, with lights and special effects and the Jumbotron lit up like the strip. The opening ceremonies with all the cowboys and cowgirls made her heart full.

Even though they were in a less than ideal situation with the police and FBI present, it made for some excellent seats. She and the others had a bird's eye view of all the action, especially the bucking chutes.

Slade and Rossen roped well, and then Slade bulldogged in almost record time. The night was going smoothly and well, and even the fact that Slade rode a saddle bronc and a bull didn't completely spoil the festive atmosphere for her. She found that night that if she got up and walked up the stairs and back and forth along the walkway behind the seats where she could watch and walk at the same time, she could make it through his bull ride relatively calmly, then go back to her seat and relax. The agents and men could watch her as she went, and knowing Slade wore a bullet-proof vest under his competition shirt helped.

The ride back to the hotel with Sean, Treyne, and Dante was uneventful, but even knowing there were agents there beside them as they exited the truck in the crowded parking lot and headed for their rooms, there was a heightened sense of awareness. The entire town, it seemed, was full of rodeo fans, and they warily threaded their way through groups of belted and booted revelers in cowboy hats and Wrangler jeans. Pretty girls, often in not quite enough clothing, and an over abundance of alcoholic beverages, made the party atmosphere over the top. The idea of security in all of this was daunting.

As they entered the lobby a cowgirl beside them

bumped into Treyne, sloshing whatever was in her glass all over the front of his shirt. She laughed and leaned into him to apologize, giving him a close-up view of the ample cleavage hanging out of the top of her tight tank top, before moving on.

He shook his head. "Good luck getting any sleep around here tonight." He sounded a little disgusted with the whole lot of them as he attempted to wipe flat beer from his shirt.

Their foray through the hotel wasn't much better and Treyne was right, even locked securely in her suite they were well aware of the activity going on all around them.

Rob, Ruger, andCooperhad gone with Slade, Rossen, and Sean to bed down their horses, and when they all came in an hour later the parties were still going wide open.

The next afternoon Slade bought Isabel her first pair of cowboy boots. In all this time together she'd only used her riding boots, and his gift was the perfect souvenir of the greatest rodeo in the world. Thinking it would be much easier to hide her gun in the folds of the fabric, she also bought some western skirts to wear with her boots from the same little shop. She had kept the gun in her shoulder bag so far, but it would be far more convenient in a skirt pocket.

They were just leaving with their purchases when she heard someone call her Carrie. Everyone around her tensed to attention, and when she turned to see who it was she rolled her eyes and sighed. Stupid Geoffrey approached, decked out literally from head to toe in the most outlandish cowboy outfit she could ever have imagined, wooly chaps included, topped off by a huge ten-gallon hat along the lines of Hoss from the old TV show, Bonanza. He was obviously not a dangerous criminal and she could almost feel the others relax. The innocent countenances of all the Rocklands was almost too much for Isabel and she was hard put to keep a straight face.

Geoffrey came right up to her and when he attempted to hug her she pressed herself against Slade's side as Geoffrey said, "Oh, Carrie, I'm so glad I've found you! I've been searching for months. I'd almost come to believe you'd been kidnapped. I was devastated when I saw you at that little track clear out in Wyoming and then lost you again. That's why I came here to see if I could find you because I knew you were with a cowboy there."

His mindless chatter came to an abrupt end when he saw the wide gold engagement ring on her finger. His face immediately fell, and his lip began to quiver as he blurted out, "You're married?" His loud question and obvious emotion created an instant scene.

As he started back in with almost wailing pointless chatter this time, Isabel stepped up to him and patted him on the back, not denying his assumption. "Don't cry St . . . , Geoffrey." She patted some more, looking around her until she caught Dante's eye and mouthed "Help!" Turning back to Geoffrey, she said impatiently, "Geoffrey, stop fussing and let me introduce you to my new family." He let out a huge sigh and his whining became louder than ever.

Isabel patted and shushed and 'There, there'd' until finally, she said, "Oh, Geoffrey, for Pete's sake! Stop this! You're embarrassing us all! Here, stop sighing and wipe your eyes. For heaven's sake, you're an adult." She started digging through her shoulder bag, but Slade beat her to the punch when he handed Geoffrey a handkerchief.

Geoffrey took it and turned to say thank you until he realized it was Slade, who still held Isabel's hand, offering it. Geoffrey glanced at their entwined fingers and went off into another sigh that ended in a wail that was all but theatric. At this point Dante stepped in. Putting his arm around Geoffrey's shoulder, he steered him off in another direction.

As they left the others could hear Dante trying to calm him saying, "C'mon, Geoffrey, ya'all need to buck up. I'm sorry, man. I've tried to tell you for years now that I didn't think she was going to marry you. I'm sorry you had to find out this way." The conversation faded with distance and all the Rocklands and Slade broke out in amused grins. Their mirth began to take on a life of its own and by the time they entered the arena, she had no doubt that Geoffrey would be mimicked around the Rockland dining table for years to come.

As Slade hugged her tightly and left her at the top of the concourse to go get his horse he said, "I see what you meant about the stupid hat club."

The second night of the rodeo went off without a hitch as well with Slade and Rossen doing very well in all of their events. When the third and fourth evenings also came and went with good performances, but uninterrupted, Isabel began to wonder if somehow the authorities had been misinformed. In the evenings after the rodeo, Special Agent Gray touched base to see how they were doing and find out if they had seen anything of interest. Thankfully, the earpieces she and Slade wore had remained comfortingly silent.

The fifth night Slade was thrown from his saddle bronc before the eight seconds and took a no score. So far in the standings they were in 3rd place in the team roping and until this bronc, Slade had been leading in the all-around. Isabel was enjoying the rodeo, but had to admit her heart had jumped right to her throat when Slade had come flying off, and that night they had the liniment out again. As she worked over his back in the sitting area of her suite, she thought back to those times when she'd first dealt with this whole bucking stock issue. It seemed like forever ago.

They knew there were agents embedded around them, either in the crowd or in the arena staff. They had been trying for days to see if they could pick them out. Making a game of it helped to make the whole thing less menacing somehow.

Special Agents Gray or Keary were in the command center van and she knew of two others who sat close by them, but who the others were was a guess. There were several people around them who could possibly seem out of place, but it was hard to tell. So far, there was only one out of place for sure. The bearded man with the tinted glasses several rows back had to be FBI. Every time they went up or down or even looked back he was watching. It should have been comforting to know she was that closely guarded, but it was actually disconcerting.

As far as seeing Tony Delvechio or any of his people, she had seen virtually nothing to arouse her suspicions until the evening of the seventh round.

Isabel was having a tough time figuring out how the rankings were tallied. Slade was competing in four different events. He was going up against seven other contenders for all-around cowboy, and they were all competing in at least two events. Even though there were only two other cowboys who were really in the running, she was too new at this and felt a little confused as she tried to figure out Slade's standing.

Rob was trying to help her sort it all out as their little cavalcade made its way down the steps to their seats just a few rows from the bottom. Her hand bumped someone else's on the handrail, and as she looked up to apologize, she came face to face with evil. There was no other way to describe what she was seeing in the deep dark eyes before her. Instantly she knew this was one of the men after Judd.

She sucked in her breath, and the skin on the back of her neck tingled as the piece in her ear broke its silence for the first time. "You're all right, Isabel." It was Special Agent Gray's calm voice. "We see him. Act natural and continue on to your seat. There are four agents all around you. They have your back. You're okay. Go sit down."

Her heart was beating almost out of her chest, and she couldn't help but search the arena floor for Slade's dark head as she continued on down the stairs. Slade had been warming up his bulldogging horse, and she knew he must have heard the agent's comments too because he stopped at the rail in front of them to find her. His green eyes met her blue ones and she could feel his silent question across the space. With all the self-control she possessed she gave him a reassuring smile and continued to her seat as he went back to loping slow circles. That evening when he made it back to the hotel his hug was long and tight.

Over the next two days she and Slade saw four more men they felt must be involved with organized crime. It wasn't just that they looked completely out of place in their obviously new cowboy garb. There was something about them, some unexplainable impression of menace that made her skin crawl and her heart rate jump in fear when she saw them. They had seats all around them and, in fact, one of them was actually sitting within ten seats of the bearded agent.

It was incredibly frightening. The rodeo that had been an adventure had now become an arena of fear. Even those few moments of Slade's bull rides were nothing in comparison to this. Only when she was

295

actually in her seat in the arena or securely locked into her hotel room with Special Agent Keary was she finally unafraid.

The evening of the ninth round she was too nervous to even leave her seat during Slade's bull ride but decided that was a mistake. She only compounded fear with fear. By the time she locked the deadbolt and safety latch on her room that night, her nerves were completely frayed. Never had she felt anxious like this. Even those last couple of days before leaving California didn't come close. She prayed several times, knowing even as she did that she wasn't focusing but she couldn't help it.

In talking to Special Agent Gray that night, she asked if they'd noticed the man seated near the bearded agent. He assured her everything was under control and that she was handling things better than they'd expected, then rather abruptly ended the call.

She lay awake for what felt like hours before finally resorting to calling Slade to talk. Feeling guilty for disturbing him on the night before one of the biggest days of his life, she called his phone. She didn't even have to explain what was going on and knew from his voice that he hadn't been sleeping either. Two minutes later when he knocked on her door, with Rossen and Sean in tow, just his presence calmed her somewhat. Keeping their voices low, they talked to her for a few minutes and finally Slade asked her if she'd like a priesthood blessing.

He added, "I've been in the same boat all evening

and they gave me one. I can't even put into words how much it's helped." Slade's quiet sincerity strengthened her spirit every time. It always had.

Thrilled at the idea of some relief from the tension, she said, "I didn't know you could give blessings to people who weren't sick." A blessing hadn't even occurred to her. It should have.

Slade squeezed her hand as he sat beside her. "The priesthood's power can help in all kinds of situations. Think of the variety of situations that Christ himself dealt with. As far as being sick, I think that's just what I've been, sick at heart."

She turned to Rossen and Sean. "Would you mind?"

Dependable as always Rossen answered, "We'd be honored."

With Sean's help, Rossen blessed her that she would be strong enough to do all she needed to do, to not hesitate to follow the promptings she felt, and to remember she could trust in God. The last thing he said was almost uncanny, "Our Heavenly Father is over all. He's aware of you and your needs and He'll send his peace like a river." The peace that crept into her heart was nothing short of miraculous. Tears welled in her eyes as the feelings of anxiety and doubt fled to be replaced with a warm, sweet calm that flowed like a current into her heart and mind. With such peace she was finally able to get a good night's rest.

Chapter 14

The evening of the last round as Isabel came out of her hotel room in her western skirt and boots, Slade spun his finger to indicate he wanted her to twirl for him. She felt like a princess under his appreciative gaze as he said, "You're the prettiest cowgirl I've ever seen." He kissed her softly and held her in a long hug that she didn't want to end.

With his cheek against her hair he said, "This is almost over, honey. I truly believe it is. One way or another we're going to be able to put this Judd mess to rest. We'll be able to go home and move on with our lives." He kissed her again tenderly. "Then can we finally get married?" His eyes had never been so green.

She pulled his head back down. At length she answered, "I can't wait."

As he turned to go start getting his horse, she caught his arm. Looking into his eyes again she said, "Slade, I need you to not think about Judd right now, or even about me. I need you to focus on this rodeo. Focus and enjoy this evening. You're going to become the World Champion All-Around Cowboy in a few hours.

Please don't let these other things interfere with that. You love to rodeo. Love it more than ever tonight." She kissed him once more and then almost against his mouth, she said, "I'm going to."

And she did love the rodeo that night. The peace of the night before was still in her heart, and she was able to relax and enjoy the evening, though she was more attentive to everything around her than ever before.

Slade bulldogged in his second fastest time ever. Then he and Rossen roped their steer in 4.1 seconds, their own personal record and fast enough to put them over the top into first place and make Rossen the new World Champion Team Roper.

Slade missed spurring his saddle bronc out, which didn't matter because two seconds later he was thrown and received a no score.

Isabel wasn't sure what the all-around standings were exactly, but she realized with that no score, if Slade was to become the next World Champion All-Around Cowboy, it was now dependent upon how he did on his bull.

Tension began to mount and in spite of her prayers and the blessing of the night before, her stomach tied itself in knots. She fidgeted all the way through the tie down roping and the barrels seemed interminable. Finally, the bull riding started. The other cowboy who was Slade's only real competition for all-around made a decent ride and Isabel knew that if Slade no-scored or got a low score, he'd place second. She wasn't even aware she was chewing her fingernails until Treyne leaned over and gently pulled her hand from her mouth and said, "You're gonna draw blood." He smiled at her and she put her hands back into her lap. Of course Slade's ride would be the last bull of the night.

She could see him below her, putting his bull rope on a huge brindle bull. Rossen was there beside him, helping him, and taping his hand and wrist. She tried not to think about it, but she kept remembering that bull ride in Salt Lake City that had ended with him nearly being killed.

Finally, completely at a loose end, she couldn't stand it any longer. As he climbed onto the chute to stand over the bull, she stood up to walk up the stairs to pace. Stepping over Treyne and Ruger, who stood to let her pass without taking their eyes off of Slade, she made it to the stairs and had climbed several steps when suddenly the piece in her ear crackled to life.

Special Agent Gray's mild voice instructed, "Isabel, I need you to turn around and calmly walk back down the stairs to the hidden gate. Let yourself through, and go down to the room and lock the door. Do it now. There will be agents right behind you. Go now."

Strangely, she was more nervous about the bull ride than about this latest development. She hoped Gray had had the presence of mind to turn off Slade's earpiece. As she turned to go down the stairs, she noticed the bearded agent coming down the stairs right behind her and was relieved to see that Slade was indeed oblivious and focused on the bull beneath him.

She made it to the hidden gate at the bottom of the stairs and pushed back the yellow drape to reveal the latch. Opening the gate, she went down a short flight of stairs to the arena floor level and glanced back at Slade. Their eyes met for a split second that lasted an eternity, then suddenly her world turned upside down.

Just as she made her way into the tunnel she was hit violently from behind and knocked to the ground. Stunned, she turned, pushing her hair out of her face, trying to figure out what was going on. The bearded agent had slammed into her. As he put his head up, without the tinted glasses, she was horrified to realize it was no agent, it was Denzel Judd! Now that they weren't hidden by the glasses she would know those mean eyes anywhere.

He had dyed his hair and grown it out, and grown the beard and she hadn't even had an inkling. The last months had aged him years. He looked awful. He was snarling at her as he hauled her up to begin dragging her brutally down the dirt alleyway that led to the bowels of the building and the pens that held the rodeo stock.

****

Slade settled onto the bull's back, being careful to keep his feet up and forward. He took his wrap with the end of his bull rope and pulled himself toward his hand. This bull was huge, almost filling the chute. He had his

302

seat and looked up to signal he was ready and instantly realized something was wrong. The moment he glimpsed Isabel below the hidden gate, his gut knotted in fear.

"Isabel!" Her name escaped his lips just as she was knocked to the ground from behind.

That same instant the bull reared up and slammed into the panel in front of him, smashing his feet and legs and nearly hitting him with its head. Rossen slapped him hard in the face and hissed, "Marsh! Focus! Now!"

Mentally hauled back to the fact that he was seated atop 2000 pounds of rodeo bull, he thought to himself, *Eight seconds. That's all. Just eight seconds.*

He instantly nodded for the gate, letting the instinct of years of experience take over as the bull exploded out of the chute. Violently it bucked and spun, his body automatically counter-balancing and adjusting, his subconscious knowing exactly what the raging animal would do next. It plunged left for two spins and then went right, whipping erratically down in front as it kicked wickedly out the back, lashing to the side and plunging into another even tighter spin followed with a bone-jarring reversal.

It whipped its head so far back around that its horn smashed Slade in the thigh before it plunged its head between its front legs again in another mighty kicking buck. At that point, everything began to blur. It seemed he rode for a lifetime before hearing the horn.

Finally!

With the whistle, he brought his free hand down to release his wrap as he fought to stay in the middle of the bull's back. Free at last, he timed its stride and sprung off and to the rear, almost landing on his feet in the dirt. Up instantly, he whirled, trying to find the bull, and ducked out of its way as it spun to come back after him. His world was a kaleidoscope of bull, clowns and officials while he was trying to orient himself in the arena. In the background was the deafening sound of the crowd and the announcer. The fact that he had just won the world title never crossed his mind.

Realizing he was across the arena from where he'd last seen Isabel, he tried to gauge whether or not he could beat the bull across. The bull made the decision for him as it came racing down the dirt, scattering bull-fighters and officials in its wake. It was a deadly game of dominos as man after man jumped up the fence when the bull pounded past.

Desperate to get to Isabel, Slade waited until after the bull went by, then sprinted across the arena. Halfway across the bull spotted him and it was a race to the death with Slade winning by one stride. Reaching the alley gate, he went up and over as the bull smashed into it with its massive head. Two seconds later, as it took off back down the arena after an official, Rossen jumped down from the chutes and went up and over the gate after him.

The Rocklands and Dante had been so intent on Slade's bull ride, they didn't even realize something was wrong until he and Rossen went flying over the gate. Looking around they were mystified about the whereabouts of Isabel until they realized the hidden gate was open and there were two people standing below it, one of whom was putting a pair of handcuffs on the other.

****

Judd had caught a handful of hair where he was dragging Isabel by her left arm and her head was pulled back and to the side. She struggled to try and keep her feet and couldn't see where they were going or what was going on behind them. When she saw the door to the secure room as she was dragged past it, helpless to try and lock herself in, she began to pray fervently.

Judd was snarling and swearing at her as they made their way with her stumbling at his side, trying to loosen his hold. It felt like forever, but it must have only been a few seconds because she heard the crowd go wild back in the arena after Slade's ride. They sounded strangely far away. At some level it registered that he must have made it safely through.

She could hear shouting in the alleyway behind them and shots rang out. It was an eerie mix of normal gunshots and the peculiar whistle of a silencer that reverberated in the iron tunnel and seemed horribly close to them.

The bucking horses in the pen Judd dragged her past began to mill around nervously. Through all of this her earpiece remained strangely quiet.

Repeatedly she tried to reach her gun, but from this position she couldn't even reach her pocket. Finally, she jerked her hair out of Judd's grasp and was able to see what was going on behind her.

Five men and Keary were in a running fire fight in the tunnel under the arena. One man was down, back near the entrance to the tunnel, and the others were either trying to run and shoot, or were trying to take cover behind the upright metal I-beams protruding from the outer wall. In the melee, it was hard to tell who were FBI and who were criminals. As she heard a bullet whine past her to clang wickedly against the steel tunnel, she assumed the ones aiming at her and Judd were not the agents.

Judd picked up the pace to a stumbling run, and at one point she accidentally tripped him and they fell headlong. As he dragged her back to her feet, she realized in his other hand he too held a gun.

She heard a loud clank back in the tunnel and felt a fresh surge of fear as she realized they were running up the same tunnel the pickup men turned the bulls into after they were ridden. As if to reinforce her fear, Special Agent Gray's usually calm voice rang in her ear, "Those of you down in the tunnel, there's 2000 pounds of angry beef pounding down your back door! Get out of the way!"

Isabel looked back and if there was any question as to which were FBI, it was cleared up immediately as three of the six figures left the shelter of the I-beams and raced across the alley to climb the fence on the other side. Two of them made it to safety as the bull raged down the lane, but he caught the third one half way up the fence and tossed her high into the air with his horns. Hardly seeming to notice the woman he'd flipped so violently, he then lowered his huge head and kept on coming up the alleyway.

Still looking back, Isabel began to scream frantically at Judd, fighting him like a wildcat, as it raged closer. The thugs in the alley realized too late and before they could react, the beast was upon them. It hit one without even pausing, knocking him down to run right over the top of him, and caught the second one with his horn. The bull threw its head angrily and sent him flying like a rag doll right over the nearby fence and into the pen of bucking horses beyond it. They shied violently, and circled their pen like a living wave, the man disappearing under its crest. Even in her panic Isabel felt sick.

Not waiting to see more, she turned from the sight of the crushed bodies to tear at Judd's hands, almost feeling the bull's breath as it bore down on them. Steeling herself for the impact, she pleaded, "Please God, help me!"

As Judd dragged her past another pen next to them, a long-horned roping steer hooked a horn through the rails, catching him in the side. He stumbled, and lost his grip and she cried out in relief as she lunged desperately for the fence, trying to climb as fast and as high as she could. Her feet tangled in the length of her skirt and in complete panic, she pulled herself to the top of the fence by sheer arm strength even as the bull knocked her feet to the side as it slammed into the fence she hung from.

Clinging to the very top of the fence, she saw the bull knock Judd down directly below her, and then circle back around to return and repeatedly smash him into the dirt with its head. It was the most horrific thing she'd ever seen and heard, but she couldn't make herself look away. After what seemed an eternity the bull lifted its head, seemed to glare up at Isabel for a long, long moment, pawed arena dirt that flew up over its back, then trotted off further into the tunnel. Moments later in the distance she heard a metal gate slam shut.

The alley suddenly became breathlessly still and quiet. Even the stock seemed to be waiting. Isabel carefully stretched her feet down to a rail and glanced over her shoulder. Four people lay in the alley, eerily still, and the other two clung to the top of the fence down the way. She saw movement and realized Special Agent Keary was attempting to sit up. From the corner of her eye she saw a man between her and Keary who she'd first thought dead or unconscious, silently extend his arm with a gun in his hand, taking careful aim at the wounded woman. The agents on the fence couldn't see him from their angle.

Isabel knew what she had to do and she didn't hesitate. Her hand slipped into the pocket of her skirt. She gripped her gun, pushed the safety aside, aimed and shot in an instant without even pulling her gun free of

308

the fabric.

A split second later two other shots rang out. There was a metallic ding and the echoing whine of a ricochet and the bucking stock began to plunge and rear in their pens. The gunman she had shot at didn't react and terror shot through her as she realized he would now turn the gun on her.

When he slowly lowered the gun and slumped further to the side, she started to cry. She was suddenly overcome with weeping and she could feel herself shaking. The storm of emotion was so uncontrollable she couldn't even climb down. She tried to wipe at her eyes with her shoulder while still clinging to the top of the fence as people poured into the alley.

Slade and Rossen arrived first. Right behind them were the rest of the Rocklands and Dante, and what seemed like thousands of FBI and law enforcement, followed by a pick-up man looking for Slade.

Slade ran straight to Isabel while Rossen came more warily. When Slade approached her, Isabel struggled to control her emotions, feeling like her entire universe was going to shatter. She was completely overwrought, but she knew Slade was needed back in the arena and didn't want him to feel guilty for having to leave her.

He tried to help her down from the fence but she couldn't make her hands let go. Finally, he softly said, "It's all over. Everything is okay." He pried her fingers loose, lifted her to the ground, and turned her back to the lifeless body of Judd to envelope her in a hug.

After a long moment, against her hair he asked, "Are you hurt?" She shook her head where it was buried in his chest and they simply stood like that until the pick-up man approached.

He sat on his horse, looking all around in amazement. Finally, he said, "Marsh, they're waiting for you in the arena. Ya'll gotta get back in there, man."

Slade turned to him without letting go of Isabel and said, "I'm needed here. I'm sorry, they'll have to do it without me."

Isabel pulled back from him and silently shook her head. Mustering all her self-control, she lifted her chin and firmly said, "No, we'll all go. We can't miss this."

The pick-up man stepped down. "Take the horse, Marsh. Hustle!" Slade looked down into her eyes and she did her best to smile at him and nudge him away. With one last squeeze, Slade legged onto the horse and galloped back up the tunnel again, scattering agents and cops.

Isabel turned to go back, wondering if her legs would carry her. Although the first trip down this lane had felt like miles, it was actually only a couple hundred feet back into the arena. Rossen and Dante and the others fell into step beside her, which was good because she needed their strength to walk.

As they passed him, Gray tried to stop them, saying, "We'll need to ask you some questions before you go."

Rossen made a sound of disgust and took her elbow, ushering her past the agent, and said with disdain, "You've got it all on surveillance." He waved at the video cameras. "You almost got her killed! You've got that on tape too." Gray opened his mouth to speak and then shut it again, as to a man the Rockland men and Dante all moved to surround her and they headed back inside. Her determination to handle this kicked in and she tried to focus only on Slade and what he'd just accomplished.

Isabel's breath caught in her throat as they reached the arena. The lights were all down except the spotlight that followed Slade and the horse as he galloped the perimeter. All the work and risk and danger, all the miles and strains and injuries had come to fruition, and he had indeed reached his goal. He was now the World Champion All-Around Cowboy. The announcer was giving some background on him and some of the achievements and sacrifices he'd made this year in his quest for the title. The story of his life-threatening wreck brought it back in an instant, but at this moment it all felt worth it. As he finished his ride to thunderous applause, Isabel's eyes filled again. This time they were happy tears.

He turned the horse into the center of the arena, took off his hat to wave it at the crowd, then putting it back on, he rode out of the spotlight for good and back down into the tunnel.

The announcer made some final remarks, effectively ending the National Finals Rodeo for another year, and the lights started to come back on. Loud, rocking country music began to play and people started climbing the stairs to leave the arena as if nothing was amiss. Everything was so normal it was bizarre.

The relief in the tension was such a let down it was almost numbing and Isabel began to shake again. She leaned against a nearby gate post and gave in to the emotional maelstrom and the tears that had only been made more poignant by the tender feelings from Slade's award.

Slade returned the horse and thanked the pick-up man. Then he came back and with all the after rodeo crush going on around them, he took Isabel in his arms and just held her, smoothing her hair gently and whispering comfort and hope to her—telling her how proud he was of her and about what a great future they were going to have—how he would keep her and their children safe for the rest of forever.

For the longest time he just held her and kissed her. They'd made it. They'd survived Judd and the mob and the bulls and the injuries and literally everything that had come at them, but they'd made it. Slade was the World Champion All-Around Cowboy, and Isabel was at long last free to move on with her life. They both were. And the rest of their life would be all the more sweet because of what they'd been through. They'd made it.

Finally, as the sweet, sad strains of "This is Where the Cowboy Rides Away" came on over the PA system, Slade tenderly kissed her temple one last time, and

312

spoke with his cheek against her silvery-gold hair, "Come on, Isabel. Let's go home."

Epilogue

Ninety days later, Ebony Wind had been back at home at Wind Dance Farms for more than two months and the Thoroughbred breeding season was winding down just as it always did in late March. Isabel still missed Eli, Dante and the others in California, but she knew in her heart that Wyoming was where she wanted to be. Other than a visit every few weeks and a lot of phone calls, she'd left the farm in Eli and Dante's capable hands. She still owned half the farm, but no longer needed or wanted to be in on the daily management of it. Dante was engaged, and she gave him her grandfather's house as a wedding present.

As the last snow was melting from the wildflower beds and the wind off the Peace River held the tangy scent of sage, Slade and Isabel Marsh sat in their home office watching a video conference call with the FBI. Special Agent Gray had invited them to sit in as he reported on the closing details with his staff.

He admitted to Isabel that until she had mentioned the bearded agent to him the second to last night, they hadn't realized it was Judd and he added, "To be honest, we didn't think he was smart enough to pull off what he did by himself. He surprised us all, obviously."

The final night of the rodeo they had apprehended nine men including the elusive Tony

Delvechio, both at the rodeo and in a simultaneous raid of another home they had had under surveillance there in Las Vegas. Two of the criminals had died of injuries sustained from the bull and horses that night. The rest had either been tried and successfully convicted, had plea bargained to lesser charges, or were bottlenecked in the system awaiting trial with overwhelming evidence against them.

Judd had died without making provisions for his estate, so his house had reverted back to Isabel as his daughter. It was slated for demolition because it held such bad memories that Isabel never wanted to see it again.

The only agent who had suffered more than minor injuries had been Keary. She'd broken her pelvis and gotten a concussion when the bull had hit her and thrown her with its head. She was mostly better and wanted to come back to work. She swore she wasn't working near any more bulls, so Gray threatened to assign her to a drug case on a crab boat in the Bering Sea with only his bland smile to prove he was kidding.

In conclusion Gray commented, "The weirdest thing about this case is that in the tunnel when Keary was coming around after being tossed by the bull, the surveillance cameras show one of Tony's thugs attempting to shoot her. He was stopped by multiple shots from three different people. He actually would have eventually died of injuries from the bull, but in his autopsy they found a fresh gunshot wound from a .25 caliber bullet. The coroner swears it happened at the same time, but none of my agents or any of the perpetrators carried a gun that small. We've watched the tapes over and over and have never figured out where that shot came from, but have reason to believe it was the shot that saved her life. We finally just marked the file 'shooter unknown,' and shelved it. It's the only loose end of this whole case."

As the video conference call concluded, Slade and Isabel sat for a pensive few moments remembering that fateful night. They talked solemnly for several more minutes, then Slade excused himself and went into their bedroom. Following a few minutes later, Isabel found him in her closet looking in the little black case she kept on the top shelf.

When she realized what he was doing, she turned to him and searched his eyes, afraid of what she would see there. There was no sign of the disgust or repulsion she feared. Instead, his voice was gentle when he asked sadly, "Why didn't you tell me?"

She looked down and admitted, "I'm not even sure how to feel about it. I certainly didn't want anyone else to know."

He put the pistol away and pulled her close and whispered, "He said you saved her life. That's a good thing."

She looked up into his eyes. "I shot a person, Slade. I never dreamed I'd have to do something like that. The only way I've been able to deal with it is that I knew at the time I had to stop him." She inhaled a shaky breath and hid her face against his chest.

316

He wondered aloud, "Are you going to tell Gray?"

She shook her head and answered without looking up, "I didn't intend to. Would it help anything, or just ruin my reputation and cost the tax payers a lot of money?"

He tipped her head up to kiss her. "You make a good point. I still wish you would have told me. That's quite a burden to carry alone. I wish you would have felt you could trust me."

"I trust you completely. You know that. I just didn't want you to think differently of me." She gave him a tenuous sad smile. "Do you?"

He shook his head. "I respect you more than ever." Then he gave her a small grin. "And I am never going to mess with you." He put his arm around her shoulders and pulled her close as they walked out of the room.

She stopped him at the door to ask, "He knew, didn't he?"

After a moment's hesitation, he nodded. "Yeah, he knew."

The End

About the author

Jaclyn M. Hawkes grew up in Utah with 6 sisters, 4 brothers and any number of pets. (It was never boring!) She got a bachelor's degree, had a career and traveled extensively before settling down to her life's work of being the mother of four magnificent and sometimes challenging children. She loves shellfish, the out of doors, the youth and hearing her children laugh. She and her fine husband, their family, and their sometimes very large pets, now live in a mountain valley in northern Utah, where it smells like heaven and kids still move sprinkler pipe.

To learn more about Jaclyn, visit **www.jaclynmhawkes.com**.

Journey of Honor (excerpt)

He pulled up and got off his horse and was just about to speak when he heard the sound of a cocking gun. The wagon flap moved and the barrel of a pistol appeared, followed by Giselle's head. When she realized who it was, she dropped the muzzle of the gun and took a deep breath and then whispered with her accent. "Oh, Mr. Grayson, you frightened me. I thought you were Henry Filson. What are you doing?"

That's exactly what he was asking himself just about now. "Uhm, you're not going to believe this, but I've come to see if you would consent to marrying me." He put up a hand. "It's just to be able to get you away in the morning, and we'll have it annulled when we get to your valley. It's either that, or stay here and deal with Filson and a trial, and waste more time getting started west."

She looked totally confused for a minute, and then said, "Just a moment." Her head disappeared back inside the wagon cover and he could hear her whispering quietly to someone and then a bare foot and lower leg appeared through the flaps. He realized she was getting out.

He went forward to help her down and she turned to look at him with big eyes in the darkness. She was wearing a nightgown covered with a long robe and her hair was loose and hanging around her shoulders. She was even prettier than when she'd been all dolled up and he questioned again to himself what in the world he was doing, while he waited there to see if she was going to laugh or cuss him.

He was completely amazed when she looked up at him in wonder and asked in a soft, sweetly Dutch voice, "You'd do that for me? Really?"

He didn't know what to say to that. He'd never experienced anything in his life that would help him figure out what to do in this situation. Finally, he just said, "Uh, yes. I would. But honestly, it's not being totally unselfish. Without you and your grandparents, we can't leave either until we find someone else to take your place. The army won't let trains of less than twenty wagons start out."

He paused for a minute and then decided that being absolutely forthright was in both of their best interests. "I give you my word to be a gentleman. I wouldn't expect anything other than your help in getting underway. You needn't worry."

She laughed a sweet laugh at him in the dark and said with her intriguing accent. "Worry? You have just taken a huge load of worry off of me! I don't doubt that I can trust you. I knew that the moment I saw you on the hotel boardwalk. And I fully intend to help all the way across this great journey. I will be glad to. I am more grateful to you than I can say right now. I would love to marry you to get started in the morning. I would be thrilled!"

For a second, he thought she was going to come right up and hug him. Just when he felt relieved that she didn't, she actually did. Just as quickly, she pulled back and looked up at him with a sober face. "Tell me what you need me to do."

Still a bit shaken, he simply said, "Be ready to go into town a little before sun up. We'll meet with the sheriff, get married and be back and ready to leave at first light."

All she did was look up at him with those wide eyes and say, "Okay." With that, she turned around and climbed back into her wagon without a backward glance at him. He walked away in the moonlight in a stupor. He got clear back to his own wagon before he remembered that he'd ridden his horse to hers and he had to go back and get it. Gathering his reins, he was turning to go when she poked her head out again.

Feeling a little sheepish, he said, "Sorry. Forgot my horse."

The Outer Edge of Heaven (excerpt)

Luken Langston pulled his pickup truck into the parking spot in front of the bunkhouse and shut off the engine in the lavender gray light of dusk. Opening the door and stepping out, he stretched his tired back and reached back in for his leather work gloves and the rope that lay coiled on the seat. He slapped the rope against his dusty pant legs and boots and breathed deeply of the evening smell of river bottom and beef cows. To some that may have been a questionable smell, but to him it was home in its purest essence and he loved it.

His stomach growled and he wondered if there was any real food in the bunkhouse fridge or if he'd have to either settle for junk, or head back up to the main house before crashing tonight. He'd been up since four thirty that morning and was too tired to go for food, even though he'd skipped dinner. Maybe there was some fruit left, or some milk. Fo lived on milk, so there should be some. Or maybe that was backward. His boots sounded loud on the wooden porch boards as he took the two steps.

He tossed the rope onto one of the hooks inside the door of the bunkhouse, threw the gloves onto the shelf above it and reached to unbuckle his chaps. Hanging them beside the rope on the hooks, he pulled his shirt off over his head in one single motion. He dumped it into the laundry hamper next to his bunk as he kicked out of his boots and spurs, grabbed clean clothes from a drawer and headed for the shower.

Thirty seconds later, he decided a hot shower was the greatest invention known to man and resolved to sleep right there under the pounding, steamy spray. This had to be the purest form of heaven.

The need to sleep there cooled with the last of the hot water and he got out, dried off, and wrapped the towel around his hips as he stood at the sink to shave. The aftershave he slapped on helped to wake him up enough that he decided he would go in search of real food, even if he had to go up to the house. It had been a grueling evening.

He usually let the hands have Sundays off except for the barest minimum of feeding chores, but this afternoon he'd had a whole herd of heifers go through a break in the fence and get into a grain field. It had been a pain rounding them all back up, moving them alone, and then repairing the fence. The field would never been the same, at least not this year.

Slipping on a clean pair of jeans, he walked out of the bathroom, shirtless and bare footed. He was half way to the fridge when there came a light knock and then the bunkhouse door opened. A beautiful stranger with blonde curls and long legs stepped inside and called out for Fo. She didn't see Luke there in the half-light and came in several more steps, calling as she came and then abruptly pulled up when she finally saw him. Both of them were speechless for a second and then she stammered, "Oh, I'm so sorry. I didn't know there was anyone else in here. Please forgive me."

The Most Important Catch (Excerpt)

North Carolina

As their meeting with the coaches ended, Robby Robideaux stood up and moved toward his friend Jason to touch base about what time they were going to be leaving for the airport in the morning. He absent-mindedly accepted a courier envelope a waiter held out to him, slipped a finger under the seal, and opened it as he turned back to his conversation. "Seven forty-five? That should be long enough to make it through security, if we only have carry-ons. I'll pick you up." He glanced down at the papers that he'd pulled from the envelope, swallowed a gasp, and hurriedly shoved them back inside. *Holy Toledo!*

He looked up, hoping no one else had seen the suggestive photos of a woman with far too few clothes on that he'd pulled from the seemingly innocuous express envelope. Geez, these things usually came in heavily perfumed pink letters or in elegantly wrapped packages and he knew not to open them, but this one had taken him by surprise. He'd expected business correspondence this time.

Jason looked at him sympathetically, and Robby rolled his eyes and shook his head as he bent to retrieve the piece of paper he'd dropped in his hurry to hide the pictures. What

324

were these women thinking? Didn't they listen to the news at all? Just this week there were two reports of women who had been assaulted by professional athletes. Not that he was that kind of a guy, but these women didn't know that. They didn't know him from Jack the Ripper! Were there no nice girls left in the whole wide world?

He checked to make sure the plain paper he was seeing didn't feel like a photo before he turned it over. It was a note and he would have just shoved it back in as well, except that it only said five words that literally jumped off the page at him. "Meet me on the balcony."

The hair on the back of his neck stood on end as he resisted the urge to even turn his head to glance at the balcony overlooking the main dining room where he was standing. Even the fact that he was a 240 pound All-Pro football player didn't stop his dread at the thought of another stalker. He hated this! How had she even known he was going to be meeting here? And, what courier service had delivered this to him?

Stepping to his left where he was far enough underneath the balcony to keep anyone above him from seeing him, he set the note carefully on a table beside him, knowing it would be dusted for fingerprints, and pulled out his phone. This meeting had been only head coaches, their staff, and a handful of the most senior players. He glanced at his phone as he went to call security. He never let anyone near his phone, but he still wondered if someone had managed to plant something in it again to track him and listen in on calls. It seemed absolutely paranoid, but it had happened to him twice before.

His suspicions were confirmed when he'd no sooner asked for security than there was a disturbance on the balcony above him, and then glass shattering and the sound of a women's heels rushing out the back. He ran a hand through his hair with a sigh, hoping this was just a one-time fluke. The last thing he needed right now was another psycho female.

Illinois

As the heavy metal doors shut with a clang behind her, Kelly Campbell squinted in the brightness of the late afternoon sun. She turned to glance at the austere tan building she had just left. It was only a psychiatric hospital, and she was a nurse, not a patient, but sometimes that building felt more like a prison. She took a deep breath and tried to rid her nose of the nasty institutional smell of commercial disinfectant, but even the thickness of the air here in Chicago wasn't enough to kill that odor.

She rolled her shoulders and headed for her car, wondering if this was really all there was. She'd spent years getting her RN and finding what she thought would be a fulfilling career, but just two months of this job was beginning to make her question if she'd made a mistake.

At first it hadn't been too bad. She knew helping these mentally ill patients was a worthy work, and when one of the seemingly sharp, young doctors had started asking her out, it had been a rush. But it was a short lived one. Dr. Peter Holmes was handsome and for a short while she'd thought he was completely charming, but now she was beginning to wonder. There was something strange going on here at this facility, and it involved him. She just hadn't figured out what it was yet.

To buy these or any of Jaclyn's other books, please visit spiritdancebooks.com or call 1-855-648-5559

www.ingramcontent.com/pod-product-compliance
Lightning Source LLC
Chambersburg PA
CBHW070210260626
47160CB00002B/504